A MANOR OF SPEAKING

Frampton Hall

By

Rory Clark

Copyright © Rory Clark 2021
This book is sold subject to the condition that it shall not, by way of trade or otherwise, be lent, resold, hired out, or otherwise circulated without the publisher's prior consent in any form of binding or cover other than that in which it is published and without a similar condition including this condition being imposed on the subsequent publisher.
The moral right of Rory Clark has been asserted.
ISBN-13: 978-1-9196221-0-1

This is a work of fiction. Names, characters, businesses, organizations, places, events and incidents either are the product of the author's imagination or are used fictitiously. Any resemblance to actual persons, living or dead, events, or locales is entirely coincidental.

To Dilly with all my love.

CONTENTS

CHAPTER 1

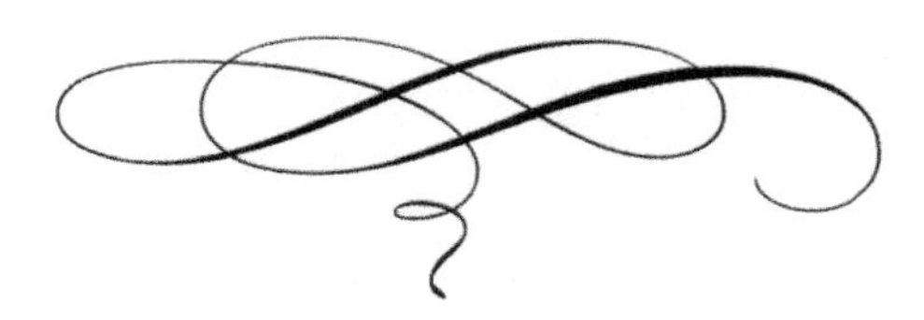

He had made his considerable fortune from lavatory paper. Or, as he liked to put it, from wiping peoples' arses. It was all a far cry from when Sir Charles Buckley, eighth baronet lived in Frampton Hall where his wealth had been inherited over many generations as members of the landowning gentry.

Tony Stoke was a self-made millionaire and proud of it. He originated from a village just outside Dartford where his father had been a bus driver for London Transport and his mother cleaned houses for the better off. He was one of three children and the only one to have achieved any success in life. He had developed an entrepreneurial flair from a young age and after some modest business ventures accumulated enough capital to buy a share in a paper making factory. It was this investment that would eventually form the basis of his considerable wealth.

On first impressions he was an unremarkable looking man and you would not immediately come to a conclusion that he was both a successful businessman and rich. Tony Stoke was in his late fifties, about 5'8" tall, solidly built with thinning grey hair and a penchant for wearing gold jewellery.

Whilst it would be fair to say that he was not an imposing looking man he did have a force of personality and driving ambition that was plainly obvious. One could tell that he was someone who was used to getting things done and done in the way that he thought best. He was concerned about his appearance and whether he was formally attired in a business suit or casually dressed for relaxation, his clothes were of the latest fashion label.

Quite unlike Sir Charles who seemed to have only possessed three suits, two tweed ones which he had inherited from his father, and a dark suit that he wore to London or to funerals. I couldn't help but keep comparing the old with the new. Frampton Hall under Sir Charles' stewardship had been a different world to the present arrangement with Tony Stoke and from the beginning I had not intended to be part of it.

As well as Tony Stoke there were a number of his family who had accompanied him to Frampton. His wife, Vanessa, or Ness as he called her, was an attractive looking woman about ten years younger than her husband. She had at some time been an air stewardess.

They had two children, the eldest a girl called Louise, or Lou for short, and a boy called Richard, or Dick, both of whom were mostly away at university. The Stokes had a liking for abbreviating names.

To complete the family arrangements Tony's parents, Mr and Mrs Stoke senior had come along for the ride.

I had not initially wanted to stay at Frampton Hall when the confirmation came through that it had been acquired by the Stoke family. At an early stage in the negotiations I had met Tony Stoke at his request to talk about certain matters to do with the estate. It had not got off to a promising start.

'Hi, I'm Tony,' he said with an estuary twang to his voice. 'You must be James or is it Jim?' he asked. Being used to somewhat more formal matters on anything to do with Frampton I would have thought that perhaps Mr Stoke and Mr Aden would have been more appropriate.

'James Aden,' I replied shaking his hand.

'Well I hear you're the bloke to talk to about the ins and outs of the Frampton place,' he said continuing, 'you've probably heard but I'm thinking of investing in it, you know something for the future and that and maybe something the kids would be interested in.'

'I had heard that the trustees were carefully considering your proposals,' I agreed.

'It's not just about the business side of it that I'm interested in, I've always wanted a bit of the land, you know the countryside and a bit of history.'

It was quite evident that I could make some assumptions with certainty. Firstly, that he had a lot of money, secondly that his interest in the estate would be driven by a business brain rather than one of stewardship and thirdly owning a bit of land and some history may be more challenging to him than he realised. It would depend upon his ability and wish to become part of landowning society.

'One of the things I've always wanted since I was a boy,' he continued, 'was a duck pond.'

I thought of the gracious lake that lay in a fold of the parkland in front of Frampton Hall and could not with any stretch of the imagination describe it as a duck pond.

I supposed that during the years since he was a boy his aspirations may have grown in parallel with his fortunes. Anyway, depending on how negotiations proceeded Mr Stoke was going to acquire a lot more than his wished-for duck pond. In its entirety the Frampton Hall estate covered ten thousand acres, it included a complete village, a number of farms and a huge stately pile that had over forty bedrooms.

'Well, Mr Stoke,' I continued, 'you will certainly be acquiring that.

As you know the estate is being divided into lots as it is highly unlikely that anyone could either afford or want to buy the whole. What lots do you have in mind?'

'Call me Tony,' he said, 'everyone calls me Tony. Well, I was thinking about most of the whole bleeding thing. I might flog a few bits off once I've had a proper chance to look at things - as I've got the cash I might as well spend it. We'll see. I'll have the big 'ouse and some land that's for sure.'

He must indeed have amassed a considerable fortune I mused, we were really in Russian oligarchs' territory.

CHAPTER 2

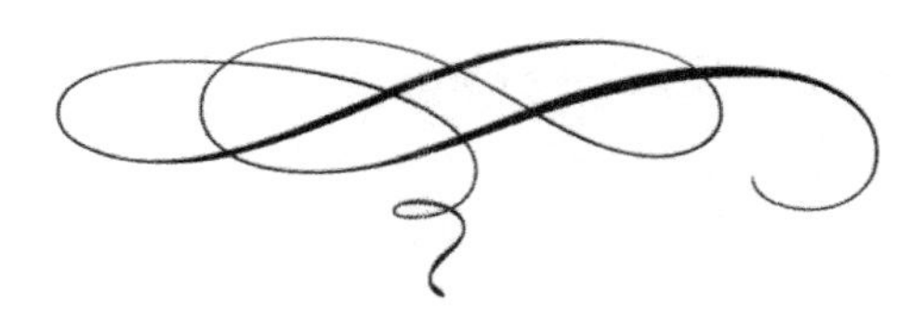

Sir Charles' death had been quite unforeseen, sudden and a terrible shock not only to his family and friends but also to all those that lived on the Frampton estate. His son Sebastian and daughter-in-law Serena were distraught to the point where they were helpless in dealing with the matters that needed urgent attention.

The first priority was to arrange his funeral. Mr Hole, Sir Charles' butler of many years agreed to undertake the task of arrangements which seemed appropriate as he was the one person who had spent more time in Sir Charles' company than anyone else. Hole was also a man of meticulous detail and having run the household organisation of the Hall over the decades was familiar with Sir Charles' personal matters. Sir Charles had, it transpired, also made known to Hole some particular wishes that he wanted carried out at his funeral.

In the main these were easily incorporated into the event but one matter had caused Hole some consternation. Sir Charles had insisted that his funeral should be a modest local affair and in keeping with his attitude to expenditure, which veered between the careful and spendthrift, had noted that he would prefer to avoid the cost of a hearse and black Daimlers. Hole could drive his coffin down to the church in the Morris Traveller.

Mr Hole was in a dilemma. He was used to carrying out Sir

Charles' wishes but, on this occasion, felt that the instructions by his former employer were unbecoming of the dignity that should be afforded to a member of the gentry. In particular, as Hole pointed out, the coffin would not fit in the back of the car unless the rear doors were left open which would then need to be secured by some string. This might have been appropriate in the case of transporting a large crate of chickens back from the market but not appropriate for transporting the eighth Baronet Sir Charles Buckley to his final resting place.

'I'll speak to Sir Sebastian about it,' I told him, 'I think that on this occasion we may need to disregard Sir Charles' wishes and take the matter into our own hands'.

Sebastian had inherited the baronetcy immediately on his father's death but he was uncomfortable being addressed by his title. He had not moved into the Hall but was still residing with Serena, his wife, at Bulls Place Farmhouse on the estate.

I drove down to see him and to discuss some other details regarding the funeral. When I arrived, I was reminded that he also shared some of his father's attitudes towards extravagant spending as I noticed his Reliant Robin in an open fronted barn at the house. Although he and Serena now owned an Audi estate car and a Range Rover, in his bachelor days he had preferred the economies of the three wheeled fibreglass contraption. He found it most convenient, he said, when he was living in Cambridge and working as a professor at the University. It was easy to park and the vehicle tax was lower. Fortunately, marriage had somewhat enlightened his outlook and I only hoped that he would not revert to previous form in considering his father's transportation to the graveside.

I knocked on the door and was greeted by Argonaut, Sebastian's enormous Irish wolfhound.

'Come in,' Sebastian shouted from within the kitchen.

I found them seated at large pine table having a cup of tea. Serena stood up and asked, 'Would you like a cup? It's only just brewed.'

'Yes, thank you that would be lovely,' I replied.

They were a good-looking couple even if not quite what one expected as gentry. Serena was a former model, a striking beauty with Ethiopian origins. Sebastian had inherited some of his father's looks, tall and thin but no moustache and a more learned ambience almost to the point of an eccentric professor.

'How are things up at the Hall?' asked Sebastian. 'I am aware that we are rather leaving you and Mr Hole to sort the details out. I'm sorry but as you know we're just not very good at some of these more practical matters and you and Mr Hole seem to know so much more about these things.'

'I know, it's perfectly all right,' I assured him, 'it's all so far going to plan and really Mr Hole's dealing with more of the arrangements than I am. In fact,' I continued, 'there is only one aspect of the funeral arrangements that is causing concern and we really need your view on it.'

'By all means,' Sebastian said. 'If there's anything we can do then you must let us know.'

'The problem we have is that, as you are probably aware, your father did leave some instructions with Mr Hole over his funeral wishes. Most of those are straightforward and easily complied with but one of the more difficult instructions has come to light. I am afraid that your father requested that he is driven to the church in the back of his car rather than a hearse. To the very end he was clearly intent on saving the estate money and wants Hole to drive him down there in the Morris.'

'Oh,' said Sebastian, 'well I don't see any harm in doing that. A car is a car after all.'

'Well to some extent I can see your point,' I continued, 'but the main problem is that the coffin won't fit in and we would have to tie the doors closed with some string. We feel it isn't very dignified.'

Fortunately, Serena piped up. 'Of course, you can't take it down in that funny old car,' she said, 'that would be ridiculous. Sebastian we must at least have a proper hearse. Besides there's a steep hill up to the front of the church and what would happen if the coffin fell out. It would be an unspeakable disaster.'

Sebastian wavered but he could see the sense in Serena's remark.

'I agree, I think Serena is right,' he said, 'we must do the funeral properly and I'm sure my father would concur with our view on this occasion.'

Surprisingly all the arrangements rather quickly slotted into place and on the following Friday the funeral was held. It was a beautiful early summer day and the Suffolk countryside was looking its very best. Skylarks were calling high above the rolling acres of wheat fields, verges of vibrant cow parsley swayed gently in the breeze alongside the lane leading up to the church and the scent of cut grass filled the air in the newly mown churchyard.

Frampton church was a massive mediaeval building which had been constructed when the prosperity of the wool trade was at its highest. The Buckley family had their humble origins in the area five hundred years ago and as they progressed from tenant farmers to wealthy land owners their sheep flocks grew larger and larger, resulting in their fortune made from wool. They acquired much land, built Frampton Hall and in an effort to ensure their place in heaven contributed greatly to the building of the great wool church. Buckleys had been buried in their private tomb for hundreds of years.

As was to be expected the church was crammed with people. The majority were made up of tenants from the estate but there were also members of the Buckley family and some of Sir Charles' close friends. There were not a lot of Buckleys left. Charles was a widower and an only child and Sebastian was his only child. There were a few distant cousins but the baronetcy title was perilously close to coming to an end. At that time, I did not realise how close that would become.

The service was conducted by our new vicar and it must have been rather daunting for him to have the church so full. He had only been in the parish for six months and had quickly become a well-respected and liked member of the community.

Our previous vicar, Reverend Sidebottom had been a bad choice and turned out not to be very reverend after all.

Frampton, as you would expect, still adhered to the old-fashioned values and a system where the gift of the living, that is to say the appointment of the vicar, lay in the hands of the manorial lord Sir Charles.

With the departure of Reverend Sidebottom a number of suitable candidates had been put forward by the Bishop and Sir Charles, together with some of the members of the parochial church council including myself, considered the proposals and then interviewed a shortlist of three. I remembered the interviews quite clearly. They had been conducted in the dining room at Frampton Hall on a freezing cold day the previous November. I think it was marginally colder inside the house than outside despite the fact that Hole had plugged in a small electric fire at an attempt to make the place more comfortable. Bearing in mind the size of the dining room was not much different to that of a sports hall, the single bar electric fire did little to raise the temperature.

It had been quite clear, certainly in Sir Charles' mind, that the current incumbent was going to be offered the job from the start.

The first applicant the Rev Smith-Parker had appeared much more suitable on paper than he did in person. The PCC and Sir Charles in particular were looking for a traditional type of vicar and although the Rev Smith-Parker had the right credentials, in person there was a lot less to be desired. For a start he had a rather limp, damp handshake, a thin squeaky voice which we felt might be challenging for the size of Frampton church and his main interest outside his pastoral duties was stamp collecting. The decision was made that he was not the vicar to embrace life in the very traditional country parish of Frampton.

The second candidate was a lady vicar and although I cannot be sure I was pretty certain that she was only on the list in order to tick some boxes in regard to political correctness on the selection forms. Quite unlike the previous interviewee we were sure that her voice would be heard throughout every nook and cranny of the church. She appeared a dominant and powerful woman with a handshake as firm as a vice and I could imagine that she would have the residents of Frampton quickly knocked into shape. However, her major misgiving was that she did not drive a car and used a bicycle as her sole means of transport. She would have an awful lot of cycling to do if she moved to Frampton.

The third contender and the man who became the current vicar was the Rev Clifford Webb who was Sir Charles' epitome of a rural priest. He was a family man in his late forties and had always held a living in a rural parish. His greatest attribute in the baronet's view was that he rode to hounds, although I'm not sure that the Bishop would have put that at the top of his list. He was jovial, forthright and yet compassionate which seemed to be a mix that would fit well with estate life.

Indeed, the Rev Webb and his family quickly settled into their new life and he proved to be very popular with nearly everyone on the estate.

Sadly, the funeral was his first opportunity to address nearly the entire population of his parish ensembled and one could see that he was both nervous and excited at the prospect. The presence of the Bishop in the congregation must have added to his state of nerves.

My wife Sophie and I took our places in one of the front pews opposite Sebastian and Serena and members of the Buckley family. The service was conducted formally as Sir Charles had wished and included the wonderful hymns of 'Thine be the Glory' and 'I Vow to Thee my Country' which were sung with great gusto and to tremendous effect filling the church with enthusiastic singing. The internment of the body took place immediately afterwards attended only by family and close friends and staff.

Others made their way gradually back to the Hall where Mr Hole had arranged caterers to provide afternoon tea. The main staterooms had been opened up and looked quite magnificent with the afternoon sunlight pouring through the huge bay windows. It was indeed very rare for the house to be used in the way that it had been designed for, entertaining a large number of people on a grand scale.

Sir Sebastian and Lady Serena having succeeded to the title, hosted the wake with a certain amount of trepidation. This was now their house though they had not yet moved in and although Sebastian had been brought up in it as a boy, he had never truly felt the affection for it that his father had. I wondered how he was going to handle the mantle of his inheritance. He lived in an academic world in which he was comfortable, recognised and he enjoyed. His grasp on business matters and indeed even normal day-to-day life seemed vague at best. Of course, he knew most of the estate tenants and the Buckley relations and he wandered around dutifully greeting as many as he could. However, he did not have his father's presence or confidence and I suspect he found the whole business uncomfortable even allowing for his obvious sadness at this time.

Sir Charles had instructed Hole as to the menu for the afternoon. The caterers provided platters of delicately sliced cucumber sandwiches, bowls of pickled eggs, Victoria sponge cake and Earl Grey tea served in bone china cups and saucers. The French windows were open and many people milled about outside on the terraces admiring the garden. We could have been in a bygone era as apart from the occasional and distant aircraft, nothing seemed to have changed there for centuries and Sir Charles' stewardship had ensured its survival to the present day.

CHAPTER 3

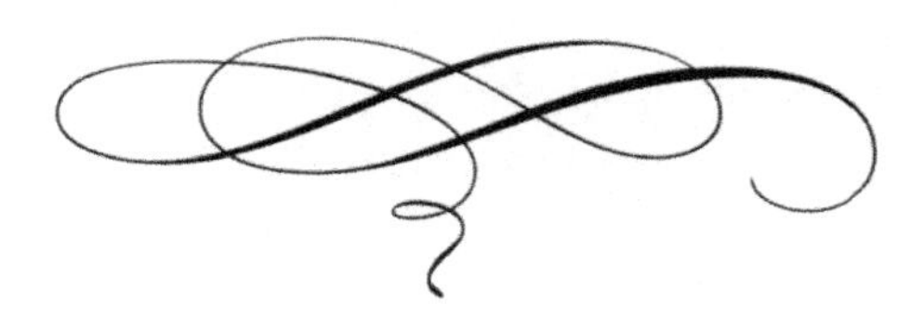

Since Sir Charles' death Mr Hole had been residing in his butler's flat which was located in the East Wing of the house across from the stable yard and Mrs Jubb, who was the housekeeper come cook had stayed on in her flat in the West Wing. That arrangement had been put in place by Sir Charles who occupied the main part of the house and thought it would be a sensible security precaution to have the three of them stationed at strategic positions. It had some semblance of merit but in reality, the three were particularly hard of hearing and it was more likely to be one of Sir Charles' poodles that would become aware of any intruders.

Until quite recently there had been a multitude of other servants including footmen and maids fulfilling the work of a busy household. But with only one person to look after, two full-time members of staff seemed sufficient despite the size of the house and as staff retired or moved on to other positions they had not been replaced. There were a number of ladies from the village who came in each day to rearrange the dust. Whether Sebastian and Serena would want to reinstate a large household had yet to be discussed.

The question of their move from Bulls Place Farmhouse to the Hall had not been mentioned either. Everyone concerned had assumed that this would be a straightforward matter of getting a removal firm to transport their belongings from one house to the other which was, after all, simply a mile away.

But Serena seemed reluctant to move straight away and Sebastian was rather indifferent. Bulls Place Farmhouse had been completely renovated and furnished to their taste within the last couple of years and it was an extremely warm, comfortable and friendly house that would quite simply be most peoples' dream home. It had professionally landscaped and designed gardens, with stables, barns and ten acres of paddocks so one could see why they were in no hurry to leave it.

Frampton Hall was also beautiful but in a very different way. It was not warm, it was not comfortable and whilst it was not unfriendly it certainly did not have any feeling of homeliness about it. The place was vast. There was a suite of formal state rooms across the South Front and along the West Wing together with various servants' flats and functional rooms like pantries and kitchens most of which were disused. It also had more than forty bedrooms and an unknown number of bathrooms, miles of passages and sixteen staircases. The great charm of the house was its architecture, its furniture and above all its collection of art. The house had evolved over centuries. It was predominantly a mansion built in the early eighteenth century and a succession of baronets had acquired possessions with which to fill it. It reputedly contained one of the finest private art collections in the country, if not the world and I doubt one could ever get bored living a whole lifetime within the surroundings. I spent a lot of time in the house as part of my job as the agent and every time I went into it, I saw something new which attracted my interest.

Sir Charles had never wanted to invest in modernising the house.

It would not have been possible to modernise it in any structural way as it was grade one listed and in any case one would not want to change the structure or layout of the house. But it did have a very antiquated heating system, a limited and out of date electrical system, temperamental plumbing and only two telephones. It would take a certain shift of attitude to embrace living in a house like Frampton Hall. Surrounded by the grandeur and formality was a privilege in many ways and there were areas of the house that were more intimate and homely which may have appealed to Sebastian and Serena.

Sir Charles' study was one such place and a few of the bedrooms were what one might describe as more ordinary. But you still had to get from one to the other and certainly during the colder months you needed to a wear a coat or at least some kind of jacket when moving about the house. This was despite the fact that there was a heating system, a remarkably inefficient one, that cost over a hundred thousand pounds a year to run. It resembled something from the mechanics of a transatlantic liner with miles of steel pipes and a great monster of a boiler in the cellar that clanged alarmingly every time it fired up.

Some difficult decisions needed to be made as it was clear that a considerable amount of money was going to be required in order to modernise the house to make it a bit more comfortable for them.

I had suggested to Sebastian that we set up weekly meetings which had been the norm when his father was alive and I would arrive at Sir Charles' study with an agenda of matters to discuss. Sebastian was less enthusiastic about this and was content to chat about things on the telephone as and when needed, with sporadic face to face meetings when the discussions were more detailed. For the interim period this seemed workable to me but I thought that once he moved into the Hall and took over the proprietorial interest in all the goings-on to do with the estate then something more formal would be required.

For the time being we pursued Sebastian's plan as he was, after all, now the boss. On this occasion being a matter of deliberation Sebastian and I met in Sir Charles' study to talk through the way forward. Although the estate would effectively carry on as before, decisions needed to be made about the house. In fact, there had been a lot of deliberations about the move six months or so before Sir Charles died. But because of Sir Charles' health which had been deteriorating quite quickly at the time, all discussions were put on hold in reality because he hadn't wanted to move out. At the time I sensed a feeling of relief on Sebastian and Serena's parts as though they felt it was their duty to move rather than something that they wished to do.

Hole preceded me down the corridors from the East Wing to the study, the steel inserts of his shoes clattering like a pony, followed closely by Sir Charles' standard poodles, Monty and Napoleon. They clearly missed their master and although Hole was taking care of them admirably, they seemed to have lost their spark. Hole left a tray of coffee and biscuits on the desk and the dogs settled down on a rug beside the late baronet's chair. It felt very strange without him being there but Sebastian and I thought that by holding our occasional meetings in the study it would give some kind of semblance of continuity, even if circumstances had changed so dramatically.

Sebastian was already seated at an oval mahogany table rather than at his father's desk. It seemed an appropriate compromise. He stood up and we shook hands.

'Hello, James,' he said, 'good of you to come up and rather force the meeting. I do appreciate the work that you're doing to try and keep things running and quite realise that I'm not being particularly decisive.'

'It's completely understandable,' I replied 'your father has not long died which makes it difficult for you and you're probably not in quite the right frame of mind to make big decisions'.

'I'm afraid I'm not', he said,' but I can see that we can't just leave things as they are. You seem to be dealing with the estate matters perfectly well as you have been for the past few years but I am finding the thought of we should do to the house quite overwhelming.'

'Well I suggest you and Serena concentrate on two things to think about with this house,' I continued, 'firstly, when you are going to move into it, and secondly, what you want done presumably before you move in? We have to think that the potential benefits of some modernisation will make it more comfortable for you. We have only got to look at the wiring and plumbing to know that it's well past its sell by date. It's an ideal opportunity to at least find out some costs of doing some upgrading and if we're going to go ahead then it's sensible that they are carried out before you move in.'

'Yes, I suppose it is,' he said 'though I really can't see Serena and myself actually going around the house saying where we want plug sockets and light switches and whatever else we need. There must be thousands of the things.'

'No, 'I agreed 'I'm sure you wouldn't want to do that and any good electrical contractor will produce a plan that you could then look at. You probably only need a few rooms that the two of you will use regularly and you could just focus on those perhaps?'

'Well okay,' he said hesitantly, 'perhaps you could make a start by getting some ideas and prices – I suppose we'd better look at the heating system and some of the plumbing while we're at it.'

'Right,' I said 'I'll look into it and get some people to quote. It may be that we split areas and price for different parts of the house at a time because I imagine the costs will be quite substantial.'

'Where do you think the money is going to come from?' Sebastian asked.

'Well, we will need to talk to the trustees but there is a reasonable amount of cash on deposit and quite a sizeable share portfolio,' I explained, 'and failing that we would need to maybe look at selling some assets.'

'When you say assets,' Sebastian asked, 'do you mean part of the estate or maybe some paintings?'

'Either or both I suppose,' I replied 'but to some extent we will need to be led by the bank and the trustees. There is also, despite the trust planning, still going to be quite a sizeable chunk of inheritance tax to pay.'

'Have we any idea what the tax implications are as yet?'

'We do have a rough idea' I confirmed, 'that at the end of the last financial year we anticipated that if nothing much else changed the would be a tax liability of fifteen million.'

Sebastian gasped, 'Good heavens, how on earth will we find that sort of money?'

'We need to put it in context of assets,' I explained, 'considering the total value of the estate and contents of this house that amount of tax although uncomfortable is manageable.'

I pondered for a bit on the thought that Sebastian really had no idea with regard to business matters. He had his salary as a professor at Cambridge and he also had a huge income from the trusts that his father and grandfather had set up. Sebastian inevitably took that for granted, which possibly most people in his position would, but it amazed me that he did not take a greater interest or comprehension of where the money came from and how it all worked.

'There are also the more mundane estate matters that I used to talk to your father about, which I've mentioned before and perhaps we should start engaging you in more of those?' I asked.

'Yes, I'm very happy to hear a bit about what's going on,' he said 'but I think in the main I will just leave it up to you, certainly for the time being.'

'I won't bore you with the minutiae although you might think this is but I suppose the only immediate thing to talk about is the summer fete which is on the autumn bank holiday.'

'Oh yes,' he sighed, 'I had completely forgotten about that. To what extent do I need to get involved with it?'

'Your father sat on the fete committee,' I explained, 'so he had an input into quite a bit of the detail. However, they really will understand the circumstances so I'm sure that the committee will not expect you to partake. But people will expect you to present various cups and prizes on the day.'

'That's absolutely fine,' Sebastian agreed. 'I will make sure that Serena and I have the whole day free to help out. Of course, if there is anything that you need us to do then just let me know.'

'Certainly, I will,' I said, 'and I'll be in touch should I need anything.'

CHAPTER 4

The Frampton fete was one of the highlights of village society during the year and an enormous amount of work went into it from all sections of the community. The estate played a pivotal role not least because it was held on the recreation field owned by the estate. Sir Charles' presence would of course be missed but business would carry on as usual and I would no doubt have more to do than in previous years.

My more immediate concern was to think about the possible improvements that were necessary in the house. The thought of how we were going to logistically manage the work was giving me sleepless nights. The rewiring was going to be the biggest headache and any new wiring would have to be very carefully hidden. One couldn't just make grooves in the plasterwork and then touch them up with a bit of Polyfilla. The formal rooms had ornate plasterwork many with gilt finishes and hand carved freesias which were of an antiquity and quality that would take careful craftsmanship to protect.

I contacted a fellow land agent who worked for the National Trust and obtained some useful contacts from him as to the sort of companies that might be able to help. The first stage of the operation was to instruct a knowledgeable building surveyor to draw up the schedule of works that we were planning.

In due course an appointment was made for a Mr Ron Short from the recommended firm of Snail, Boxall and Holder, apparently leaders in their field, to carry out a survey and make a detailed specification of how we were to go about it.

Mr Short was indeed short but he had an amazing enthusiasm for tackling the minute details of how things should be done.

Hole showed him into Sir Charles' study where I had taken up temporary residence at the table leaving the desk untouched.

'Mr Short to see you,' Hole announced, 'and I have bought some coffee and biscuits.'

'Thank you, Mr Hole that is very kind,' I replied.

'Good morning Mr. Short,' I greeted him.

'Mr Aden good to meet you. What a beautiful morning in such a beautiful setting.'

'It is indeed,' I replied 'and thank you for coming to see us. We have a rather difficult task ahead.'

'Not at all,' he commented, 'this kind of job is an absolute peach. I adore the challenges of working in such special buildings and I can't wait to have a look at what it entails.'

'That's excellent news,' I said, 'it's certainly going to be a challenge.'

Sir Charles' poodles had come in with Hole and settled on their rug as usual, emitting various types of doggy smells none of which were pleasant.

'Are those your dogs?' asked Mr Short.

'No, they belonged to the late Sir Charles – I hope you don't mind them. I'm afraid they rather wander around looking for him as they don't really have a master any more. Mr Hole the butler looks after them but he is not really a dog person. Do you mind dogs?' I asked.

'Oh no, not at all,' he said, 'in fact the opposite - as a sort of hobby I breed English bulldogs.'

'Do you?' I enquired, reflecting on how often owners look like their dogs. Mr Short had that bulldog appearance with a similar shaped head but perhaps not such heavy jowls.

'I usually have two litters a year,' he continued, 'and as well as breed them I judge them.'

'Are you a recognised person then in the bulldog world?' I asked.

'Yes, indeed, if you were to mention my name, they'd know me or of me. I judge at Crufts.'

Personally, I wasn't very fond of bulldogs and thought that their pushed-up noses, heavy breathing and slobbering was not an attractive asset in a pet. However, it wasn't the time to embark on discussions about breeding bulldogs.

A thought suddenly occurred to me.

'I wonder whether you would be willing to come and judge our dog show at the Frampton fete,' I asked, 'that is if you are free on the August bank holiday? It's nothing very advanced.' I explained, 'More along the lines of the dog with the waggiest tail that sort of thing. It would be rather a coup to have a Crufts judge there!'

'Well if I'm free I would be very happy to come along and help,' he said, 'I'd have to let you know when I get back to the office.'

'That's very kind, it would be an enormous boost for the fete's credentials,' I said. 'But I suppose we now better move on to the immediate matter in hand.'

I explained what, in an ideal world, Sebastian and I had discussed and that we wanted a suitable new electrical wiring system installed throughout the house together with an appropriate telephone system.

'You don't have to do much to improve the existing telephone system,' I explained 'as we only have two telephones, one here in the study and one in Mr Hole's office. The wiring is a much bigger problem and in parts of the house that aren't really used I think it's probably some of the original lead wiring.'

'I'm used to all this,' he said excitedly, 'I can feel a real sense of a project here.'

'As to arrangements,' I continued, 'I will be on hand should you need me and Mr Hole will show you around the house. I gather from your letter that you are going to need to be here for about a fortnight?'

'Yes, I have allowed two weeks work to survey and come up with the plan and then after that I'll return to the office and draw up the detailed specification which you can then put out to contractors for quotations.'

'Are you staying somewhere locally?' I asked knowing that his office was in Reigate. 'Yes,' he confirmed, 'I have booked at the Angel Hotel in Bury St Edmunds as we have a special rate with that chain of hotels.'

I rang through on Sir Charles' telephone to Mr Hole's telephone and asked him to come and join us.

Hole appeared some while later and agreed to show Mr Short around the house.

'If you can give me a brief tour to start with that would be very helpful,' Short asked, 'and once I have an idea, I'll be able to just get quietly on with it.'

'Very well sir,' said Mr Hole, 'where would you like to make a start?'

Fortunately, we had some rather old but quite accurate plans of the house which I'd discovered in the estate office and had copied them for Mr Short's use. Having found them was quite achievement otherwise we would have had to commission yet another survey which would have taken a great deal longer than Mr Short's inspection and added thousands to the cost. I left them to it, but before leaving asked Mr Short if he had made any arrangements with regard to his lunches.

'I have as it's the first day brought some sandwiches. I am a man of habit and always have a cheese and pickle sandwich and a pork pie.'

'If it would help,' I remarked, 'I'm sure Mrs Jubb, the housekeeper would prepare you something each day for the next two weeks or if you prefer the risk of the village shop then you could nip down there – they make sandwiches.'

'Oh, I wouldn't want to bother Mrs Jubb although that's kind of you to offer, I'll drop into the shop on my way through each morning.'

I returned to the estate office in the village to try and resume my routine duties. It was a strange time as most things were carrying on as normal but there was the addition of dealing with all sorts of things to do with Sir Charles' death, not least managing the inheritance tax situation but also the move of Sebastian and Serena to the Hall and the resulting improvements required.

I was brought back to the present by the most appalling deafening crash outside in the Square. I looked out of my window and with horror saw that Mrs Arbuthnot had reversed her Bentley into the scaffolding surrounding the baker's shop which was being reroofed.

Some of the scaffold poles had fallen onto the roof of her car and there was general commotion with people rushing out of the bakery. I could see Mr Cartwright, the baker, trying to take some control of the chaos.

I sped out of the office to see if I could help. Fortunately, nobody appeared to be injured and Mrs Arbuthnot was still in her car looking rather indignant. She was not a lady who scared easily and was one of the few people, she once told me, who had flown a Spitfire over Frampton Church. She should not really still be driving let alone flying I thought, as I knew she was over ninety years old. But ladies like Eugene Arbuthnot did not give up their independence easily. I could see her carer sitting in the back seat who seemed far more alarmed by the circumstances than her employer.

Eugene Arbuthnot did not live on the estate but in a moated mediaeval hall some four miles away. However, she did have close associations with Frampton not least that she had been a friend of Sir Charles. Her family had lived in the same house for several generations. There was still a Mr Arbuthnot who was even older than her and had reportedly received a telegram from the Queen. But he had not been seen for some years due we supposed to his frail health. Mrs Arbuthnot did not subscribe to frail health either from her point of view or that of her husband. He was, she said, simply bored with society and preferred to stay at home. The carer, who was quite clearly her husband's carer, was referred to rather grandly as her maid. Whether the carer knew that or minded I never knew.

Eugene Arbuthnot had been raised in an affluent family although there seemed to be no knowledge of where their money had come from or indeed what her father and grandfather had done to acquire their money. Being brought up in the nineteen forties and fifties she once told me that she had been to finishing school in Switzerland, was a society debutant, had a lively and interesting life until she met Mr Arbuthnot whom she regretfully married and from then on it went downhill.

I think that was probably rather unfair of her bearing in mind that she had not got married until later on in life and therefore the energy to pursue such exotic pastimes such as flying aircraft and racing classic motorcars would have been exhausted in any case. There were no children and they continued to live in the manner to which they had become accustomed resolutely clinging to the nineteen fifties. Hence the Bentley which was a relic of that era.

The case in point was clearly a relic now as the roof had been dented badly by the scaffolding and I doubt it was worth repairing. As I reached the car the carer was being helped out by Katie Cartwright, the baker's attractive young daughter who worked in the shop. Mrs Arbuthnot was intent on extricating the car from the jumbled mess causing further consternation amongst the bystanders.

I went to see her.

'Are you all right Mrs Arbuthnot?' I enquired.

'Of course I am,' she exploded, 'I just got myself in a bit of a pickle and need to get the car out.'

'I think it would be unwise to do that just yet,' I ventured, 'because if you move the car the rest of the scaffolding might fall down. Why don't you get out and we will wait for assistance before you move it?'

I knew one of the reasons that she didn't want to get out was because although mentally alert and reasonably active, she did have trouble walking which is why she brought her maid with her on shopping expeditions to the village. In normal circumstances Mrs Arbuthnot would drive from shop to shop with the maid sitting in the back of the car who would get out and collect the groceries before they returned home. However she couldn't sit there all morning waiting for help to arrive so she did indeed, with her maid's and Mr Cartwright's help, disengage herself from the Bentley.

'Come over to the estate office,' I suggested, 'and sit down while we arrange for someone to take you both home.'

In due course I took them and their groceries back to their house and arranged for the scaffolding people to come and assess the damage and make it good. We then extricated the Bentley and Mr Cartwright kindly drove the car to her house with me following.

She never did get the roof repaired and is still driving it, probably the only person in England motoring around in a Bentley with puddles on its roof.

CHAPTER 5

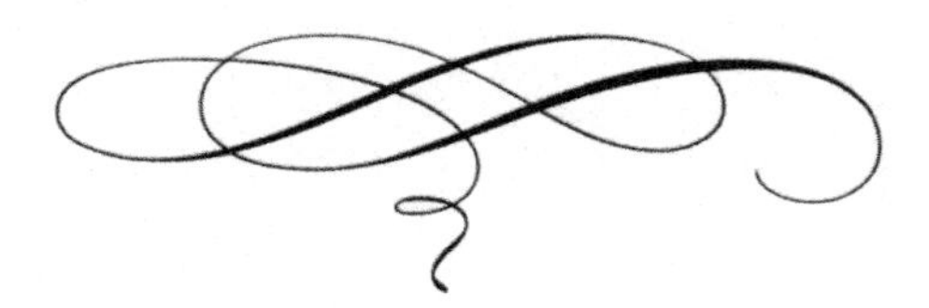

Once I'd sorted out Mrs Arbuthnot, I returned to the office to make some notes for Mr Short as I realised that I had forgotten to include some additional improvements which may as well be carried out at the same time.

The most important one concerned the cost of the insurance of the Hall and its contents. We had an astronomical premium to pay for obvious reasons but the cost was hugely increased because we did not help ourselves. As it was, most of the very valuable art wasn't insured at all.

The main liabilities were fire and theft as any fire damage to the house would be extremely expensive to repair due to the size of the place and the quality of the building and its interior decoration. The contents were even more of an issue. We had an inventory of probably most of the contents, certainly the most valuable ones, but I doubted it was very accurate in terms of values put against the listed items. The Buckley collection of art was one of the finest in the country and it was conservatively valued at a hundred million pounds. There was another ten million allocated to furniture and seven million for various specific collections such as one of porcelain, another of enamels and a third one of silver.

The premiums would be substantial in any case and understandably so but we were deemed higher risk because of the security and fire arrangements that we had in place. Or, to put it bluntly, that we did not have in place.

Sir Charles had agreed to having smoke alarms fitted in all the state rooms and those rooms that either he or the staff used. They were not very sophisticated and hardly better than those available at your local do-it-yourself shop but at least they were something. What the house really needed was an electric main operated smoke detection and sprinkler system and we were forever being pushed by the insurance company to get one fitted.

The security arrangements weren't much better. All the ground floor windows had internal wooden shutters which Hole used to close at night. He would attach a cowbell to them by means of a little hook presumably in the hope that anyone breaking in would set the cowbell ringing which should alert someone in the house. It was a pretty useless idea as unless somebody was either in that very room or one close by the ringing of a cowbell was highly unlikely to summon the alarm. In order to get any insurance at all we had to confirm as a condition that house would always be occupied by at least one person which in itself caused difficulties as there were only the three of them living there. Fortunately, Mr Hole and Mrs Jubb didn't venture very far but in theory it meant that they could not both go out same time unless they knew Sir Charles was in residence. Now that he had died the situation was even more fraught which was one of the reasons that I set up a temporary office in the study and flitted between there and the estate office.

I set out my thoughts in a memo to Mr Short as it seemed an opportune moment to include some fire and security systems in the rewiring of the house.

I drove back up to the Hall in the estate Land Rover to give Mr Short my memo. When I got there, I found Hole looking very flustered and most unlike his usual composed self.

'You look harassed Mr Hole,' I remarked.

'Ah Mr Aden,' he replied, 'indeed some of the things I have to do here are quite beyond the imagination.'

'Oh dear, was has happened?'

'I'm afraid that Monty has brought in a live rabbit from the garden which he chased down the corridor and I now believe it to be either in the Yellow drawing room or the Wedgewood room.'

'I'll come and help,' I said, 'have you asked Mrs Jubb to assist?'

'That I did but she was not overly helpful saying that I shouldn't have let the dogs in through the French windows. I had been out on the lawn letting them have shall we say, a chance to relive themselves.'

'Well these things happen, don't they? Those dogs are incredibly quick. I'm surprised that they didn't kill it.'

'I originally thought it was dead,' continued Mr Hole. 'When Monty dropped it in the corridor it just lay there but suddenly got up and shot off in the direction of the drawing room.'

'Let's go and have a look and see if we can find it. Where are the dogs now?' I asked.

'I've shut them in my office as I thought that there might be a commotion if one of them found the rabbit again. We don't want blood on the floor.'

We went off to search for it. I followed Hole along various corridors until we reached the place where it had last been seen. In passing I wondered why butlers of a certain age developed a particular style of walk, plodding, with slightly bowed legs and whether it was simply an acquired habit.

There was no rabbit to be seen. There was a considerable amount of furniture that it could hide under or indeed inside, and as the adjoining doors were open, it may well have hopped through into the next room. I knelt down on the floor to peer under the beautiful-gilded Chippendale furniture and under the flamboyant Louis fifteenth cabinets but to no avail.

'Let's look in the Wedgewood room,' I suggested.

There were fewer hiding places for it in there as most of the furniture consisted of glass cabinets mounted on the floor.

'Well I have no idea where it's gone,' I said, 'I suppose it could have gone down the passage and into another room.'

'I suppose it might have,' Hole agreed despondently.

'We might have to leave it,' I suggested. 'We could spend all day looking for it and still not find it. I'm sure we've both got better things to do.'

'We can't just leave it surely?' said Hole.

'It won't do any harm,' I remarked, 'it's not likely to chew anything.'

There was nothing else we could do and the rabbit could be more or less anywhere by now.

I left my memo for Mr Short and went back to my car.

Before driving off I thought I would have a quick walk around the gardens as we had, only last year, rabbit fenced the immediate gardens to keep them out. The grounds of the Hall were suitably complimentary to the house and its interior. They were immaculately kept by two full-time gardeners as Sir Charles had a keen interest and obtained much pleasure from what he described as his gardening hobby. He didn't actually do any gardening as such but he used to discuss at great length the plans for planting, what was growing where and how the plants were thriving with his gardeners on a daily basis.

The large sweeping lawns were kept mown to a precise height and were beautifully rolled to achieve a striped pattern, reminiscent of Lord's Cricket ground. Flower beds with annuals were organised formally in arrays of differing colours and a superb sunken rose garden maintained to provide glorious scent from spring through to autumn.

It was no hardship to be walking around the gardens on a warm summer's day even if I was supposed to be looking for a hole in the netting. There was no sign of either of the gardeners but I presumed they were in the walled kitchen garden which was a quarter of a mile away on the other side of the house.

It took me an hour to walk around the boundary but I couldn't find any signs of rabbit activities. I would have to have a word with the gardeners at a later date to see if we could set up some traps. With some reluctance I drove back to the estate office to tie up a few loose ends before I went home.

Home was a small farm just off the estate that had been left to my wife Sophie by her uncle a few years ago. I wanted to get back a little early as two Suffolk rams were being delivered that evening. We owned a flock of mule ewes which we kept on the farm and crossed them with Suffolk rams to produce a useful type of lamb for the market. Sophie really ran the farm with the help of a couple of farm men, the Flatt brothers, who lived next door to each other in a pair of semi-detached farm cottages. They did a reasonable job for us despite the fact that they hardly uttered a word to either Sophie or myself and never between themselves. They were practically indistinguishable from each another except that one of them had a habit of farting, often and loudly, without apology. They were nonetheless exceptional stockmen and because they had done the same jobs year in year out in accordance with the seasons, knew exactly what to do and when to do it.

I would like to have been able to spend more time on our farm but with a full-time job as agent of Frampton estate I could only muck in every now and then. Sophie divided her days between looking after our young daughter Emma and keeping track of what was going on outside.

The arrival of the new rams was worth getting home in time for as they were going to be responsible for the prosperity of our flock. We had purchased them direct from a breeder of pedigree Suffolk sheep at no small expense and although Sophie had chosen them, I had not yet seen them myself.

I was in time to watch the sheep being unloaded from a livestock trailer. The Flatt brothers were nowhere to be seen which didn't matter as they would have only offered a series of grunts no matter how impressive the new rams appeared.

Sophie was chatting to the chap who had brought them.

'They look very fine animals to me,' I said, 'really beautiful confirmation.'

'I'm glad you like them,' said Sophie. 'My husband hasn't seen them before,' she added to the breeder.

'You'll have fine proper lambs out of these two,' he assured us. 'I know you've paid a lot of money for them but they'll be worth every penny, mark me words.'

I certainly hoped he was right as they had indeed cost a lot of money, far more than we usually paid for a ram. We had made the decision the previous autumn to alter some things on the farm. One of those was to lamb all our sheep in March rather than twice a year in January and March so as to cut down on the work. The other was to increase the size of the flock and its quality. Sophie was doing less on the farm than when we were first married because of Emma but she did oversee everything that went on. She managed the accounts and ever-increasing paperwork. Farmers were fortunate to be able to claim grants for all sorts of things on their land but the rigmarole of applying for these things was detailed and complicated. Sometimes it seemed as though she spent more time in the farm office than she did outside on the land. There must exist a huge army of civil servants who fiddled around with the paperwork or computer inputting at the other end. It wouldn't be long before every time a chicken laid an egg, we would have to declare it and apply for a document from Defra before we were allowed to eat it.

We said goodbye to the breeder and watched the two rams explore their new paddock. They soon had their heads down, munching the grass and their journey to their new home appeared not to have unsettled them.

It was a lovely evening so I suggested to Sophie that we should saddle up our horses and go for a ride around the farm. Our housekeeper, Mrs Painter would look after Emma whilst we were out.

My horse, Grehan, was a pretty dark bay mare but she was getting a bit old and had recurring problems with her tendons. She was still a lovely ride but she couldn't be ridden fast or do any jumping which was a shame because she had been a good hunter in her time. Sophie had a dreadful little mare which as far as I was concerned was an absolute menace and unpleasant to ride. It would shy at everything, was forever pulling at her bit and if anyone got too close to her, she would immediately kick out. Sophie had been given her by a friend and thought her friend would be very upset if she got rid of the horse. I suspected that the friend must know what the thing was like hence giving it away and would not be the least bit surprised or upset if we had shot it. Whenever I suggested that course of action, I gathered that was not going to be the case.

The warmth of the early evening was a delight despite the wretched horse and one could smell the warmth of the earth and dried grass as we rode around the headlands of the fields. At the far end of the farm was a piece of woodland and although we did not own it there was a bridle path running through the centre. The chattering of birds and slight breeze in the trees were the only sounds to be heard apart from the movement of the horses. I reflected on how lucky we were to live in such a beautiful part of the country and more importantly to be able to get out and enjoy it.

We were out for about an hour before returning back to the house to have supper and do bath time duties with Emma. Mrs Painter was very accommodating and looked after Emma if we needed but it was ritual that I enjoyed getting Emma ready for bed each night giving her a bath, reading a book to her and teaching her about the animals in her books. They were treasured moments to enjoy before tucking her up in bed for the night.

The following morning, I saw the Flatt brothers out in the yard as I was preparing to leave for the estate office.

I greeted them. 'Come and have a look at these new rams.'

They followed me over to the paddock to cast their eyes over our new acquisitions. 'Good-looking animals,' I suggested. One of them grunted, the other stayed silent. The Flatt brothers, not the sheep.

'They should improve the quality of next year's lambs,' I continued, 'let's just hope they square up to what has been promised by the breeder.'

I left them to contemplate the potential of the two animals and went on my way to work.

My secretary Anne was already in.

'Morning James,' she said, 'how are you today?'

'I'm fine thank you, Anne, and you?'

'Good thanks. I think I've got a busy day ahead though, as I need to help the Carnival committee with some letters to go out and there's a number of tenants who I need to chase for late payment of their rent.'

'Oh good. Thanks for doing that,' I said. 'I don't think any of them are in any sort of financial trouble it's just they take a delight in being tardy with paying. One or two of them especially find it is a strenuous and emotional event to open their cheque books.'

She laughed. 'Especially Mr North,' she continued, 'he is always the last to pay and yet I saw him driving a new car yesterday. When I mentioned it to him, he said that he had to get a new car to make full use of his tax reliefs.'

Preston North, to give him his full name, which sounded like a railway station, was a friendly old rogue. It was extremely difficult to get him to part with any money in so far as we were concerned. Because he was such a jovial and likeable character it made it almost impossible to get annoyed with him, a trait that I'm sure he exploited.

I had once asked him about his Christian name as it was unusual. Apparently, his mother had originated from Lancashire and having married Mr North senior and moved down south, she managed to persuade her husband that in fondness for her north country upbringing their children would have the names of Lancashire towns. Preston, who was the eldest had a brother called Burnley and two sisters called Morecambe and Clitheroe. It was some consolation to her children that she had not named them after rivers in Lancashire or they might have been burdened with such names as Ribble, Hodder or Lune.

As we were talking about this he arrived in the square in his new car.

'Quick,' I said, 'let's go out and have a word with him,' so we rushed outside to greet him.

'Morning Preston,' he turned around and looked over.

'Ah morning James, morning Anne, you both all right?' He looked rather smart wearing a fine suit which was not his normal weekday attire.

'Very well thanks Preston, where are you off to, you look bit dressed up for shopping in Frampton? You're usually in a boiler suit not a lounge suit.'

'Aha you got a sharp eye James,' he said laughing, 'I am having a day off. I'm taking the misses over to Newmarket and we going to have a look round the horse racing museum. On the way back we're stopping for lunch at that new French bistro in Bury St Edmunds. L 'Escargot I think that's how you pronounce it.'

'Goodness you are splashing out a bit specially with your new car.'

Preston laughed again. 'I've a heart of gold you know that and I like to look after the missus. She's a good wife, works hard as she should and every now and then she deserves a treat.'

It sounded to me as he was talking more about a pet rather than his wife but he did have a rather traditional attitude.

'On such matters,' I continued, 'Anne tells me that the rent is still outstanding. I hope you've kept enough back to be able to pay us?'

'She's a tittle tattle in't she,' he joked, 'yes I hadn't forgotten it but unfortunately I'd run out of cheques.'

I chuckled. 'That's the first time you've used that excuse,' I said, 'but perhaps when you're in Bury for lunch you can pick up a new cheque book and then solve the problem!'

'Now that's a good idea,' he said, 'but I think the bank is already sending me one out in the post. Now look here, I'll pop in tomorrow and I'll settle it.'

'Well that was a timely meeting and saves you one less letter to send out,' I said to Anne.

'Yes,' she said, 'he's a funny chap, isn't he?'

We went back into the office and set about our tasks for the day. I had rather a mixed bag on my list. I needed to go up to the Hall and speak Mr Short to find out how he was getting on, I wanted to go and see how the foresters were progressing with thinning the Oak Plantation out on one of the farms, I had to inspect an empty cottage in the village as the tenant had moved out so we could organise its re-letting and there was the usual stack of paperwork to wade through. At some point I also needed to see Sebastian to discuss with him what he wanted to do about a lot of his father's personal effects. Somebody had to go through his clothes and personal belongings and also his study and files. It was really up to Sebastian to do that but I could easily see that it would all just get left and stay cocooned for years.

I noticed as I went out to the Land Rover that one of the tyres seemed to have developed a slow puncture. Another job to put on the list. It didn't appear too bad so I drove up to the Hall and went to search for Mr Hole who I eventually found in the kitchen talking to Mrs Jubb and the brigade of ladies that came up from the village to clean.

'Good morning everyone.'

Various greetings of morning Mr Aden they replied.

'Has anyone seen Mr Short this morning?' I asked, 'as I wanted to go and have another chat with him.'

It appeared that the most likely place, or at least where he was last seen, was in the Chinese bedroom or what was called the Queen's suite which were on the first floor in the West Wing. I sighed as I would be gone for least half an hour venturing into that part of the house.

I asked for a cup of coffee to be taken through to the study whilst I checked through the morning's post. I had assumed responsibility for opening the mail addressed to Sir Charles or to Frampton Hall and then distributing the contents either to members of staff, Sebastian or the relevant professional advisers. The present situation was slightly in limbo because although Sebastian was now the master of the estate and the beneficiary of the various trusts, there was still a lot of property and correspondence to do with Sir Charles which was in the main being handled by the executors of his estate.

CHAPTER 6

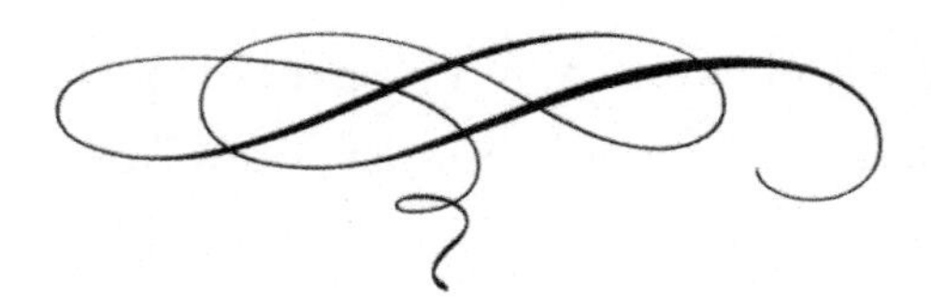

It was amazing what you learnt about somebody after they had died. The most illuminating information came through junk mail, as presumably the recipient had at some point signed up to the products that these people were selling. There was the expected quantity of brochures about field sports and country clothing, gardening and matters to do with horse racing but there also seem to be an inordinate number of catalogues about home baking equipment. I don't think the late baronet would have known how to boil an egg let alone embark on any home baking.

I sorted the post out into piles for the respective people, the majority being placed in the recycling bin.

I went to find Mr Short, by then we were Ron and James, as predicted in the Chinese bedroom. He was peering intently under the bed, which was an elaborate monstrosity which, not surprisingly had originally come from China. In general, I had in mind that Chinese people tended to be vertically challenged and therefore the size of bed bore no correlation to my image of their national height. It was reputed to have been acquired from some long-ago Emperor when one of Sir Charles' ancestors had taken a tour of the Far East and purchased a number of pieces of furniture and works of art with which to embellish the family seat.

'Morning, Ron,' I said presuming that it was his pair of legs sticking out from under the bed.

There was a muffled cry and some wriggling before he appeared.

'Morning, James,' he replied, 'sorry about that but I think there is a dead animal under the bed. I just can't see what it is but it looks a bit like a rabbit to me.'

'Oh, my goodness,' I exclaimed, 'how on earth did that get up here?'

'It does seem a bit unusual,' he agreed.

'Yes, it is a bit but I do know where it came from,' I explained, 'one of the dogs brought in a rabbit last week and it disappeared in the Yellow drawing-room. Mr Hole and I searched high and low for it but couldn't find the thing anywhere. Clearly it's made its way all the way up here trying to find a way out. I'll let Mr Hole know and he can get one of the cleaners to remove it.'

'Oh I see,' he said.

'How you getting on with the survey?' I enquired.

'Actually, surprisingly well. The plans you provided are extremely helpful and I'm pretty much on target for completing my work by the end of the week.'

'Ah that's reassuring,' I said. 'I know Sebastian is keen to get some prices together for the work before he makes any further decisions about the future.'

I left him to his measuring and plotting and on the way out popped in to let Mr Hole know of the whereabouts of the rabbit. I rang Sebastian from my mobile phone to update him on the survey progress. I also asked if I could drop in to discuss what we could begin to do about some of Sir Charles' possessions.

'Oh, that's good news,' he said, 'yes by all means call in but can you leave it until later as we are just about to start our yoga class.'

'Oh, okay,' I said a bit taken aback. I thought I remembered him once mentioning that Serena and he were devotees of a yoga group but I assumed that was only when they were in residence at their Cambridge townhouse. Anyway, it fitted in well with my schedule and I drove on towards the oak plantation to see the foresters.

Across the estate were numerous blocks of woodland which were scattered throughout the tenant farms. Although the farms were let, the woodlands remained in hand primarily for sporting reasons but also as the woods were managed for timber production. This particular woodland was a couple of miles to the west of the village which required driving down some pretty country lanes through a ford and then up along a track to one of the higher points of the estate. High in Suffolk of course is a relative term but nonetheless when I pulled up at the entrance to the wood I got out and looked around.

The view was lovely. One could see for miles across the undulating arable countryside and the gentle breeze wafted through the corn with a delightful whisper as it ruffled the crops. The tall tower of Frampton church sat proudly and squarely in the midst of the estate, not only a monument to the Christian faith but also a reminder of how the productive East Anglian soils had created wealth over the centuries.

Some of the mature oak trees in the woodland were hundreds of years old but in the main they had been planted in the late nineteenth century and our present task was to thin a selection of them to allow the rest to grow on to maturity. It was a particularly good plantation and Frampton was known for its attentive woodland management, unlike so many other woods across the county. These oak trees had long straight stems with very little epicormic growth giving them a premium value to the sawmills. Richard Watson our head forester was a man known throughout the timber world for his expertise at producing excellent timber. He was a taciturn soul, rather unkept in appearance and I suspect that in differing circumstances may well have preferred living a hermit's existence deep in the wood.

I heard the chainsaws some way ahead of me. I waited to hear a tree fall, which made a great deal of noise as it crashed through the surrounding trees and then a thud as it landed on the ground. Once the chainsaws had stopped, I shouted a good morning.

Richard Watson stood up slowly putting his chainsaw on the ground. The two men with him shouted a greeting and I clambered over the crushed undergrowth to meet them.

'Alright, Mr Aden?' he enquired.

'It's a fine day,' I replied, 'and you seem to be getting on well?'

'We've got some cracking good logs and I'd go as far to say probably some of the best we've ever have had off the estate. Beautiful these clean long stems.'

I agreed with him that these would be quite sought after. I must remember to tell Sebastian to come and have a look as he was interested in the forestry probably more than anything else on the estate.

The forwarder had already extracted and stacked considerable amounts of timber neatly arranged beside the main ride through the wood. There must have been well over a hundred tree butts.

'How much more have you got to do?' I asked.

'I reckon we're about halfway through,' Richard suggested looking at the two men.

They nodded. 'Provided this good weather holds then that would be about right,' one remarked. 'It'd be nice to get them all out while the ground's still so dry.'

I agreed. I could sense they wanted to get on with their job and left to it and taking a detour through the wood via a particularly enchanting deer lawn. Sophie and I picnicked here sometimes when we had first come to Frampton. It was a sizeable clearing in the wood which was kept roughly mown. Almost in the centre of the plantation, it had a real sense of isolation and tranquillity. To one side was a high seat, a platform about twelve feet off the ground accessed by a narrow ladder. It was used by the keepers from which to shoot deer, which although very pretty creatures to admire caused havoc to young trees and neighbouring crops. They were culled to maintain a sustainable population.

By the time I returned to the Land Rover the slow puncture had become more enthusiastic and the tyre was completely flat.

'Oh bugger, what a bloody nuisance,' I said to myself, 'I'll have to change the wheel here.'

There was short length of scaffold plank in the back of the Land Rover specifically kept for this purpose. Changing a wheel on soft ground needed some kind of surface to put the jack on otherwise it would simply bury itself into the soil. It was straightforward enough to change but inevitably by the time I'd finished my hands were covered in grease. I had to go back to the estate office to wash before nipping down to see Sebastian.

'Anne, could you just ring that tyre place in Bury and see if they've got a Land Rover tyre size 235 – 70 R 16 please. I had a puncture and if they've got one in stock, I'll get it sorted this afternoon.'

'Will do,' she said.

'Thanks, I'm just off to see Sebastian now but should be back at lunchtime.'

Sebastian was sitting in the garden when I arrived, at a large round teak table shaded by an umbrella. He looked up.

'Hello James, come and sit down,' he offered.

'Thanks,' I replied.

'How's your day going?' he enquired.

'Quite busy actually,' I said 'I've seen Ron Short up at the Hall, he hopes that his survey and report will be finished either later this week or early next week. It means I can get on with getting some prices for this upgrading work. I've also been up to the oak plantation where they're thinning and I think you'd probably enjoy going to see what they are doing. There is some very good quality timber coming out of there.'

Sebastian nodded. 'Yes, I'll go up and take a look. I might take a trip this afternoon as it's such a lovely day and a beautiful place for a walk.'

I agreed.

'I need to speak to you about a rather sensitive subject I'm afraid.'

He looked at me inquiringly.

'It's to do with your father's personal belongings. At some point you're going to need to make a decision about what to do with them. Presumably, this is something that maybe you and Serena will do. Perhaps Mr Hole could be involved?'

He sighed. 'Yes, it is something that needs doing I suppose. I've been putting it off. It's a bit emotional and it'll be difficult and in any case it's rather dull and depressing. Besides which I shall have to make all sorts of decisions about what to keep and what we do with things that we don't want. It all seems a bit of a chore.'

'I think perhaps Mr Hole might the best person to help you with things like clothes. And if you want, I'm very happy to help you go through papers in the study and that sort of thing.'

'That would make a great difference thank you. I suppose I'd better set up some times to do it. I'll start with Mr Hole and then maybe once we've done all that with the clothes and so on, you and I can sort through the study.'

'Great I will let him know that you'll be in touch so that he can put aside some time.'

In most households the closest surviving relatives would obviously have to do all this as a matter of course but it was a little different if you had loyal long serving members of staff. Hole for instance had been more than just a butler, he was really a manservant to Sir Charles and looked after his clothes, brushed his shoes, and had access to his diary for reminding his employer of engagements.

In terms of business and estate matters, even down to personal bank accounts, then as agent I was privy to most personal details. Sebastian really needed to concentrate on private correspondence between his father and his friends and family and any other issues that I had not been party to.

That was some progress, I thought, as I made my way back to the office. How quickly it would all happen goodness only knew but it was definitely in Sebastian's hands now.

'James,' Anne said as I went in the front door of the office, 'I've rung the tyre depot and they have got those tyres in stock so you can go this afternoon if you want. Apparently, they're not very busy they said.'

'Thanks, I'll just grab a sandwich for lunch then go over to Bury. Is there anything you need from there?'

'Not that I can think of,' she said. 'Only if you've got time you could go to the bank for me as we need some petty cash.'

'Okay, I'll do that if you let me have the cheque for whatever you need and I'll pick it up.'

It was only a twenty-minute drive to Bury St Edmunds but I got caught in some roadworks which considerably slowed me down. I was waiting in the queue for a frustrating ten minutes to then drive past a mile of cones with precious little going on behind them. The only apparent civil engineering work I could see was a small hole in the road about the size of a dinner plate.

Particularly irritating if one was in a hurry. Fortunately, I had no fixed appointments.

I went to the tyre depot first on the basis that if I had another puncture than I would be in trouble.

Despite them telling Anne that they weren't busy, by the time I got there inevitably I had to wait. As far as I could remember every time I had visited Tonga Tyres I had the misfortune of wasting half an hour of my life in their waiting-room. We had tried various tyre companies in the area over the years but they all seemed the same when it came to price and quality.

They also provided the same standard waiting-room for their customers. A counter covered with oil-stained pieces of paper, a wall calendar depicting impossibly attractive looking women in various poses involving a tyre, a selection of unmatched uncomfortable chairs and a coffee table strewn with well outdated copies of *What Car* magazine. This particular branch had the benefit of a coffee machine which, as I found out, gave you, for the benefit of a one-pound coin, a vile cup of dirty brown liquid. I couldn't tell whether it was coffee or the contents of the mechanics' handbasin. It tasted like the latter.

Next stop was the bank where things were much more accommodating. I managed to park right outside the door and nip in to cash the cheque. I must have missed the lunch hour rush as there was nobody else in there. Having had the good fortune to park so centrally I decided to stroll along to the bookshop and look for a couple of new books. There was nothing more relaxing than being able to read for half an hour in the evening before turning off the lights.

My mission is accomplished I set off back to Frampton taking an alternative route home to avoid the roadworks. The way took me through some beautiful Suffolk countryside and two of its many pretty villages. The first I came to was Cavendish which like Frampton boasted another stately wool church and a delightful village green with many fine timbered cottages built around the perimeter. Following the road towards Frampton I then passed through Long Melford, a somewhat larger village than Cavendish but nonetheless as striking. It had an even more impressive church, a huge green and a substantial country house which was the seat of a family that owned the estate bordering Frampton. The historical interest and importance of the area was unselfconsciously never far away and wherever one looked there was a continuity to it. To be working as part of the evolving history through the means of managing one of the greatest estates was a privilege.

CHAPTER 7

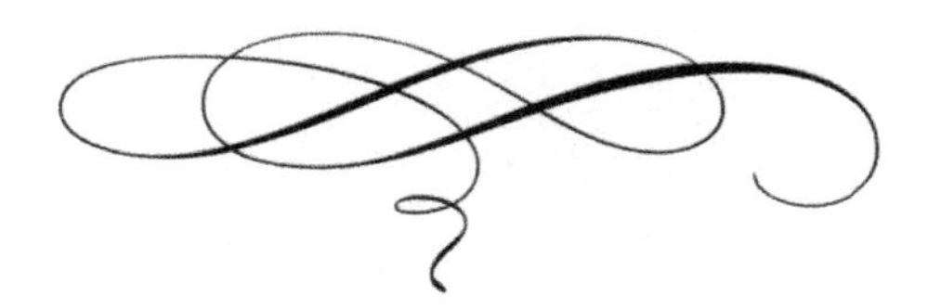

I did not usually go into the estate office on Saturdays as we had enough to do on the farm but on this particular Saturday I had to go to the bakers as we had run out of bread. Being practically next door and having my office key with me, I went in to check the post. Most of the letters were regular mundane missives and to be expected but one particularly luxurious white envelope caught my attention. It was addressed to the estate of Sir Charles Buckley Bt. and looked as though it contained a smart invitation. I opened it. It was an invitation from the senior steward of the Jockey Club to attend a dinner which was being held in order to raise money for the Injured Jockey's Fund. I would ask Sebastian if he and Serena wanted to go but I thought it was highly unlikely as they had no interest whatsoever in horses or horseracing. If they didn't want to go then perhaps Sophie and I could, representing the estate.

As I drove back to Cordwainers Hall I reflected on the situation with regard to Sir Charles' racehorses. With everything else to do we had not paid much attention to their future. There was a stud on the estate situated just beyond Frampton Hall where Sir Charles had taken a keen involvement in breeding racehorses. He also had four horses in training at a yard in Newmarket. In the scheme of all the things that needed to be done the horses were a fairly low priority and besides, I personally liked seeing them around. But this invitation reminded me that we would need to make some changes, probably rather difficult ones, as Sebastian would want to sell them.

I knew a little but not a lot about racing but I imagined that the trainer would be willing to help find a way forward. The horses in training would be easy enough to deal with I expected as they could be sold easily but dismantling the stud would be more complicated and rather sad. Apart from seeing all the horses go it would make the stud groom and the two stable lads redundant. It was another item to put on the list to discuss with Sebastian next week.

We were collecting a second crop of hay at home which had already been bailed and needed picking up and stacking in the barn. We still used the small bales which suited our farming system and over the years we had perfected our routine. Sophie would drive the tractor and I would stand on the trailer and stack the bales whilst the two Flatt brothers passed them up with pitchforks. Our farm machinery was basic, primarily because it was a grassland farm and relatively modest in size. We relied on a Massey Ferguson 165 and couple of Masseys 135s. The trailer was a four wheeled one rather like the back of an articulated lorry and pulled by our biggest tractor the 165. The baler had a sledge behind it which left the bales in groups of eight enabling Sophie to drive from batch to batch whereupon the Flatt brothers would pass them up to me to carefully stack. As the stack grew the more effort was needed for the men to pass the bales up and we usually managed to get ten layers high before it became too difficult.

Although it was the most satisfying of tasks especially in pleasant weather, it could never be described as jovial. Sophie was in the tractor so couldn't really hear what was going on apart from shouting when we were ready to move to the next batch of bales and the Flatt brothers liked to work in silence with the occasional grunt or fart. I was able to decipher some of the grunting but usually it was more a case of guesswork. Nonetheless it was fulfilling to see the harvest, as it were, being gathered and safely stored in the barn. This later crop did not have quite the same delightful scent as the first crop that we cut in late May nor was it of the same quality but it was certainly worth making especially if we suffered a particularly long cold or wet winter.

We completed two loads and then stopped for some cheese and pickle sandwiches that Sophie had made with the delicious fresh bread that I had collected earlier from the bakers. Even in the more relaxed setting the Flatt brothers still said nothing but I presumed that they listened to whatever Sophie and I were talking about. I did wonder what made them tick. They had lived on the farm all their lives and worked for Sophie's uncle before we moved there. Their parents had worked for Sophie's grandfather so there was a long connection but one that would cease when they retired as they were both bachelors.

Once the third load was stored, we called it a day. Sophie and I wanted to spend some time with Emma and the Flatt brothers went off to look at the sheep. At this time of year one or both of the brothers would go around all the sheep to check that they were in good health. Occasionally there would be some matter to attend to such as a lame sheep or more unpleasantly a lamb with fly strike. Probably the most unpleasant job on the farm was dealing with a lamb with fly, where eggs had been laid in the wool, especially mucky wool, and the maggots hatch and start to eat the flesh of the animal. This all had to be cleaned and cut away so that the area could be treated. Any sign of fly strike had to be acted upon promptly as the maggots would spread quickly and cause severe damage. We tried to prevent such outbreaks by keeping the sheep and particularly the lambs as clean as possible and also by dipping or spraying with chemicals that repelled the flies.

Apart from those two common illnesses checking the sheep was merely a matter of driving around in the Land Rover making sure they seemed alright. Usually some had escaped or were stuck in a fence, because no matter how well fenced the fields, sheep seemed to have a knack for finding their way out. Even if they were perfectly happy and had plenty of grass, for some reason they needed to make an attempt at freedom. Or perhaps it was simply that the grass was always greener on the other side of the fence.

On Monday morning I had arranged to see one of the tenant farmers. We felt we had a lovely and privileged life the way we lived at Cordwainers but in relation to the Buckley's it would have been considered quite modest. Put either of those into the context of Joe Harrison and it took on a different slant.

He had asked me to go and inspect his windows as allegedly the frames were so rotten that they were in danger of falling out altogether. Anne had duly made an appointment.

Joe was a bit of an oddity in almost every way one could imagine. For a start he was an agricultural tenant who had gradually given up his land year by year until he was left with his present farmhouse, yard and about ten acres. In all honesty we would have preferred him to give up the lot but he had security of tenure. Joe was a nice enough sort of chap, in his early sixties and divorced with no apparent children. If you went into his house you could see why. He always looked in remarkably good health and was a skinny active man.

One activity that he clearly did not engage in was house work. The kitchen and particularly the floor were so dirty and disgusting that I felt I needed to change my shoes at the door and put wellies on before going inside. It was marginally less dramatic if the weather was dry but it's the only house I had been in where the occupant would throw the butt of his cigarette on the floor and stub it out. What's more, he left them there. It was littered with them.

A number of cats inhabited the work surfaces which I supposed was better than the alternative which would be rats, and two or three old dogs resided under the table and were chewing some bones when I arrived.

I knocked on the door.

'Come in Mr Aden,' he shouted.

I entered and purely by habit wiped my feet on what looked like a doormat before realising that that was of course a waste of time. If anything, matters deteriorated and I swear that I saw two rashes of dried-up bacon and a slice of toast lurking on the kitchen table covered in a green tinge.

'Like a cup of tea Mr Aden?' he asked.

Being forewarned therefore forearmed I was ready with 'that's very kind of you Joe but I've just had one before I left the office thank you.

One would need to develop a constitution of some magnitude to cope with eating or drinking anything in his house and I suspect it may take several years of acclimatisation. I certainly did not want to take the first step on that journey.

'Let's have a look at these windows,' I suggested, 'and if they're as bad as you say then I'll get someone out to measure up.'

We went outside and I produced a penknife from my pocket, opened the blade and slid it into the joints of the window frames. They were indeed mostly rotten and must have been for some time. As landlords we were responsible for such repairs and despite the state of the interior there was no reason why we should not replace them. It was particularly frustrating because Joe Harrison's holding, being occupied on an old type of tenancy, had a rent that was based on the acreage rather than the value of the house. The result was that he paid about a thousand pounds a year when a house of that size in good condition in the village would have fetched five or six thousand pounds without the land.

Every time we did something for Joe, I tried to get him to improve something from his side of the bargain.

'Joe, I have to agree the windows are in a state so I'll get someone out to measure up.'

'Thank you, Mr Aden,' he said, 'you know I don't like to trouble you too much but I think they've really gone past it now.'

'I agree, that's fine, we will do it. Let's do a deal, as we will sort out the windows for you, do you think you might make a start on tidying up your yard?'

Much to my regret as agent, Joe Harrison's farmyard was on the side of the public highway through the estate and was clearly visible to passers-by. It did not reflect well on us but we were unable to do much about it. The house looked half decent from outside and so did the traditional brick and timber loose boxes beside it. There was also a large open fronted cattle barn which had been erected by the estate in the early nineteen seventies and that was in passable condition. The issue arose that since then Joe had embarked on a series of building projects which he erroneously described as tenants' improvements but in both legal terms and in common usage of the English language could never have been described as improvements.

His main building components were corrugated iron sheets which appeared to be somewhat randomly attached to old telegraph poles further adorned with old plastic fertiliser sacks of different colours and several miles of baler twine. If it was either windy or raining or worse, both, then the din of all this stuff being shifted by the wind and battered by the rain was abysmal.

'Do you really need all these old tin sheds?' I asked.

'Oh yes Mr Aden,' he confirmed, 'they're me livelihood.'

'But what do you keep in them?' I asked.

'There's all sorts of things. Some are used for keeping the cars in, some are used for cattle, another one has often got machines stored. There's hardly any spare space here,' he assured me.

'Well what about all this stuff lying around the yard? Looks like it's just rubbish – plastic bags, old tyres, bits of scrap metal.' There were even a couple of old tractors and a car which could never possibly work again.

'Well some of it's a bit of rubbish,' he agreed, 'some of the bits I like to keep for parts.'

'Parts!' I exclaimed. 'What on earth would you get off those things that could possibly be of any use to anyone let alone you?'

'That's where you're wrong Mr Aden,' he continued. 'I've often found a little bit of a mechanical thing I can take off one of those tractors. That one's still running,' he explained pointing at a rust-coloured pile of metal which had a couple of wheels hanging off it.

It was a pretty useless expectation to be honest, but I had to have a try. Nothing had changed since I had been on the estate and I don't suppose it ever would. I just felt I couldn't let it go unnoticed when I had the occasional foray there to attend to some repair work. I couldn't help myself raising the issue.

I drove back to the village and into the office.

'James, Sebastian's been on the phone,' Anne warned me as I entered.

'Oh, right any idea what he wanted?'

'No, I didn't quite get what he said but seemed to be something to do with his father's trousers.' She looked at me quizzically.

'Perhaps he's been speaking to Mr Hole about what to do with Sir Charles' clothes,' I explained.

She laughed. 'Who knows in this place.'

I rang Sebastian who had, apparently, just finished his Monday morning yoga class.

'Are you passing by James?' he asked which effectively meant could I call in.

'Yes of course,' I said, 'what time suits you and I'll drop by on my way up to the Hall. I have got a couple of other things that I need to ask you about if you don't mind?'

We settled on two o'clock as it gave us both a clear hour should discussions take that long.

Discussions in fact took considerably longer and even then, we didn't finish them. Sebastian had wanted to talk about which charity shops they should send his father's decent clothes to which then led to a discussion on his father's patronages. Sir Charles had supported various charities and sat on a lot of committees, most of which had been in touch with me to enquire as to whether Sir Sebastian would be willing to stand in his father's footsteps. Sebastian and I got around to talk about some of them making a few decisions as to yes or no, mostly no, but really we needed to conclude the subject. There had even been one or two that when Sebastian had declined the invitation had been re-offered to me as a representative of the estate.

There were a wide range of subjects covered in such charitable interests. Lots of course were to do with the immediate vicinity of the village and Sebastian has agreed to take on all of those, such as chairman of the parish council, the chairman of the village hall committee, member of the parochial church council, the Frampton

Art Society, the Frampton fete, and patron of the Frampton tennis club. There were endless requests but in the main quite un-demanding, only really requiring his name on the notepaper rather than much active engagement. Sir Charles had his favourites and put more effort into some than others. The ones further afield were more to do with Sir Charles' interests rather than what might be considered his responsibilities and would probably fall by the wayside. He had several positions to do with horseracing and had at one-time been a steward of Huntington racecourse, was a past president of the Eastern Shires Agricultural Association, sat on the committee of the Historic Houses Association and had been an honorary member of the Standard Poodle Club of Great Britain. There were many others, some of which were only just appearing out of the woodwork.

It was to be expected that Sir Sebastian would only take up the mantle of those positions if the cause interested him. He didn't for instance have the slightest interest in standard poodles and hadn't even offered to take Monty and Napoleon when his father died. Highly unlikely that he'd sit on some committee that dedicated itself to the well-being of the breed. Likewise, anything to do with horses was out and he was cautious about getting involved with the Historic Houses Association as his attitude to historic houses was somewhat removed from passionate.

I broached the matter of the racehorses, only suggesting that I should speak to the trainer in Newmarket to obtain some initial advice. Sebastian heartily agreed. By the end of the meeting which had gone on longer than either of us intended, I think the only decisive action agreed was what to do with Sir Charles' old trousers.

CHAPTER 8

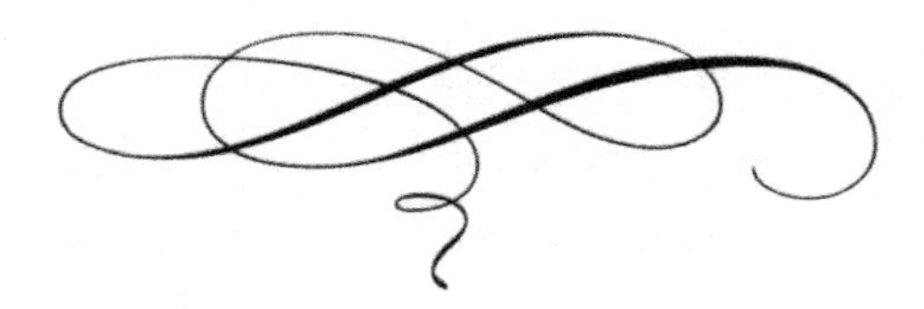

As well as Anne there were two other staff in the estate office. Gail and Brenda. Gail was in her early forties and dressed as she as if she was in her early twenties. She was an assistant to both Anne and to some extent to Brenda who did the accounts. Gail was a bit flighty and her main interest outside work appeared to be having her clothes removed. She was good at her job and, by all accounts, having her clothes removed. It was because of her that our previous vicar the Reverend Sidebottom had served less than two years in the parish before the scandal broke.

All Saints, Frampton had a particularly comfortable vestry which for some reason benefited from a somewhat unsteady Victorian chaise-longue. This particular piece of furniture became crucial evidence closing the Rev Sidebottom's tenure at Frampton. Although details were never made clear the gist of Mrs Sidebottom's version was that Gail was doing what she did best and more besides with the Reverend on the chaise-longue in the vestry. At the time I remember thinking it sounded more like a game of Cluedo than the misgivings of a parish priest. During some activity in the vestry one of the legs on the chaise-longue snapped off and one can only assume the scenario, but the Reverend Sidebottom broke his arm and due to the pain was unable to get his cassock back on. An ambulance was called and Mrs Sidebottom managed to add two plus two and got four which brought about the demise of our vicar.

It was extremely annoying for us because it brought the scandal into the heart of the office. Gail was very tight-lipped about the matter and appeared to rise above the tittle tattle in the village. It was not a novel experience for her in any case and unfortunately, I think that Mr Sidebottom had been lured rather than the other way round.

I had been reminded of this incident when I walked into the office that morning as Gail was sporting an outfit which exposed her bare midriff and a pierced belly button. Additionally there was an adornment of a tattooed snake appearing to encircle the piercing. It was not really what would be deemed suitable estate office wear even though it was a warm day. On the positive side I had been assured by some of the younger tenants that like the scion drawing the sailors onto the rocks, they were apt to pay their rent promptly by coming into the office to get a glance.

Brenda was more composed and balanced the office dynamics as well as the accounts. Although she resembled an energetic spaniel, by nature she was rather sedate.

The estate office was always busy because there was such lot going on over the whole estate at any one time. In addition, we had some of the estate management responsibilities for the Buckley's estate in the Scottish Highlands. The Strathard Estate north of Inverness. It extended to 40,000 acres making it four times the size of Frampton but considered relatively modest in terms of Scottish Highland estates. It was large enough to warrant a resident factor, as they refer to land agents in Scotland although most of the accounts and procedural matters were dealt with in Frampton. Angus McKay was the factor and I worked closely with him giving me a particular benefit of being able to hold some meetings up at Strathard.

In addition to the usual business we were involved in winding up the late baronet's affairs and preparing for the future.

We had a further piece of work at the time, which was to sell Moss Farm, an outlying smallholding separated from the majority of the estate by the main road. The tenant, one of the oldest at eighty-five had resisted leaving the farm where he had been born. It was in a terribly sorry state but Albert White was a dogmatic old man who was always in the right and would never change his ways nor accept other people's opinions. Notwithstanding that, he was a lovely man to visit not least because he had interesting stories to tell from years gone by.

It was one of the last houses on the estate not to have any mains water or sewerage systems. The lavatory was of the bucket and chuck it variety, housed in a small redbrick outbuilding behind the house, the tap in the kitchen was a hand pump that drew water from a well underneath the brick floor of the kitchen into a stone sink, which was in itself large enough to also serve as a small bath. Which it did.

Modernisation had been offered many times in the past but it was always politely declined on the basis that he had got this far without it so thought there was no need for a change or the disruption.

It had been painful to see him struggle during the last few years, especially in the winter, with his seventy acres and small herd of suckler cows. He did have some help as he was simply too old and frail undertake all the jobs especially when dealing with strong healthy cattle. The farm was antiquated and even the machinery was of a bygone era although surprisingly it still worked. Everything was meticulously tidy and one could sense that Albert maintained his pride.

Eventually he succumbed and his niece persuaded him to move into a care home in Bury St Edmunds as he became unable to look after himself. I visited him there shortly after his arrival and he was visibly distressed at having been removed from his family home.

Some months later I returned as I needed to ask some questions about the property, few records of which we could find to help us in preparing the details for the forthcoming sale. Much to my surprise Albert seemed much more alert and happier. He told me that he wished he'd moved into the nursing home years before as he'd now experienced the comforts of modern living and in particular did not have to go out into the garden to use the loo.

Gail had taken on the responsibility of getting the details together for the sale of Albert White's farm. It was very rare for the estate to sell any property but we had a large tax bill to face for death duties and the farm, being dilapidated, needed a lot of money spending on it so it seemed a sensible choice. Gail, for all her faults, was a very gregarious and engaging person and an ideal person to get the property on the market and drum up some enthusiasm from potential purchasers.

We had sought the services of a local estate agent, Crockett and Co. who would market the property on their website for a small fee, although we would prepare the sales particulars and show people around the property. Damien Crockett was well-known in the area for his ability to negotiate sales and I suspect that he and Gail got on like two peas in a pod. He certainly had a lot to say for himself which was helpful if you were in the marketing world. He dressed in a shiny suit and rather pointed shoes and looked totally out of place when he came to look around the farm. Gail assured me that despite this he had taken great interest in the property and she had no reservations about him doing an excellent job for us.

Gail had also offered to sit on the fete committee representing the estate and reporting back to Sebastian and myself when needed. She was probably not the best candidate for the job as although most of the men on the committee of a certain age enjoyed her presence her reputation made some of the wives a little wary. On the plus side she did know practically everybody in the village and was very adept at persuading people to take part or offer raffle prizes. The committee chairman, Mr Partridge, I knew quite well as he kept a few sheep in the churchyard. They ate the grass saving the expense of a lawnmower which had always appealed to Sir Charles. If he needed any help with his sheep then he tended to engage my assistance which was inevitably a frustrating business. He embarked upon projects with great energy but little knowledge with resulting chaos. Many times I had chased his four pet sheep through the village as he failed to secure the boot of his car when moving them from field to churchyard.

As the committee chairman though he did a brilliant job and he rushed about the place with great importance and fluster encouraging people to do things. He earned his living as a building society manager in Bury St Edmunds but lived in the village and was involved in several of the community groups. His delegation skills were exceptional and consequently his chairmanship succeeded. Between him and Gail they energised what appeared to be at least half the village inhabitants into taking part in some way or another. The proceeds of the fete would be shared by two worthy causes one being All Saints, Frampton and the other being the Alms House charity in the village, the Lamplight Close Trust.

One of Gail's inspirational ideas, and something which had not been tried before at the village fete, was to hold an auction of promises. They included all kinds of offers from the promise of half a day's gardening to valeting a car, a day's fishing on the nearby lake and somewhat unusually half a tonne of farmyard manure. With

Sebastian's approval the estate offered a week's holiday at Strathard in Scotland. Rumours that Gail had offered an evening of her company were I think unfounded and certainly didn't appear on the auction list on the day.

I had been discussing the latest with Gail in the office when Anne had phoned through.

'James, it's Angus McKay on the telephone from Strathard,' she said.

'Hello, Angus,' I said, 'how are you up there?'

'Well we're quite gud,' he replied in his Highland lilt. 'So far the summer's been kind to us.'

'Excellent and I'm glad,' I said, 'it's a wonderful place to be during a good summer.'

'You'll have to come up laddie, and that's why I am ringing really. There are a few things I'd like to go through with you and it may be better face-to-face.'

'I'm always happy to make the trip up north,' I confirmed. 'Especially if it can be tied in with a bit of fishing,' I laughed.

'There is no problem there as you know,' he chuckled.

'That's kind of you Angus, we will have to look at diaries. What are the things on your mind?'

'It's really to understand what Sir Sebastian wants to do with the estate in a general sort of way,' he explained, 'and that relates to my second point which is that a piece of fishing is for sale, the stretch on the river that we do not own and I think this is a rare opportunity to acquire it.'

'That sounds very interesting,' I said, 'whereabouts is it?'

'It's the lower beat between Anshabeen and Meig,' he explained.

I knew roughly where he meant but I would have to look on the map to be precise, or better still walk it with him.

'Let's fix a date,' I said reaching from my diary. 'And if there are any other things then let me know so that I can be prepared if necessary.'

'Well the third thing we need to consider is the Lodge, as I think there will be some quite substantial repairs needed to the roof. Again, you can look at that when you come up.'

I provisionally organised a date with him but as I guessed that Sophie would also like to accompany me wanted to check with her. Likewise, it was courteous to also check that Sebastian had no plans to visit.

That was something to look forward to I thought, provided the plans fell into place. The plans did fall into place and in fact we had to go sooner than expected. Angus McKay had rung again to say that somebody else was interested in the fishing and although the vendor had offered us first refusal, he wanted a decision sooner rather than later.

I went to see Sebastian about it.

'I realise that this isn't the ideal timing,' I admitted to him, 'but I suspect this is a once-in-a-lifetime opportunity to acquire these fishing rights.'

'Yes,' he said, 'it's not ideal but I can see the logic.' Sebastian knew the Strathard estate surprisingly well and the exact stretch that was involved.

'In fact, it's always seemed a shame not to have the fishing on that piece of water,' he said, 'it's such a beautiful part of the estate and that length of the glen is beautifully wild and remote.'

Although Sebastian never said so, I had a strong suspicion that he felt more passionate about Strathard than he did Frampton.

Frampton of course was the ancestral home and provided the money generating asset behind the family's wealth. Strathard on the other hand was a much later acquisition. The Buckley family had purchased it in the late eighteen hundreds as a sporting estate which was a common activity by wealthy English families at that time. Strathard soaked up money like a sponge and needed Frampton income to support it but from Sebastian's point of view I could see that he loved the remoteness and it would appeal to his sense of tranquillity and isolation. He usually managed to spend a month a year up there and although he wasn't particularly interested in sporting, he did enjoy the occasional foray out onto the riverbank.

'If we can afford it and the price is right then I think you and Mr McKay should see if we can get it,' he said. 'Apart from anything else it means that we wouldn't have strangers visiting that part of the estate.'

I agreed that we would see what we could do. Acquiring the fishing would reduce the number of visitors although anyone could walk anywhere on the estate under the right to roam laws in Scotland.

The following week Sophie, Emma and I drove north in Sophie's Audi estate car. When we were visiting purely for a couple of days then we tended to fly to Inverness but we had planned to make a short holiday of it. As well as dealing with any business at Strathard we would then head out to the West Coast. The car seemed easier and less expensive than flying and then renting at the airport.

It was a long drive and by preference we like to leave at sparrow's fart and stop for a decent breakfast somewhere up in Cumbria. Pre-Emma days we would make the hike in one go but it was unfair to expect her to sit in a car for over twelve hours. We stopped overnight in Stirling before continuing at a more leisurely pace for the final three or four hours towards Inverness. The House of Bruar was a welcome diversion for coffee and a browse through their shops and a chance to be relieved of considerable amounts of cash in a remarkably short time.

In consolation though they probably had the best public lavatories along the hundred and ten mile stretch between Perth and Inverness.

It was a joy driving to Scotland as the scenery improved the further we travelled. As we headed north the gentle landscape of Perthshire pastures and wide meandering rivers became more rugged as it merged into the Cairngorm Mountains. Once over the high pass at Slochd summit the road started to descend towards the Moray Firth revealing one of the finest views in Scotland. The first glimpses of the Northwest Highlands in the distance.

Once over the Kessock Bridge and onto the Black Isle we were on the last leg of the journey taking us deep into the North Western Highlands.

Strathard estate was in Sutherland and was typical of what had originally been built as a Victorian sporting lodge for the gentry. Little had changed over the years for some very obvious reasons. Because the countryside was sparsely populated it was an unspoilt natural landscape with a few areas of forest planting. The cottages tended to be croft houses which although ravaged by the Highland clearances in the nineteenth century now provided housing for people that worked on or near the estate. The house itself, Strathard Lodge, although unchanged in appearance since being built was surprisingly comfortable inside and a great deal more so than Frampton Hall.

There was a decent heating system which had been installed by Sir Charles. He was fond of hind stalking during the winter and liked to spend New Year in the Highlands. As his visits coincided with the worst of the weather, he had taken the unusual step of spending some money to keep warm. The wiring was better than Frampton because twenty years previously there had been a fire caused by some faulty electrics. Whilst the damage was limited, rewiring was forced upon him by the insurance company and the Highlands and Islands Fire Brigade. The effectiveness of the fire brigade was modest so avoiding a fire in the first place was paramount.

The Highlands and Islands Fire Brigade in Strathard consisted of two part-time firemen, who were employed by the estate as farm workers, and a water bowser attached to which was a hose and pump. Housed in a shed on the way up the glen in a rather remote woodyard it would not have been particularly rapid in its response. In all probability I expect the insurance company carried more weight with regard to the insistence of a new electricity supply.

The final half-hour of the drive was undoubtedly the most spectacular. Once we left the main road north of Inverness, we took a single-track road which headed towards the west coast but came to a dead end at Strathard Lodge. The road followed the river closely along the bottom of the glen and occasionally climbed where waterfalls indicated a change in height of the valley floor. This lower part of the glen was quite open with lush green fields either side of the river but the steep rocky mountains were ever visible in the background. We were driving through the neighbouring estate of Strathbeck which was owned by another English aristocrat, similarly acquired in the late eighteen hundreds. This estate was softer than Strathard and it wasn't until we passed the hydroelectric dam on Loch Ard that we arrived on estate grounds.

Almost at once the scenery changed and the lush green meadows by the river gave way to rough grazing and rock faces. The weather was beautifully warm and the clear light illuminated the landscape with absolute clarity. We followed the loch side until we re-joined the river that fed into it and up the glen towards the village of Strathard. It was really more a cluster of houses than a village although it did have a sparsely used church and a primary school. The entire village was owned by the estate although most houses were rented out as the estate staff had dwindled in number over the years.

CHAPTER 9

The road carried on through some dramatic mountain scenery as we continued further back into the mountains. At times the road hung to cliff edges with sheer drops down to the river. Occasionally red deer could be spotted on the distant slopes. It was above all a stalking estate. Finally, the lodge came into view, a typical Victorian building embellished by several round turrets with conical roofs. It lay in isolated splendour on the far shore of yet another loch, this time a natural loch reportedly one of the deepest in Scotland. We finally bumped over the last cattle grid onto the gravelled drive between the sweeping lawns and rhododendrons to draw up outside the front door.

We were not expecting to see Angus McKay until the morning. The housekeeper was expecting us.

'How lovely to see you,' greeted Mrs McLeod.

'And you too, Mrs McLeod. It's great to be here again and in such glorious summer weather.'

'It's been very kind for several weeks now,' she said, 'but come away in and let's get away from these midges.'

That was the single drawback to being in the Highlands in summer. A beautiful evening could be ruined by clouds of midges who within a few seconds would be in your ears, up your nose and plastered all over any exposed skin.

We were ushered inside and shown to our rooms which we had stayed in often before. Our master suite had a connecting door into a small bedroom where Emma could sleep. Mrs McLeod had kindly prepared a dinner for us which was equal to that of any fine restaurant in the Highlands. Scottish smoked salmon followed by venison cutlets and Scottish shortbread with ice cream. It was an entirely appropriate meal for the setting.

'This is absolutely delicious,' Sophie said and I agreed. 'You shouldn't have gone to so much trouble although we are delighted!'

Sophie continued, 'We are perfectly happy to clear up and put everything in the dishwasher so please Mrs McLeod don't feel you need to stay. We can see you in the morning.'

'Och well,' she replied, 'if you're both very sure then I'll do just that. I've some scones to bake for the sale of works in the village hall at the weekend. You know where everything is so help yourself to whatever you want and I'll see you in the morning for breakfast. And would you like breakfast at about eight o'clock?'

'That would be perfect thank you,' I replied.

'I'll see you then. Have a lovely evening.'

Mrs McLeod lived in the lodge cottage further down the drive so we had the whole house to ourselves. Although it was nowhere near as big as Frampton Hall it was still sizeable but more homely. It had eight bedrooms and various reception rooms including a lovely oak panelled study or smoking room as Sir Charles called it, a large drawing room, a billiards room and a more intimate sitting room which is where we settled for the evening. Emma was tired after the journey and was perfectly happy to watch some children's television while Sophie and I made some plans for the rest of the week.

We would stay at Strathard for two days and attend to estate matters with Angus and hopefully get a bit of fishing in whilst we were there. After that we would head to Ullapool and take the ferry out to Stornoway and explore the islands of Lewis and Harris having booked a holiday cottage about ten miles out of Stornoway.

As instructed, we helped ourselves to a glass or two of Glenard malt whisky which was distilled in the local town equidistant from Inverness and Strathard, savouring the peaty flavour which somehow always tasted better in Scotland than anywhere else.

After the most restful night's sleep we were duly down in time for breakfast which was as to be expected at the lodge an elaborate cooked affair with an inordinate amount of choice. Despite there only being the three of us Mrs McLeod had organised the selection in heated silver dishes covered with domed tops along the Georgian mahogany sideboard and it felt very much as if we were staying in an upmarket hotel. Shortly after breakfast Angus McKay arrived and came into the dining room.

'Hello, hello, how good to see you both,' he said to Sophie and myself. 'I can see you bought the wee bairn with you. Well how delightful.'

'Yes, how lovely to see you as well,' we answered in unison. We had spent many times at Strathard since working for Sir Charles and had grown to know and like Angus. He had a reserved, slightly distant courteous Highland manner but once you got to know him, he was affectionate, charming and witty.

'I'm hoping that you might teach her to cast a fly.' I laughed knowing that Angus was an expert salmon fisherman and probably as good as any ghillie on the rivers thereabouts.

'Of course, we'll have a go. There's no point you coming all your way up here unless you're going to put a fly on the water. Business is business but we all need a bit of pleasure.'

We all laughed.

Emma was looking at Angus. She would not have remembered him from our previous visit.

'Why is that man wearing a skirt?' she asked looking slightly perplexed.

Mrs McLeod entered the dining room at that point and there were great guffaws of laughter.

'Why is everyone laughing?' Emma enquired.

'Well,' said Mrs McLeod, 'it's a thing that men do in Scotland. Men wear skirts but they don't call them skirts. In fact, they'd be very cross if you do. They're called kilts.'

Emma didn't look particularly impressed but had the grace to say, 'it's a very pretty pattern.'

His kilt was blue with red stripes and he explained that it originated as the McKay tartan from Strathnaver although I don't think Emma was overly concerned as to its origin.

'Well you are looking in very fine form, Angus,' I said, 'it's lovely to be here again. And looking forward to having a look at the river later on. What have you in mind – shall we attend to some of the business matters this morning and then go down to the river?'

'Aye let's do the business work first and then take a wee trip out. I've had a word with the vendor of the fishing rights and he said we could try it out for ourselves. We need to get a few salmon out of it to make sure it's worth the money.'

We laughed. 'Fantastic. We brought our rods but I'm not sure that we've got the necessary flies,' I mentioned.

'Och no matter, there's plenty here. We'll have a look in the rod room and see what we need before we set out.'

I left Sophie and Emma to finish their breakfast and occupy

themselves for a couple of hours while Angus and I went down to the estate office. It was a small building which presumably once housed a range of stables that had been converted into the office located about half a mile from the lodge. The steading in which it stood also comprised of the deer larder, where the carcasses were brought in to butcher, a barn where the Argocats and various bits of machinery were stored and a cottage where a ghillie lived.

We looked through the various quotes for the reroofing of the lodge that needed imminent attention and I confirmed that I had previously obtained Sebastian's go ahead with the works. Sebastian appeared surprisingly relaxed about spending money at Strathard. We then got down to discussing the possible purchase of the fishing. In Scotland it was possible to own the land through which the river flowed, including the trout fishing, separate to another person owning the salmon fishing. The salmon fishing on a good river, was usually worth more than the river itself but clearly it was better to own both.

'Sebastian has agreed to buying the salmon fishing provided that it was a reasonable price,' I explained to Angus, 'as you know he is very fond of Strathard and enjoys spending time here. I think he would also like to limit as much as possible the public access to the estate so that is a contributory factor.'

'Well that's good to know,' said Angus, 'and although we get plenty of hikers, they seem not that problematic. They tend to go for the Munroes slightly to our western boundary.'

I agreed. Whenever I was at Strathard I very rarely came across anybody else unless they worked for the estate. To secure this purchase would not only be a wise financial move but also provide some extra decent fishing. Whilst the stalking was the biggest attraction on the estate having some salmon fishing was huge bonus.

There was plenty of trout fishing available in the river and in the lochs and more so in the dozens of lochans up in the hills, but they were not really of any financial benefit.

We dealt with the less exciting estate matters during the morning in the office and then after bite of lunch Sophie, Emma and I climbed in the Land Rover beside Angus. Our route took us back down the glen road past the loch for three miles and then we left the paved road and turned down a track. The first mile or so were relatively straightforward but we began to climb higher back into the mountains to a pass that lead us into the next glen. The going got steeper and rougher the higher we drove and at times the Land Rover seemed to scramble to keep a grip on the surface. The views were breathtaking. At the top of the pass one could see mile after mile of emptiness. We paused at the highest point and climbed out of the vehicle.

'I never tire of this view,' Angus sighed looking around him.

We agreed. There was a faint breeze mercifully keeping the midges away. It whispered softly through the heather and rough grasses and as always in the mountains the faint sound of water tumbling down the rocky burns. We had the good fortune to hear the mewing of a pair of golden eagles circling over an impenetrable rocky outcrop.

Resuming our journey, we continued down into the next glen. It was as near as remote as anywhere one could get in the Highlands. This glen was softer than Strathard, the valley floor was wider, grassy and it seemed the hills were of a gentler sweep before the land rose in height to the peaks. This was the stretch of glen that we had come to fish. The river meandered majestically like a silver ribbon along its length. Occasional rapids and deep pools made this some of the best salmon fishing in the region. Angus had selected some rods and flies from the lodge and he was kindly acting as ghillie for the two of us.

He had brought fourteen-foot Spey rods and was adamant that his chosen flies, the Munro's Killer, a Willie Gunn and the Silver Stoat were just the job for the business. He drove as far as he could and then we abandoned the Land Rover and proceeded on foot carrying our gear for about half a mile downstream to his first choice of pool.

One of my friends who had an impatient nature the best of times could never understand anybody's passion for fishing. 'Why,' he said, 'would anyone want to put on a pair of large rubber boots and stand in a river for hours on end waving your arms.' For those people that have a passion for fishing it is not just the thrill of trying to land a fish but it is also the opportunity to study the water carefully, the insect life and with luck your prey. It was also about being in some of the most beautiful undisturbed countryside that few people would ever experience.

Our afternoon was filled with adventure and although I had no luck Sophie was able to get a fish on the fly though disappointingly was not only able to land it. Emma was taught the rudimentary skill of casting but soon tired of it and went to search for pretty stones on the riverbank. At least we had tested the purchase before we bought it on behalf of the estate.

Angus joined us for dinner that evening and Mrs McLeod put on another feast with fresh crab starter followed by a rib of beef and raspberry pavlova for pudding.

'We certainly live like the laird when we stay here,' I remarked. 'Thank you both so much for entertaining and looking after us as usual. It has been an absolute delight.'

Sophie agreed.

'Aye we enjoy having you here,' said Angus, 'it's good to have the chance to share some professional thoughts and ideas. It's a very insular job being a factor on this remote Highland estate.'

'I am sure it is,' I said. 'In some ways I would love it, in others I think I might find the remoteness too much. And of course, it hardly gets light in the winter. You probably have to be born here to accept it.'

'It's alright,' said Mrs McLeod. 'We all get along and make our own community though it can be a bit bleak especially in the winter as you say. But I wouldn't swap it for anywhere in the world.'

'It certainly does have its charms,' I agreed, 'and I expect we will see some more beautiful landscapes when we get over to the Hebrides tomorrow evening.'

We did indeed discover a completely new aspect of the Scottish Highlands and Islands over the following few days. What was especially striking were the miles of empty sandy beaches on the Islands. They were a paradise under brilliant blue sky and gentle seas that rolled onto the shores. We were lucky that we had chanced upon some unusually warm weather as for most of the year although still beautiful, those Islands lying out in the Atlantic Ocean would be anything but gentle.

CHAPTER 10

Things were anything but calm when we arrived home. We had only been away six days but in that time all sorts of things had happened.

First of all, there was a letter from the racehorse trainer in Newmarket setting out some thoughts on what we might do with Sir Charles' horses. He indicated that he probably knew some people who would be interested in them and suggested we should get together to discuss.

The first quotation for rewiring the Hall had arrived and one certainly was wise to sit down before reading it. It was an astronomical amount of money at just over one and a third million pounds. We hadn't yet had any prices for the re-plumbing and heating system so I hoped that those horses might be valuable enough to cover some of the costs.

There was an agenda for a forthcoming meeting that I needed to attend on behalf of the estate in Manchester. Sir Charles' passion for forestry had led to his membership of a committee that advised the government on community tree planting. Effectively they planted new woodlands on old derelict industrial land around cities such as London, Liverpool and Manchester. Sir Charles' involvement was with the Manchester area and I had been asked to sit in his place following his death. I would have to travel up the night before as the meeting began at nine o'clock in the morning.

Finally, there was a note to go and visit John Ravensthorpe, one of the selection of slightly odd bachelors that we seemed to have residing on the estate. He was a tenant of a smallholding. Mr Ravensthorpe farmed a pig unit which I suspect was struggling as all his pigs were reared indoors and the fashion had moved to outdoor free-range methods. His holding only amounted to five acres so he was unable to change his style of farming as he didn't have enough land.

I telephoned the racehorse trainer, Sir Ian Glass and arranged to go and see him at Newmarket on the Friday once I got back from Manchester. With so much on I thought I'd better stay in the office for the next couple of days to catch up on paperwork but I would nip out and see Mr Ravensthorpe.

'Anne please could you give Mr Ravensthorpe a ring and see what time would suit him. I can pop down either later today or tomorrow morning.'

I got on with dictating some letters and signing off various cheques for repairs and other bills. The monthly outgoings on the estate were never-ending and it was at times a juggling act to balance the income with the expenditure. Farm rents which were the largest source of income came in twice a year meaning the cash flow was intermittent. In some ways it was extraordinary to think that this huge asset, the estate and its associated components, houses, farms, the village, stables, the collections of art and so on only seem to generate enough income to pay for it to stand still. There wasn't a huge amount left over at the end of the day. It was a point that Sebastian had remarked on in the early meetings we had when his father was still alive and introducing Sebastian to his inheritance.

John Ravensthorpe lived out on the road towards Bury St Edmunds. He was of retiring age and had come to the estate as a relatively young man having been brought up on a nearby county council smallholding where his father had also kept pigs. His house and unit were kept immaculately and even though his pigs did not have the freedom to wander around fields they would have been happy as he took great pride in their welfare. The farmhouse was attractive as well, pink rendered plaster walls and a thatched roof with a very pretty traditional cottage garden full of flowers. I expect the limitless quantities of pig muck were a direct consequence of the abundance of flowers in his garden.

John looked not dissimilar to Ron Short who had carried out the survey of the Hall. Except that Ron Short had a slightly pushed up bulldog shaped nose and John had a rather extended one alike to the snout of a pig. Strange how people often look like their animals. His appearance with very smooth pink skin, especially for a farmer, and bright twinkly eyes did much to enhance that observation. And for some reason he shared a common trait with most pig farmers that I had come across which was that they were most jovial of sorts.

As I arrived, he came out of his house beaming broadly.

'Good to see you James,' he said, 'kind of you to come down so soon.'

'Not at all. It's good to see the place looking as meticulous as ever,' I commented.

'Thank you, thank you James, yes well I do try as you know, but I always say a tidy farm is the sign of a good farmer.'

'Certainly, that,' I said, 'I can't see a piece of straw out of place here.'

He chuckled. 'You're too kind. Come on in and we'll have a cup of tea.'

I followed him in noticing his small grey Fergie tractor parked by the back door. Again, this was in meticulous order and appeared cleaner than my Land Rover. It was an oddity of John that he had never passed his car driving test but he had at the age of sixteen taken his tractor driving test and passed. He used the little grey Fergie like a car. To be fair he never went much further than Bury anyway, and he had had some lights fitted to it that he could also drive at night.

This led to some rather unusual sightings in the locality. He would always attend the monthly National Farmers Union meetings at the Corn Hall in Bury St Edmunds and arrived there at seven thirty whatever the weather. The little tractor had no cab so he tended to don a very heavy duty set of waterproofs which, with a hat that resembled a space helmet, looked like something out of a science fiction film. To see what appeared to be Darth Vader chugging along the A134 at ten o'clock at night in the pouring rain on a grey Fergie was somewhat surreal. I often overtook him my way home from such meetings and would give him a toot as I passed. He seemed oblivious to his unusual behaviour.

Similarly, he would arrive at parties in the same manner although most of his friends had grown used to it and it was simply what he did.

He put the kettle on and made us a cup of tea. We sat down at his spotlessly clean kitchen table. After some general chitchat he said, 'I think it's about time I hung up my wellies. I'm not getting any younger and this pig job is getting harder each year, so I'm thinking that I should retire.'

'But,' I said, 'you've had pigs all your life. You will miss the farming, won't you?'

'I will I'm sure but it's about time and I've got other things I want to do before I get past it and stuck in an armchair for the rest of my life.'

'You're not that old, you look fit and healthy and I'm sure there's a lot of interesting things you want to do.'

His eyes twinkled and he chuckled again. 'One of the things that I really want to do is a bit of travelling. Whenever I tell my friends they just laugh as they say I only travel on the tractor but you know this James, I've never been abroad.'

'Haven't you really?' I exclaimed. 'But I suppose you will have been tied to the farm.'

'That's right,' he said. 'I'm here on my own looking after these pigs and as you know I don't have any family or staff to help out. So here I've been for the past thirty odd years. To be honest I've never been much further than Bury. Never had a holiday'.

He paused. 'So, what I wanted to chat about was to ask you something. I was wondering that if I give up my tenancy here then I wonder if you can find me a house in the village? I don't want to buy anything because I've no one to leave it to and if I do a bit of travelling then think something in the village would be more secure. If I stopped at this place and it was empty for weeks on end, no doubt someone would break in and burgle it as it's a bit isolated'.

He continued. 'Officially I have to give a year's notice so I suppose that'll be the timing.'

'Oh, you needn't worry about that,' I said, 'you can choose when you want to give up. If I were you, I'd try and judge it to sell when the pigs are at a decent price. I know how the market is up and down like a yoyo.'

'That would be most useful thank you,' he said, 'and that's partly what's brought this to a head really. Pigs are as good as they've been for long time, best in ten years I'd reckon, and that's what made me think perhaps I should sell the entire herd.'

I agreed. 'You could always sell the pigs and then stay on in the house until we found you something in the village of you like?'

'That's a thought and a kind one James, thank you.'

'Have you any idea what sort of house or cottage you would like or perhaps even have your eye on a particular one?"

'I'm not sure of a particular one,' he confirmed. 'I only need something small so two bedrooms would do but I would like a garden and I'm keeping the tractor so somewhere to park that.'

I left him with the assurance that I would ask Anne or Gail to send a list of empty properties or ones that were likely to become empty in the next few months so that he could start to think about his retirement. I passed on the message to the girls when I got back to the office and then sat down at my desk to look at the agenda for the forthcoming meeting up in Manchester. I had been to one previously when Sir Charles had been unable to attend so I had some idea of what it was about. I organised some accommodation in a hotel reasonably close to the offices where the meeting was to be held which was pretty near the city centre.

The following afternoon I drove to Manchester leaving earlier than I needed as I thought it would be interesting to have at least a brief look around the city. The motorways around Birmingham and Stafford were nose to tail with heavy traffic and then, despite using my satnav, finding the hotel car park was a challenge. Eventually I checked in but much later than I had intended. Nonetheless it gave me a couple of hours to walk through the city centre and find somewhere to have dinner. My hotel was in a tower block just off Piccadilly and had some splendid views of the metropolis and out to the sprawling suburbs. Being a southerner, I felt that I was very much in the far frozen north although to be fair it was a pleasant summer evening. As I wandered the streets plenty of bars and restaurants had tables on their terraces alongside the pavement.

I stopped at what appeared to be a lively and popular Italian restaurant and took a table outside. An authentic pizza and a couple of glasses of Sauvé were surprisingly delicious for the price and although I dined alone, I enjoyed the opportunity to people watch in this bustling city which was so far from removed from my usual life. The jangling bells of the trams were an added attraction emphasising the different and interesting environment.

I reflected on this relatively affluent city centre life as tomorrow, after we had the meeting, we would be visiting a site only five miles away in a completely contrasting locality where it was dangerous to venture out at night alone.

I enjoyed a relatively good breakfast the following morning. The hotel, typical of large chains, had an arrangement where a self-service buffet offered a multitude of things to eat. Eight o'clock in the morning is never quite the right time to partake of such a range of slowly congealing savouries but I was able to devour a cooked breakfast even if some of it was rather tepid and slimy. The fact that you haven't had to cook it yourself is an extravagance and whilst nowhere near the standard of breakfast at Strathard Lodge it was an indulgence of sorts.

After breakfast, having put my bags in the car and arranged that I could leave it in the hotel car park for the morning, I walked to City Hall where we were convening for the meeting.

CHAPTER 11

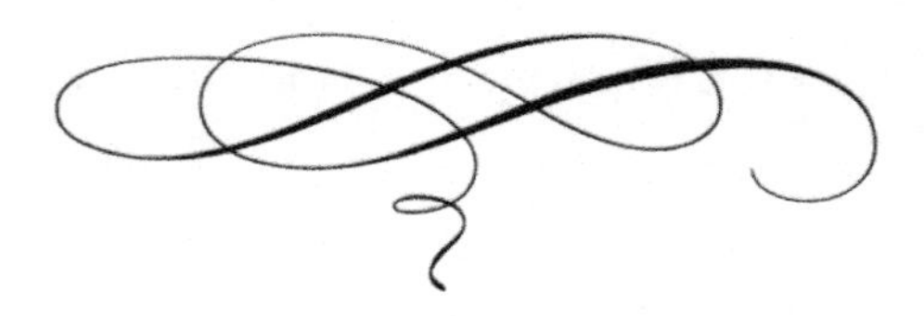

It was an interesting mix of folk that sat on the committee. There were representatives from the local community, the Forestry Commission and private woodland owners. There were a few well-meaning locals from the Greater Manchester area who for various reasons desired to have an input. Ten of us sat down at the table to deliberate the agenda. The meeting was chaired by a woman from the council who seem more intent on ticking boxes on government policy than putting any practical measures into operation. I could sense a disparity among the group. Everyone agreed that the idea of establishing a forest, although that was rather a grand word for the project, was a commendable idea. Some seemed more concerned with its promise as an intention rather than a physical presence.

I reflected how different it was to work in the private rather than the public sector. It seemed to me that in the private sector people just got on with the job. In the public sector there had to be endless debate, endless papers and meetings, before anything could actually happen. There were really three people on the committee who drove it and due to their very different personalities made for some interesting dynamics.

Foremost was Simon Stephens a wispy man from the council who looked as though he hadn't eaten a decent meal in months. He had a neat little beard and wore open toed sandals with socks. Nobody said so but I sensed that everybody found him an irritating individual as he was more concerned about risk assessments, health and safety regulations and proper procedures than the logistics of how the project would physically be achieved. However, being from the council meant he had access to various people and committees which the project needed.

The second was a lady in her early forties called Deirdre Day who, as we found out at lunchtime, was a vegan, gluten and lactose intolerant and accordingly had brought something of her own to eat safely secured in a little plastic box. She had an inherent dislike of the internal combustion engine and her interest in the project lay in providing cycle paths and walking trails for all abilities. Her strength was being able to secure funding.

The third person John Cockerill was a geologist. He had a loud voice and intent manner. When he spoke everyone else shut up. I should think he was in his sixties, probably retired and with a wealth of experience, he understood the underlying nature of the sites that were to form these new woodlands.

An unusual mix of people, together with the others on the committee, made for a surprisingly collective balanced voice. Despite all the risk assessments, cycle path demands and the disastrous state of the underlying ground conditions several of these woodlands had started to take shape.

Following the meeting we all climbed into a minibus and were taken to see the latest acquisition which was an area of about forty acres squashed between a busy railway line and a mixture of residential areas, all of which were an appalling mess. In terms of architectural history, it provided a textbook example. At the southern end of the site were rows and rows of back-to-back Victorian terraces which had no gardens at all. A little yard behind each house which originally contained the outside privy backed onto the same for the opposite terrace. Where the terraces finished there was a vast council housing estate built in the nineteen seventies. The Victorian terraces, although poor housing, did have a sense of history about them whereas the more modern houses were faceless. They looked run down, there was litter everywhere and graffiti on the walls. A remarkable number of cars had missing wheels. It was also noticeable how many people, both adults and children were out in the streets even during a weekday. At the north end of the site were a number of tower blocks, probably twenty stories high, with interconnecting concrete alleyways and bridges. Windows and balconies were lined with washing hanging out to dry. A few menacing looking dogs of no defined pedigree skulked about searching for dustbins to raid.

The forty acres that we were visiting was covered with rough scrubby undergrowth strewn with rubbish and significant fly tipping. The remnants of burnt-out cars littered the place; the scrubby vegetation was all that grew in an estimated metre depth of soil, below which was a huge quantity of arsenic and asbestos. This had been the site of an industrial chemical works and the resulting land contamination that was left behind was so poisonous that no houses could be built on it.

This sort of situation was common in areas of the industrial cities and the purpose of the project was to transform these derelict sites into woodlands for the benefit of the people nearby. It looked like an impossible task.

Having spent half an hour wandering around we climbed back into the minibus and drove just two more miles to an area that had once been an enormous landfill site taking the domestic waste from

Manchester. The millions of tonnes of rubbish were still under the ground and occasional pipes seen sticking out were releasing the methane from the decomposing waste.

However, this project which had started ten years earlier was a complete transformation. It was predominantly covered with young growing trees and open areas of grassy glades where people were picnicking or playing games. Deirdre's cycle paths were evidently well used and the council man's notices were being obeyed. The geologist had clearly worked out his ground restoration satisfactorily as the trees were flourishing.

Not only had they changed the landscape but provided both ecological and recreational benefits. It was a delight to witness such a transformation which had taken relatively little time. I could see why Sir Charles had accepted his position to join the committee and why he had spent such a considerable amount of time on assisting with the woodland creation plans.

Friday's appointment couldn't have been more different. From the rundown deprived areas of inner-city Manchester to the manicured turf of Newmarket.

I went to see Sir Ian Glass a leading racehorse trainer who looked after Sir Charles' horses and also some belonging to Her Majesty the Queen. Sir Ian was a knight not a baronet and had been given his honour in recognition for services to the racehorse industry. I was quite confident that any advice he could give me on behalf of Sebastian's trustees would be as good as we could get.

The approaches to Newmarket were impressive, meticulous with mile after mile of beautifully kept gallops, wide neatly mown verges along the sides of the roads and acres of neatly kept post and rail paddocks grazed by some of the finest thoroughbreds in the world. The studs and training establishments of the town were internationally recognised and sought after. The wealth that poured into the town through racing was evident and immense.

The town itself was not particularly smart. There were a few notable shops and restaurants and of course Tattersalls auction house and the Jockey Club estate. Most Newmarket residents were the workers in the race horse industry not the owners.

Sir Ian Glass' establishment was entirely as one would expect as befitting a leading racehorse trainer. It lay on the far side of Newmarket near Six-Mile Bottom. The road out of Newmarket was beautifully lined with mature trees and affording occasional glimpses to the railed paddocks beyond. I turned off the road through an impressive gateway to Copy House Stables and along an immaculate gravelled drive to what was in fact quite a modest house. The grandeur and wealth of the place related entirely to the stables, the paddocks and the training gallops. Horses came above all else in Newmarket and although some trainers were fortunate enough to have some very smart houses, the facilities for the horses were more relevant. Looking around me as I climbed out of the car it was impossible not be impressed by the sheer number of beautiful looking and well-kept horses grazing in the paddocks or with their heads peering over the stable doors.

Sir Ian Glass was a likeable fellow with an air of competency and decisiveness about him.

'Come in, Mr Aden,' he invited me into his house. 'Would you like a cup of coffee?'

'That would be very welcome thank you.' We sat down whilst his secretary attended to our refreshments and brought in a cafetiere of coffee, cups and saucers and chocolate biscuits. This was an office that was used to having multimillionaire visitors coming to discuss their precious investments and indulgences.

'Shall we start by talking about those horses of Sir Charles' that we have in training here?' he asked.

'That's absolutely fine,' I agreed, 'basically the situation is that Sir Sebastian, who you may have met, is not at all interested in racing. It's a shame but there we are, so he and the executors have decided that the racehorses should be sold. My job is to really make sure that we do the best we can and sell them at the right time. Presumably, we need to get the timing right? I imagine that if one of them has just won a big race then it is worth selling? If we were to sell before a race then that may not be to our advantage unless it lost. This is where we need your guidance.'

'Absolutely right absolutely, although it's always a bit of a tricky judgement as to when to sell. If you do badly in a race then the value of the horse will be considerably less. If you sold it just before when it may be running at higher odds, it'd be worth more. Do you have to sell them all within a certain timeframe?'

'No not at all. We will literally be guided by you on this, horse by horse. There is no problem over the training fees and so on, so we trust your judgement. I'm not even sure how you go about selling racehorses – is it mainly by word-of-mouth or do you advertise them in the *Racing Post?'*

'In these circumstances for the horses here we would probably find new owners by word of mouth. Whilst to be quite truthful, none of them are absolute top drawer, they are all pretty useful animals. All of them have won or been placed during the last season so they're the sort of horses that will sell by reputation. I probably even have owners in this yard who would be interested, certainly in two of them. The other two we might have to look a bit further afield.'

We discussed the sort of values that they might be worth and vague timing dependent on what races they were likely to run in and came up with a plan that, although slightly flexible, would eventually ensure that the racehorses would be sold.

'The other thing that we really need your help on please, Sir Ian are the ones at the Frampton stud, which as you know was one of Sir Charles' great passions. We haven't done anything with them at all so there are no changes and the breeding programme has been left to the stud groom. Again, Sir Sebastian isn't interested in keeping them so we'll have to sell all those as well.'

'Yes, of course I know, I've been over to the stud several times. One of the horses that Sir Charles has here in training is one that he bred. As with the others it's partly timing to do with the sale and again probably word of mouth. Really, I'm not sure exactly what stock you have over at Frampton to be honest. I cannot remember if indeed I ever did know the full arrangement.'

'I have put some lists together,' I said sliding piece of paper across the table. 'Obviously, the stud groom keeps proper records of everything. You can see the mares and how they've been bred and of course the yearlings and foals. It has all the details of the parentage and dates of birth. There are also three two-year olds which the stud groom seems to think Sir Charles wanted to put in training. I think that would be pointless now so they'll have to be sold as soon as possible for someone else to train.'

'Can I suggest that I have a look at this and study the books and so on before coming back to you?'

'Of course, take whatever time you need and would it be a good idea for you to come over and meet the stud groom and inspect all the horses?'

'That's an excellent idea and clearly I couldn't do this for you without having a look at everything. I'll come over and I'm very happy to do it for Sir Charles' family.'

'I express my thanks on their behalf to you,' I continued.

'Not at all, Sir Charles was a good friend and I enjoyed his company enormously. He and I would often spend time at the races together in one or other's boxes. He was a very knowledgeable and understanding owner and I can tell you I don't get many of those!' he chuckled.

'Would you like to come out and have a look around my yard as you're here?'

'That's kind and I'd absolutely love to although I'm not a racing person I do love my horses.'

'You've got horses then?' he asked.

'Yes, my wife and I both have hunters which we just use for hacking around the farm. We like having them about and never really want to be without horses on the place. They add something to the feel of a country home I always think.'

'Well come and have a look,' and he shouted something to his secretary before striding out through the front door.

It was quite an honour and very interesting to be shown around the immaculate yard, or in fact two yards by this hugely respected racehorse trainer. The place was run with precision and not a strand of straw was out of place. The considerable number of lads or staff were clearly respectful of their employer and practically stood to attention as we walked around and inspected the horses. They were aristocratic animals, beautifully kept and it was no surprise that Sir Ian was one of the leading racehorse owners in the country.

I took leave of the visit but not before Sir Ian had very kindly invited me to come and watch his horses in training if I would like an early morning six o'clock start to see them on the gallops. I assured him that I would love to and was very appreciative of his offer.

In the meanwhile, he would make arrangements with our stud groom at Frampton to visit and make an appraisal of the horses.

CHAPTER 12

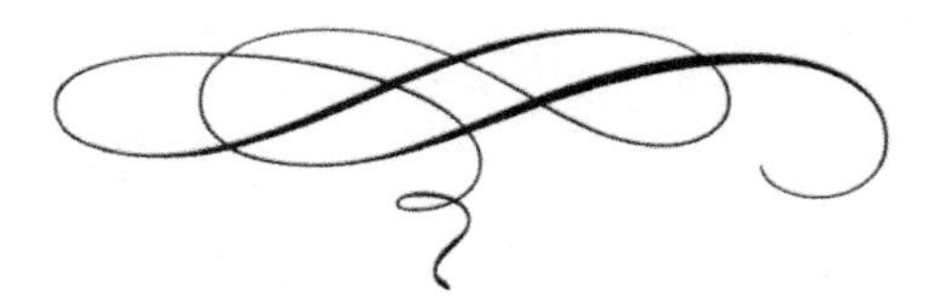

'Mrs Taverner has lost her cat,' Anne announced as I walked into the estate office.

'She's such a miserable old bat, I expect it's run away,' I replied.

'That's a bit harsh,' she said and laughed, 'but no she's not exactly the joy of any party.'

'Anyway, what have we got to do with it?' I asked.

'She's been in and asked if we could ring all the tenants in the village to see if it's got shut in one of their sheds.'

'I hope you said no, it'd take ages.'

'I did say no and she seemed a bit put out. But I did say we would put a notice up the window and also ask anyone who comes in to see if they can help.'

'It's all we can do really,' I agreed.

Evidently Mrs Taverner decided to take the task of delivering the message to all the villagers herself as she could be seen knocking on every door in the Square presumably then going off to do the same in the High Street and every other little street.

Mrs Taverner and I did not have a good relationship. She was one of those people who saw the bad in everything, the good in nothing and had a completely negative outlook on life. How she managed to remain married to the same man for thirty years was to my mind remarkable. He was either a saint or masochist because he actually seemed to enjoy being in her company. He even went, and this was how I knew that they had been married thirty years, on the day of their anniversary to put up a large handwritten placard at either end the village and tie thirty balloons to two signposts announcing their wedding anniversary.

He was as jovial as she was miserable so perhaps opposites did attract. He had a laid-back attitude to the point of being horizontal. To my misfortune any dealings I had with them to do about their rented cottage tended to be dealt with during the working day when she was at home and he was at work. He was employed in a garden centre on the outskirts of Bury St Edmunds. I am not sure what he did there but I don't think it was very taxing as he did not appear to like dealing with anything very taxing in their private lives. He preferred leaving his wife in charge of all the household and financial matters. They didn't have any children and I guessed that the cat was Mrs Taverner's surrogate child. I doubted that Mr Taverner could be bothered one way or the other, either about a child or the cat.

What he did bother about and bother about very considerably was his cottage garden which presumably because of his occupation, was quite possibly the best in the village if not for miles around. I didn't like to enquire if they got a discount for purchasing all the plants or whether he was perhaps given the leftovers that couldn't be sold. If that was the case, he must have taken a long time to get them all back to his house as he went to work on a motor scooter. They didn't have a car and on occasion the two of them were seen astride the machine, helmets securely fastened on their way out for an excursion.

They had a pleasant cottage in the village, a redbrick Victorian house at the end of a row of three. It had the benefit of the largest garden being at the end of the row giving them ample space to pursue their gardening interests. Mr Taverner also had an allotment where he grew superb quality fruit and vegetables, some of which he sold at the garden gate where he had erected a covered wooden structure displaying his produce and the prices. There was an honesty box into which the purchasers could leave their money. He was a frequent winner at the fete vegetable competition. Mrs Taverner complemented proceedings with her array of jams, preserves and chutneys. They were also for sale in the little booth and on display at the fete.

The fete, which Sir Charles' often referred to it as the fate worse than death, wasn't long away now but I concentrated on the matter in hand which was the loss of the cat.

The last time I'd seen Mrs Taverner was to discuss her request for a new kitchen. Admittedly the one they had was somewhat tired but there was nothing wrong with it and we always had to prioritise on the estate budget as to what repairs and improvements were made across all the houses. Of course, everyone including Mrs Taverner thought they should be at the top of the list but when one considered that the Taverners only paid five thousand pounds a year rent it would effectively mean that a whole year's worth of income would be spent on the kitchen. I had offered her an arrangement whereby we would agree to them installing and paying for a new kitchen and should they leave the cottage within the next five years we would repay a proportion of the cost as unexpired value. They had lived there for twenty years so it seemed unlikely they would leave within five years and I could see no reason why they would. It was an arrangement that she accepted with bad grace.

Mrs Taverner must have thought a lot of her cat. Coming to the estate office first thing in the morning and spending all day calling at houses. When I left the office for the evening, she was still to be seen in Church Street on her rounds. I hoped for her sake, and the cat's, that the results would be favourable.

When I got home that evening, I had a quick cup of tea with Sophie and caught up on the day's news.

'It's such a lovely evening,' I said. 'I think I'll go down and fix that gate in the meadow.'

'That's a good idea,' she replied. 'It's a nuisance having to get off the horses to open it. Why don't you take Emma? She can play in the stream,'

'Yes, that would be nice for a change,' I agreed. 'I'll go and put some tools in the Land Rover and come back and pick her up.'

I went outside and reversed the Land Rover to the workshop to throw the necessary tools in the back. As I opened the rear door of the vehicle a very frightened and angry orange cat shot out. For second, I wasn't sure what had happened then realised with some despair that it may likely be Mrs Taverner's cat. I could only presume that it climbed in the previous evening when I'd left the door open as I was loading some boxes of paper from the office to take to the recycling skip. There was no connection between the back of the Land Rover and the cab but even so it was surprising that I hadn't heard it when driving to and from work.

The question was what to do now? I could pretend that I hadn't seen it and hopefully it would make its way home on its own. I wasn't particularly keen to have to telephone Mrs Taverner and tell her that her cat had been knocking around in my car for the last twenty-four hours and that now it had shot off into a barn on my farm. Whether it would ever get home was another matter. I thought perhaps five miles might be a bit challenging together with the fact that it must be slightly disorientated and hungry. I returned to the house to consult Sophie over the matter.

I explained about the missing cat and Mrs Taverner.

'It just shot out of the back of the Land Rover,' I explained. 'I had no idea it was there.'

'We'd better try and catch it,' Sophie suggested. 'Then you can take it back.'

'I don't think it will be very easy to catch. It was pretty scared and it's gone into the hay barn so it could be anywhere now.'

'Let's go out and have a look.' She gathered Emma who clearly was not going to get a chance to play in the stream after all as we would no doubt be preoccupied with catching the wretched cat for a while.

As hard as we searched, we couldn't find it. Of course, it might well have left the hay barn and taken to the fields. It may already be on its way home but my conscience couldn't just leave it like that and I felt I ought to ring Mrs Taverner to put her in the picture.

It was not a task I looked forward to. The relationship was frosty at the best of times and she would no doubt assume that I had not only abducted her cat but let it loose in unfamiliar surroundings miles away from home.

I explained my dilemma to Sophie.

'She can't surely blame you for what's happened?' she said, 'after all you didn't catch the cat and take it away. It was its own fault it jumped into the Land Rover.'

'I know but she's the kind of person who will take this the wrong way whatever I say.'

'If that's the case then I should just leave the bloody thing to its own devices,' she retorted.

'Whilst I tend to agree, but knowing where it is, roughly at the moment at any rate, I feel I ought to give her the chance to come and try and find it.'

'Well it's up to you.'

'I think she sort of sees it as a child,' I replied. 'She's been quite beside herself all day trying to find it. Knocked on practically every door in the village thinking somebody shut it in their shed.'

'It's your decision,' Sophie said. 'If it was up to me, I would just let it find its own way home and hope that it doesn't get squashed on the road on its way back.'

Darling little Emma then appeared in the kitchen saying, 'Look what I've just found.'

Unbelievably she was holding an orange cat. 'Where on earth did you find it?' I asked.

'It was in the garden,' she said.

'And it just let you pick it up?' I asked.

'Yes', she said, 'it's a very sweet little cat he's ever so friendly. Can we keep it?' she asked.

'No,' I almost shouted, 'we certainly can't keep the damn thing.' Then a bit more calmly, 'Sorry Emma, we can't keep it because it belongs to somebody else and we know who it belongs to. She's been looking for it all day and is terribly sad not to have found it.'

'Oh well,' said Emma putting it down on the floor, quite used to the comings and goings of animals having been brought up on a farm.

'Quick shut the kitchen door or it'll be out again.'

The door slammed. Unfortunately, my raised voice and the slam of the door startled the cat and it darted off upstairs.

'James don't go after it,' said Sophie, 'you seem to simply frighten it. Let Emma see if she can coax it.'

Emma went in search of the cat and managed to placate it and brought it calmly back downstairs.

'I'll put it in a box and take it back to Frampton and then, hopefully no-one will see us and I'll let it out somewhere near the Taverner's house and presumably it will go home.'

'Good idea James. I'll go and find a box.'

Having with difficulty pushed the wretched thing in the box I secured it with several metres of masking tape to prevent its further escape. Placing it in the Land Rover I returned to Frampton.

It felt like driving with an unexploded bomb in the back as indeed at any moment something might go terribly wrong and it would fight its way out. I was fortunate. It didn't escape and as far as I knew no one saw me as I pulled into a field gateway very close to the Taverner's cottage. Surreptitiously I looked around me and luckily none of the villagers were out walking their dogs so I quickly cut the tape, opened the box and let the cat out.

Whether or not it immediately knew its home surroundings I was unable to tell as it disappeared at speed into a hedge.

The next morning Anne was pleased to tell me that Mrs Taverner had been into the office to say that the red alerts with regard to the cat had been turned off. Wilfred had apparently returned home about eight o'clock the previous evening, hungry and on edge but otherwise fine.

I had also returned home that evening hungry and on edge but to be fair to Wilfred I hadn't spent twenty-four hours locked in the back of a car.

CHAPTER 13

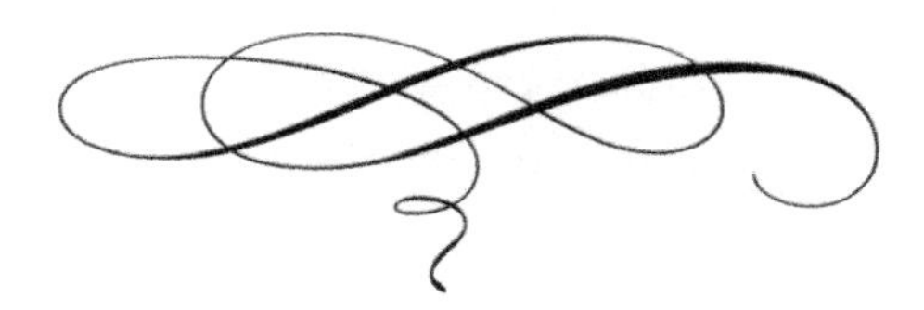

Two things happened the following day which put the cat episode into perspective. The two things that happened would eventually have far-reaching consequences.

They occurred during my now weekly meeting with Sebastian in Sir Charles' study. I went armed with the quotations that we had received for rewiring Frampton Hall and putting in a new central heating system.

Sebastian and Serena were expecting me when I arrived. It was very unusual for Serena to attend these meetings as she had no involvement with the day-to-day matters of running the estate.

I was surprised to see them both.

'Hello, it's a delight to see you here Serena,' I said, 'it's not often we're graced with your company in these matters.' I joked.

Sebastian replied, 'Well it's because we have some news to impart. It's rather personal and distressing so we felt it was right to tell you both together.'

'Oh,' I was alarmed, 'what on earth is the matter?'

'You won't know of course,' Sebastian said, 'but we have been trying to start a family for the last couple of years and there have been difficulties, all sorts of difficulties,' he explained rather formally.

Serena piped up in a controlled but emotional state. 'We now know that it will never be possible for us to have children,' she quivered and put her hand on Sebastian's arm. 'We've now been through all the tests and IVF, everything you can think of but for reasons that we won't bore you with we can't have children.'

I was shocked. I didn't want to probe into their very private matters but inevitably the position of the resident agent on an estate immerses one into all kinds of intricacies.

'I am so sad to hear that,' I said. 'I didn't realise that you had been trying and certainly didn't realise that you are having problems.'

'We wouldn't expect you to,' said Sebastian, 'but of course now that we're in this position we feel somewhat disillusioned and upset and thinking about where we want to go in the future. After all it's not just us – it's the title, the estate, the history of my family and five hundred years of inheritance.'

I looked at them with sadness. For any couple who wanted to but were unable to have children it must be a devastating experience. There was also the added weight of assuming an heir to take on all that Sebastian mentioned which must have compounded their grief.

'Sebastian, Serena,' I said. 'I cannot tell you how sorry I am to hear this. It must be dreadful for both of you and I really cannot express my feelings in any way that would give you some comfort.'

They nodded.

'I don't think that the rest of this meeting is particularly appropriate,' I suggested. 'Shall we get together another day?'

'No,' Sebastian replied. 'We have had a little time to come to some sense of this and we must go on.'

There was a knock at the door and Hole entered carrying a jug of coffee for Sebastian and myself and a little pot of tea for Serena.

'I have brought some refreshments,' he announced.

'Thank you, Mr Hole,' said Serena.

Sir Charles' poodles who were in the study as usual during our meetings, started sniffing each other's bottoms. Hole very deftly kicked one of them gently and it looked up at him in surprise. I glanced at Hole thankfully as the dogs settled down again on the rug.

'Let's get on with the business in hand,' said Sebastian as Hole left the room.

'Yes, first thing, we've had the quotations in for rewiring and the heating for this house,' I explained 'and it's not good news I'm afraid. We always expected them to be expensive but I'm afraid it's quite a lot more than even Roy Short had guessed.'

'What are the figures?' queried Sebastian.

'The best wiring quote is one point three million,' I paused as Serena gasped, 'and then the heating system is even worse at two point four million.'

They both looked shocked and taken aback.

'So that's three point seven million quid,' Sebastian worked out, 'to get the house rewired, get the heating sorted just to make it more comfortable for us to live here.'

'Yes, it is but we must bear in mind that it is a huge house, it's of national architectural importance and nothing's been done to it for really generations. Your father wouldn't spend a penny on it and your grandfather wasn't much better. It's a wonderful place and if you want to enjoy it then I think these improvements would really help.'

Serena said nothing. Sebastian murmured something about it being iniquitous but didn't enlighten us further.

'There's no need to make any decisions today,' I said, 'it's just now that we have the quotes we can plan ahead for the future. It is a lot of money but can be afforded.'

Sebastian asked if there was that amount of money in the bank.

'Not immediately,' I said to him, 'but to put it in perspective it is money that we can find. The paintings in this house are worth many times more than that amount and for the sake of say one painting you can make the place much more liveable.'

They looked at me questioningly.

'We just need to get our minds around this,' Sebastian said with Serena nodding her head in agreement. 'I've always known that this house costs a fortune to run but we are now into the realms of many millions of pounds just to keep it habitable. We need to think about this carefully.'

I agreed with them and we left the meeting all pondering about future plans and how we might take them forward. It was to be the catalyst for massive change.

I was a little uneasy and unsettled by the conversation as not only had we failed to agree on progressing the improvements, or how we would fund them but it seemed as though was going to be no further heir to the baronetcy of the estate. My first instinct was to return to the office and work out the nearest relations who could be successors either to the title or to the estate or both. It had never been discussed because like most people things were just presumed to carry on as intended. Sir Charles had always been, if not concerned, then aware that there was an heir and no spare but understandably he didn't like to dwell on the matter. He had an heir and in his lifetime that was what mattered. The present situation was a considerable blow. Sir Charles had also been an only child and the succession had always been one of those elephants in the room that no-one talked about. In defence of not having an alternative plan it would have been difficult to have had one. The family couldn't presume that Sebastian would not have children and therefore it would have been inappropriate to involve distant family members in succession, even if that was what was wanted.

Sir Charles' father, Sebastian's grandfather had a younger brother who had of course long since died but it did give a line of Buckley's, some of whom had attended Sir Charles' funeral. One of them would inherit the title once Sebastian died by default.

However, the estate and all the family possessions were another matter. They could be bequeathed to a distant relation but there was no legal requirement for that to happen. The nearest male relation on the Buckley side as far as I could make out was Sebastian's second cousin and whilst there was no animosity between them, I don't believe there was much if any contact. The situation was to remain private and there was no cause for raising expectations. Sebastian was only in his mid-forties so although this was sobering news the show had to go on. With luck he would have forty years at the helm as guardian of the estate and at some point, during the next four decades decisions could be made as to what would happen in the long term. It was a matter that was to be kept totally confidential and I returned to the estate office from the meeting in a sombre mood.

'You seem a bit quiet,' Anne said.

'Do I?' I replied. 'Yes I'm just really thinking about the quotes we've had in for the house improvements.'

'My goodness yes they are a huge amount of money,' she agreed having seen them in the incoming post.

'I think Sebastian was rather taken aback,' I said, 'at least we had some idea of likely costs but he really doesn't get involved enough to have been prepared.'

'It's a pity he's not more involved,' Anne said, 'he never really comes up to the estate office like his father used to. Serena does occasionally but usually to get some stamps or something.'

'I know but he is a true academic and I imagine it's just quite difficult to have a totally absorbing life involved at the University which he loves and then try to immerse yourself in the vagaries of owning and running a huge country estate.'

'Yes, I can see that,' she said. 'Sir Charles was completely the opposite, wasn't he?'

'Precisely,' I said, 'his whole life was the estate and the people on it, the horses and paintings and so on. It's something we have just got to adjust to.'

'I suppose we have. By the way Brenda's left a whole batch of cheques for you to sign on your desk,' she said, 'if you can get them all done, I'll send them out later.'

'Thank you, has she gone home now?'

'Yes, she went at lunchtime and shall be back in tomorrow first thing.'

I sat down at my desk and carefully went through the bills and cheques to be signed. It was our only real form of cost control in that any member of staff could order things directly but I was the only one could sign the cheques. It would have been bureaucratically burdensome for every order to come through the estate office. The stud groom or whoever, would order feed or tack or buckets or whatever on the estate account and I would see the invoices, authorise them and sign the cheques. Occasionally I'd come across one that needed questioning not because we expected any misdoings but because the invoice was incorrect in some way.

There were three parking ticket fines from Cambridge City Council, two for Sebastian's little runabout and one for Serena's Range Rover. The cars were registered with the estate hence the tickets arrived in the estate office but no matter how many times I mentioned the regularity of this neither Sebastian nor Serena took any note. It made me wonder whether they knew what the yellow lines painted on the side of road meant. It would have driven Sir Charles mad to know how much we wasted on parking fines.

There was another invoice that needed paying and as often the case with the cheque paying sessions they acted as a kind of aide memoir for me. The invoice was from the roofing company who had recently completed the job of renewing the roof of a little pub that the estate owned in a small hamlet three miles from Frampton.

Some months ago, we had agreed to spend some money at the Thread and Needle even though it would have been better turned into a house and let as such. The works had originally been agreed when Sir Charles was alive as he had a wish to support the publican Reginald Leather. Sir Charles had philanthropic views on many matters and maintaining local businesses and facilities for local people was foremost. The Thread and Needle was a pub that would have demised under normal circumstances purely because Reginald Leather failed to keep up with the times. Sir Charles liked it for that reason. It was a genuine old-fashioned pub that focused on ales and not much else. When I had first arrived at Frampton, I nipped out there for a bite of lunch one day and to introduce myself as the agent. I was surprised at the choice of menu.

Having introduced myself to Reg and asked what may be available for a lunchtime snack he replied, 'we do crisps and peanuts' and then with some attempt at embellishing the offerings added, 'plain or salt and vinegar, roasted or dry roasted'.

He paid next to no rent and lived on the premises so his overheads were obviously minimal. To be fair to him we had had several discussions over the ensuing years and he did embrace some suggestions but with a modicum of enthusiasm.

It became apparent even to him that pubs needed to sell food in order to make a living. Violet, his rather stout and lazy wife was not much disposed to undertaking any kind of activity and until the smoking ban, she sat in the corner of the room surrounded in a haze of smoke doing crosswords. More recently she had had to partake of those activities in a small shed outside but it hadn't made her any more active.

Reg enlisted the help of a girl who lived in one of the nearby houses as a cook. There had been some involvement by the estate at that point when he realised that the kitchen did not meet any up-to-date hygiene standards at all. The local environmental health officer had apparently visited and said that he wouldn't want a glass of water from the kitchen let alone anything to eat.

Sir Charles, not wanting to see the pub fail, had agreed that the estate would contribute to improving the kitchen. Once this was done Sharon, the girl from the nearby cottage, joined the team. She would do all the cooking and waitressing; Reg would run the bar and serve the drinks and Violet would take turns between puffing away in the shed and sitting on the window seat doing a crossword.

The ambitious project was only partially successful. The problem was twofold. The quality was abysmal and the choice limited. I could see it from a customer's point of view. The new choice of menu was somewhat restricted and if you didn't like chips then it would not be a happy dining experience. With these chips you had a choice of either sausages or, for the vegetarians as Reg put it, scampi. The scampi was out of a frozen bag that he got from local supermarket and the sausages were dreadful examples which may have contained a small percentage of pork but they were clearly cheap and mostly fat. Presuming one then went ahead and ordered a meal it was served in little plastic baskets which had been procured from the pound shop in Bury St Edmunds.

Notwithstanding this dismal state of affairs, the pub continued to function albeit in a rather disabled sort of way. The one thing Reg did do exceptionally well was keep his beer and I suspect that is what kept the place going. It was a man's pub and he had a loyal following of hearty ale drinkers who once they had consumed enough pints possibly found the sausage and chips did a good job of soaking up the alcohol. Local rumour had it that a glance of Sharon's breasts as she served at the tables assisted sales.

The pub now had a new roof and one hoped was set to linger on for a few more years to come. I would go and inspect it before settling the account.

I finished signing cheques and then wrote a detailed report over the proposed wiring and plumbing improvements to send to the trustees. Everyday expenditure was delegated to me to supervise but when it came to major capital works then the trustees were consulted. Sebastian's wishes would be taken into account and would drive the contract or not as the case may be, but if the work was going to go ahead then the trustees would have to agree to the sale of some assets. There was certainly not enough money in the bank account to proceed and although there was a substantial share portfolio, the trustees, I knew from past experience, preferred to keep that intact. We would have to look at selling either some land or some chattels to raise the money.

It made me wonder about property that the Buckley's owned in Canada. It had absolutely nothing to do with me and although I knew what it was and where it was the whole operation was managed in Canada under a separate company. My vague recollection was that the situation in Canada was different and the Canadian property was owned by a limited company the shares of which were held by Sir Charles and Sebastian. I presumed that Sebastian now owned all the shares and that any dividend income was going to him.

The limited knowledge that I had of the property was that it extended to a considerable 30,000 acres which sounded a lot but in reality, was mainly forests, lakes and scrubland. It was miles from anywhere on the Pacific coast of northern British Columbia and I understood that its income derived from forestry and the sale of timber. There was certainly no house there and to get to it you had to journey by boat or train to a town called Prince George and then take a seaplane and land on one of the lakes.

I did know that Sebastian had been there but that was many years ago. When I next saw him, I would mention it and at least raise the idea of perhaps diverting some funds from that to the renovation at Frampton Hall.

I drove the few short miles home that evening thinking about the many different strands that made up the agents' life on an old, landed estate and whilst it had its challenges it could never be described as dull.

CHAPTER 14

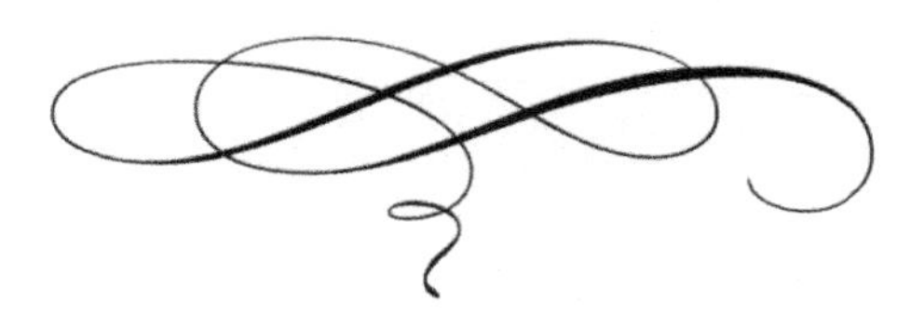

August was a busy month for Frampton as the picturesque village filled up with tourists. Many were day trippers who like to browse around the village and visit the variety of shops which ranged from the functional Co-op to craft and antique shops and the inevitable tearooms.

There was always a difference between what the residents wanted. Those that lived in the village but were not reliant on the tourist trade resented the deep influx of so many people. This influx did however produce the trade that supported many of the local businesses which in turn produced the rent payable to the estate.

Some of our shops were of notable quality particularly one or two art galleries. They often had exhibitions of paintings by well-known artists and whilst the prices might not match those of paintings up at the Hall, they were still eye watering figures. There was one good antique shop which sold proper antiques but the other two shops were catering predominantly for foreign tourists and especially Americans. They were filled with what Sir Charles described as a bric-a-brac. The proprietors would probably not have used the term bric-a-brac but a lot of their merchandise could hardly be described as antique. There was an abundance of items made of copper and brass, together with china ornaments which may have looked attractive in some settings but I personally couldn't quite put my place on them.

The tearooms and bed and breakfasts did a roaring trade. The Anne of Cleves in the Square was so popular that it was necessary to book a table for dinner and it was impossible to find a parking place after ten o'clock in the morning.

This crescendo of activity in the village was a precursor to the August bank holiday fete which was fast approaching. Preparations had gone well, according to Gale, and this year was going to include various new excitements never seen before in Frampton.

We were lucky. The weather was a perfect August day and would have been too hot if it weren't for the breeze. The village looked fabulous with bunting criss-crossing the High Street and throngs of people, locals and visitors alike, enjoyed the spectacle. Sir Charles' presence was missed but Sebastian and Serena did their best in his stead. Serena, the more outgoing of the two, laughed and joked with people she knew from the estate. Sebastian with his more reticent nature was slightly aloof but made an attempt to enter the spirit of the day.

This year the carnival floats were based on a farming theme which was an appropriate subject for the area. The imagination of the groups that had produced a float was far ranging and included at one end of the spectrum the Women's Institute, who sat on chairs singing as they were towed along the street. At the other end was the Frampton Ferret Society who had constructed a warren of see-through plastic pipes through which they dragged a stuffed rabbit followed closely by an assortment of ferrets chasing it. The Frampton Caged Bird society had a large scarecrow on their trailer and hanging from it were various cages containing, appropriately enough, caged birds. The Weavers Guild, a friendly bunch of old ladies, had a pen of sheep on their display, although I seem to recall that is what they did every year. There were twenty floats in all which was an impressive turnout. They were pulled by a multitude of horsepower from literal horse power in a pair of Suffolk Punches which had been borrowed from a local brewery to a number of tractors both ancient and modern. Jack Howdego, who ran the local garage, had been enlisted by the antiques centre to tow their float along with his ride on lawnmower.

The procession made its way along the High Street and uphill towards the recreation ground by the church. It tended to stop and start a bit partly due to the different towing abilities and varied engine capacities and because every so often something would fall off one of the floats. Fortunately, no people fell off any of the floats but nonetheless the procession halted to retrieve a ferret at one point and Mr Howdego's Panama hat at another.

Sebastian had the prestigious job of judging the best exhibition, which considering how much work most of the various societies had put into the job was always going to be controversial and awkward. He chose the Ferret Society which was a well-deserved winner and had certainly attracted the greatest interest from onlookers.

Gail was there with Mr Partridge who between the two of them and the rest of the committee had orchestrated events which appeared to run like clockwork. It was a traditional English fete and people sat around the ring on straw bales watching the multitude of different activities some of which seemed very professional, others less so.

A sheepdog trial was conducted by a well-known local shepherd as he worked his dogs around a group of eight Indian runner ducks that he eventually cornered in a pen, a chap with a Harris hawk entertained with his falconry skills although the bird was less enthusiastic and spent the majority of its time perched in a tree.

Ron Short had kindly turned up and judged the dog show with much professionalism.

The Salvation Army brass band had a tent near the ice cream van and pleasant music could be heard over the festivities as people strolled about taking part. I had heard from Gail that there had been a last-minute hitch over the coconuts. For years, a very large lady from Ipswich attended the fete but the previous week she had been hit by an errant ball whilst attending her shy. The last-minute replacement was a somewhat sinister looking man with shifty eyes and a porkpie hat.

'How is it all going Gail?' I asked as I walked past.

'So far so good,' she said, 'no hitches and the weather is perfect.'

Children ran around screaming excitedly trying to persuade their beleaguered parents to part with yet more coins to spend on candyfloss, win a goldfish, or buy an ice cream. The youths of the village and those fathers that were able to extricate themselves from their families had a jolly time in the beer tent which was run by the proprietor of the Anne of Cleves. He looked as though he was enjoying himself and perhaps sampling a bit too much of his own wares.

A lot of people had brought picnics and were sitting on rugs around the ground delighting in the simplicity of such an old-fashioned tradition. At various points during the afternoon Sebastian and Serena were called upon to judge displays and award prizes. Serena gaily presented the cups and Sebastian solemnly shook hands with the winners.

At five o'clock the fete drew to a close with its finale, an exhibition in the main ring. This year's honour was performed by a group from the Frampton Young Farmers who did a sort of show jumping event riding quad bikes. I couldn't quite make up my mind whether it looked more dangerous on a quad or a horse. In any case I doubt Gail or Mr Partridge had carried out any sort of risk assessment so a collective sigh of relief must have been sighed as the display came to an end with no deaths or casualties.

Emma had enjoyed the day, probably much more so than Sophie and me. She had been for a ride on the merry-go-round, watched the goings-on in the arena and unfortunately won a gold fish by throwing a ping-pong ball into a jam jar. As we were leaving Emma suddenly remembered that we had forgotten the goldfish just as we were going out the gate. I had hoped that we would leave it behind with the stallholder. We returned and collected the poor little fish now swimming around in a plastic bag of water. We set off to fetch my car which was outside the estate office. It was good to see so many people milling about in Church Street but somehow the eagle eye of Mrs Bumstead picked me out.

'Afternoon, Mr and Mrs Aden,' she said, 'hasn't it been a lovely day?'

'It has indeed,' I replied, 'have you been up on the recreation field?'

'Yes, I have,' she said, 'but I came home early as I always have me dinner at four o'clock and I'm looking after me little grandson for a couple of days.'

'Oh well you will have had the most of the day,' I said, 'it's all winding down now.'

'I can see everybody's drifting back,' she remarked. 'I expect they're making for the pub.'

'I'm sure a lot of them are but not us, we must get off home now.'

'Well before you go can I just have a quick word? That's why I was hoping to pick you out in the crowd.'

Oh dear, I thought ominously. Mrs Bumstead was one of those tenants who believed in a quick word which was anything but quick.

'It's me lavatory,' she went on, 'and excuse me Mrs Aden,' she said to Sophie, 'and I know it's a bank holiday and all that but it's stopped flushing. And with the little bairn here it's a real nuisance.'

For goodness sakes, I thought, I'm out on the bank holiday afternoon with my family and now presented with having to attend to some old dear's lavatory.

Anything to do with sewage was the bane of a resident agent's job. It was all very well calling the plumber but often the preliminary inspection was down to myself. Either to see if it was something simple that was easily fixed or to make sure that we got the right tradesperson organised to attend.

'I'll come in and have a quick look,' I said, 'but I'm not a plumber so it might have to wait until tomorrow.'

'Oh please do come in and see,' she implored. 'I don't think it'll wait until tomorrow. You see it's a bit overflowing.'

This was getting worse. I left Sophie and Emma standing outside her cottage with the promise that I wouldn't be very long.

The bathroom was on the ground floor at the back of the property typical of the Victorian terraced cottages in Church Street that were basically two up two downs. At some later date probably in the nineteen sixties they had a bathroom and WC tacked onto the back.

To be fair to Mrs Bumstead she had been dealing with this issue for a while as she kept calling in the office to mention it but I had kept forgetting her. There had been faint murmurings in the estate office about the condition of her bathroom possibly for a couple of months but until this moment I hadn't taken her seriously. I expected from past form that it would be a tiny matter and would probably solve itself.

'It's in 'ere,' she said leading the way through the kitchen to the little offshoot at the back.

'I'll just put the boy in the sitting room to play with himself,' she told me. I thought she should perhaps use a different preposition in her sentence.

The offshoot did not smell pleasant.

Fortunately, the loo had lid on it so I was spared some unpleasant evidence of the problem.

'When you say it doesn't flush, do you mean this handle's broken or it's not going away?'

'It's the 'andle Mr Aden. I think it's come of inside.'

I had to have some sympathy with her. She was a widow of very limited means and although she had a very supporting family, they had all moved miles away. Her husband had worked on the estate as a farm labourer on one of the tenanted farms but he had died quite young when he had been kicked by a cow. It gave him internal problems that were never resolved.

The evidence of his handiwork in the cottage was all around. He had been quite the opposite of his wife and would never call the estate for any help or repair work to the cottage. It was to be generally applauded but did rather depend on the skill of the tenant carrying out the repairs. The late Mr Bumstead, who I never knew but by all accounts, was a cheery friendly fellow, not only attended to matters such as decoration but also plumbing, general maintenance and carpentry. His skills had been honed botching up calf pens or repairing gates but if such finesse existed on those objects it didn't extend into the house.

The lavatory handle was clearly one of his repair jobs and it was a wonder that it had lasted so long as he had been dead for ten years. It appeared to me to be made out of an old bicycle pump. When I questioned Mrs Bumstead, she confirmed that I was correct.

'It's an unusual thing to use as a lavatory handle,' I remarked.

She looked at me as though she didn't agree.

'My late Fred put it there,' she explained, 'it's done the job up till now. He was a craftsman,' she added proudly.

I felt that I was been accused of criticising her late Fred's handiwork but I persevered.

'It's just that it's rather long and a bit unwieldly. It looks rather odd.'

'I suppose I've got used to it,' she said and glancing around the cottage I noticed that quite a lot of things looked rather odd but I suppose she had got used to them too.

'Let me show you', she went to action the lever, 'see it's gone all floppy,' she explained.

I was a pretty hopeless handyman myself but an occupational hazard had led me to become a semi-expert in basic plumbing. There didn't appear to be anything wrong with the bicycle pump itself so I took the lid off the system. I then saw that it was a simple matter of piece of wire that should have connected the end of the lever to the top of the ballcock had come adrift. It was easily secured.

'There,' I said, 'let's give it a try and see if it works now.'

After a couple of goes the pan emptied itself with a considerable gurgling and spluttering and gushing. Once it had settled, I gave it another pull and everything seemed to be back in working order.

'Oh you are a wonder Mr Aden,' she enthused, 'a wonderful man.'

'That's very kind of you to say so Mrs Bumstead, but I think we were just lucky on this occasion that the problem was simple to solve.'

I went to re-join my family who were patiently waiting outside but couldn't help noticing as I left that the bookshelves to the side of the fireplace in the sitting room sloped at an alarming angle.

'Those bookshelves don't look quite level to me,' I mentioned to Mrs Bumstead.

'I know,' she said. 'My Fred put them up. They are a bit wonky but the main thing is there as strong as the Forth Road Bridge,' she assured me, 'I can put anything on them and they won't fall off the wall. He always put a bit of strength in his work. He was a craftsman you know.'

With that remark I left so that we could get on with rest of our evening and return home.

CHAPTER 15

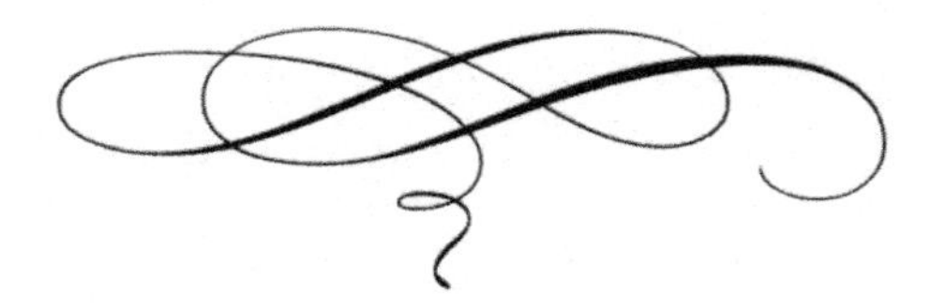

On Tuesday the weather changed dramatically. The front brought in heavy rain and thunderstorms which were a welcome delight for the parched fields and gardens. The electricity in the air produced magnificent lightning strikes and rolls of thunder as dramatic as I could remember. Torrential rain flooded down the streets. The force of it washed straight off the land into the ditches and streams which were suddenly bubbling with fury after a long hot dry spell of weather.

On Wednesday, although the weather had eased, storms were brewing in the Buckley household.

Anne put through a call in the estate office.

'Sebastian how are things with you? I hope you enjoyed the fete and seeing Frampton in all its glory?'

'Yes, I did thank you,' he replied. 'Well no, actually I didn't. I mean it's lovely to see these traditional English festivities and I am glad that we are part of them but I didn't really like having to judge things. Or pretend to be interested in organisations that make up the fabric of this village.'

I was rather taken aback.

'Sorry to hear that. It's all so much part of village life and the estate. Now, you being the Lord of the Manor it's difficult to avoid. Did Serena enjoy herself?'

'Yes, she did to a certain extent,' he explained. 'I just don't feel comfortable in the role.'

'I think it's surely a matter of time,' I said, 'you've got your father's footsteps to follow in and he devoted his whole life to the estate and all this sort of activity.'

'I know that, it's just not me.'

There was a pause then he continued, 'I would like you to come down and see me and Serena if you can sometime today. I think there are things we need to discuss.'

'Of course,' I replied, 'whenever suits you. You're the boss,' I added jokingly.

'Well yes, I suppose I am. In a way that's the point.'

I didn't say anything.

'Is eleven o'clock okay? And we can have some coffee?' he asked.

'Fine I'll see you then at Bulls Place Farmhouse.'

Rather like the ominous thunder storms of yesterday I sensed an ill wind to the discussion. Inevitably though I needed to hear what they had to say.

Before meeting them, I needed to have a chat with Albert Coppins who lived in the Market Passage just down from the estate office. He and his wife were delightful Suffolk people who like many others in Frampton had spent their whole lives in the village. He was a retired gardener from the Hall and had always had an interest in keeping bees. As far as I could make out, he was the biggest provider of honey in the village and he took great care and delight in producing jars for sale. He still kept some beehives in the old garden at Frampton Hall but most of his hives were now located near the allotment gardens. His house in Market Passage had a garden but it was not suitable for keeping bees and certainly not the number that he kept. He now had twenty hives by the allotments and we had recently been receiving complaints from people working on the allotments and those walking on the footpath nearby who were concerned that they were being pursued by bees.

I went and knocked on his door on the off chance that he would be at home. He was.

'Hello, Mr Aden,' he greeted me.

'Hello, Albert. Sorry to bother you is it a convenient time to call in?'

'Any time, any time, as always pleased to see you.'

'Thank you,' I said, 'but I'm afraid I've some awkward news for you which we ought to discuss. Don't worry,' I continued, 'it's just that we've had complaints about the bees down by the allotments.'

'People always complain about bees and yet they're the gentlest creatures you can possibly imagine,' he said. 'They ain't gonna sting you unless you trouble them.'

'I'm sure you're right,' I replied, 'but you know what most people are like, they don't even know the difference between a wasp and a bee.'

He threw his hands up in disgust.

'Well they ought to know,' he said.

'I agree but it's not going to solve the problem. They won't stop worrying about it so I think we should move them so they're slightly further away from where people might come across them.'

'What I suggest is we won't do anything rash but you have a look around – that is if you need to look as you know the estate so well – choose somewhere else that is just further away from the public. We can fence off an area for you to put them.'

'Right then Mr Aden, I'll have a ponder,' he agreed. 'I can see the sense in that and it's very kind of you and Sir Sebastian to think of me like this. It will have to be near the village though because the bees do prefer the gardens to the fields. There's more pollen in them garden flowers and vegetables than out in them fields.'

'I'm very happy for that,' I said, 'choose a few places and come and tell me so we can try and organise something.'

Having dealt with that minor concern I returned to the office and climbed into the Land Rover to drive down and see Serena and Sebastian.

I had a feeling that there was something ominous about the forthcoming meeting with Sebastian and Serena. Although Sir Charles' death had been rather sudden and I knew that Sebastian would find the significant changes demanding, there seemed to be more to it than that. It was as though he didn't want to try and embrace his new life at all and wanted to maintain a low profile and hope things would carry on as before. There were plenty of other instances where large estates had a non-resident owner, especially the estates in Scotland. But it would lead to particular problems under this scenario at Frampton. Anybody living in Frampton Hall and owning the estate would have a significant presence and would inevitably be drawn into estate life.

Despite the warm day I was invited into the sitting room and the three of us sat down in comfortable chairs with a tray of iced drinks on the table in front.

'How are you both,' I asked.

'Fine thank you,' they replied in unison.

'I hope you enjoyed the fete, it seemed to go very well I thought.'

'Yes, it seemed to be very busy and I hope it raised plenty of money for the various charities,' replied Sebastian.

'No doubt we will hear soon,' I replied. 'I think Gail is gradually getting all the figures together.'

They looked uncomfortable and slightly ill at ease. We were disturbed by a commotion at the front door and a lot of barking from Argonaut the Irish wolfhound. Serena went to find out the cause of it. Apparently, a passing cyclist had come across some lambs in the lane and presuming they belonged to the owner of Bulls Place Farmhouse had kindly come to let them know.

'Oh, they're always getting out,' Serena told us, 'I never do anything about it as they seem to find their own way back.'

'It's a bit irritating if you keep getting someone at the door telling you they've escaped when they're not your sheep isn't it?' I asked.

'It is a bit', she agreed, 'but people are getting used to it now.'

She poured some cordial for us and then looked at Sebastian as though expecting him to say something.

'I don't know where to begin,' he said, 'this is not an easy discussion and I'm sure you won't want to hear it. But,' and he paused for effect, 'Serena and I have spent a long, long time thinking about what we should do now that my father has died and what to do with the future of this estate.'

He stood up and started pacing in front of the fireplace with some agitation.

He continued, 'There is no easy way to put this, so here it is. I have decided to relinquish the title and sell the estate.'

Serena was looking intently at him and I nearly dropped my drink on the floor. I had expected bad news but not as devastating as this. I was speechless. It basically meant that he didn't want anything to do with the Buckley inheritance, the centuries-old title, the history, the hugely important status of Frampton Hall and all its internationally important contents. It was unbelievable and I couldn't take it in. To have been lucky enough to have all this given to you on a plate and then reject it seemed not only unreal but idiotic.

'Have you got something a little stronger than lime juice?' I suggested in jest.

They laughed nervously.

'I'm sure we can find something.'

'I'm only joking,' I said. 'I just can't believe what you've said.'

'I know it's a massive decision,' confirmed Sebastian, 'but we have given it so much thought and not just about what I've said but looking ahead to the future.'

'Have you spoken to any of the trustees?' I asked.

'No. At the moment this is purely between the three of us, but we needed to get you to understand our reasons about what we would do with everything before we took it further.'

I was grateful that they had taken me into their confidence.

'There are so many things to consider here,' said Sebastian, and Serena nodded. 'I'm sure we will need to have plenty more discussions but let me tell you what the main points are and why we've come to the decisions and what we intend to do in the future.' It came out in a bit of a rush.

'I'm intrigued what you have to tell me,' I said.

'Let's take the title first of all,' said Sebastian. 'Neither Serena nor I are comfortable with being Sir and Lady. It doesn't fit with our lives outside the estate which to be honest are our lives. The estate side of things are something inherited and although it seems ungrateful, and we're not, but we feel to be honest we're not interested in it or want to spend time and effort making it our lives.'

I remained silent.

'And as you know, and you are one of the very few people to know, we shall not be having any children so the title will extinguish after me anyway unless some distant cousin inherited which is somewhat pointless. They will have had nothing to do with Frampton and it would not be my intention to leave the estate to a distant relation who we neither really know nor have any common ideals.'

I was still speechless. I didn't like to mention that I had traced the possible successor to the title as I didn't want to disrupt his train of thought.

'So, if you accept that the title will extinguish and we don't want it then there must be some logic in our decision.'

I murmured an assent but didn't comment.

He went on. 'The second main issue is the house. We have a beautiful house, Frampton Hall, filled with treasures and yet it costs an absolute fortune to run it. From what I can tell we need at least the rent from ten thousand acres of land and all the cottages and houses and so on simply to run the place. In our view that's ludicrous because why pour that money into one building where just two people live when we are perfectly comfortable here? It just doesn't fit with our ideological and personal feelings.'

I was dismayed and remained in a state of disbelief. The historical importance of a family such as the Buckleys, who owned huge tranches of the British countryside was something that in my view was to be preserved. It benefited the family of course but also all the people that lived and worked on the estate, it preserved a living history, it preserved the stability in society. I recognised that there would be many people that would challenge that view and see extreme wealth in the hands of one person or one family was inequitable. My job had to be the opposite of that – my career had been spent on trying to preserve these traditional families and their estates.

'There's an awful lot to think about,' I said, 'and if it is the way you want to go forward then a massive amount of dismantling of your family's heritage needs to take place.'

'I can completely understand that,' Sebastian agreed and Serena nodded.

'Have you thought about setting up a trust such as they have at Burghley or Chatsworth? There the estate assets fund the houses and their collections which are then open to the public. So, you and Serena could step back and let the trustees manage it while still preserving everything intact for future generations.'

'We have thought vaguely about that and of course handing it over to the National Trust but that doesn't fit with our ideological responsibilities,' he said.

'You see, our intention is to set up a trust but not simply for the benefit of preserving the house which we don't really feel is warranted. But a trust that can benefit what we perceive to be more important than a building. You know that we both have involvement in a subsistence farming organisation in various countries and water provision in Ethiopia and, which you might not know about, a research project into human infertility. We feel that we would prefer to fund these kinds of missions than preserve a house which has no future use for us or our descendants of which there won't be any!'

I could understand the point of their reasoning but it was, nonetheless, a huge mental shift from less than an hour ago when I had left the estate office.

'I suppose you realise that there will be a colossal amount of persuading the trustees to agree to your ideas,' I continued, 'as you know they were selected by your father to protect both you and the estate. A lot of the property is in trust. In legal terms they own it and you are the beneficiary of the income.'

'Yes I know there's a lot of legal complications with all of this,' Sebastian agreed, 'and I have no doubt that the trustees will be not only be alarmed but also totally against the idea.'

'I think that's an under estimate,' I said, 'and to be honest I'm not even sure what the legal standing will be and if it can be unpicked. That's something for the lawyers to discuss and advise you on. All I can do is keep on doing the best I can knowing that this in the back of your mind.'

'This is more than just in the back of our minds,' Sebastian affirmed, 'it's something we've been thinking about for a long time and it's only recently when we found out about not being able to have children that it seemed to be the final thing that's tipped the decision.'

'Have you thought about alternatives whereby you keep the estate intact and maybe open the house to the public and try to make it profitable and then maybe using some of that money for your charities?' I asked trying desperately to find some kind of compromise for what they wanted.

'No, we haven't particularly thought of that scenario,' Sebastian pondered. 'I suppose it is something we should at least consider but it doesn't get over the two things already mentioned. That is, as I said earlier, the house soaks up hundreds of thousands and now with these improvements, millions of pounds and we think people are more important than buildings. And secondly neither of us have a particular wish to play the Lord and Lady of the Manor role.'

'There could be ways forward though,' I continued, 'if we could set up the whole estate to benefit this charitable trust. I accept that a good part of the money would go towards maintaining the house but the residue could go into other charitable trusts that you and Serena could run. You wouldn't have to live in the house or even take an interest in the estate. You could stay living here, low key and concentrate on the lives you want and the separate charitable trusts that benefited from any excess that the estate made.'

I was clutching at straws.

'Well we can think about it,' they both nodded, 'it's not really what we had in mind but we certainly won't disregard it. Have you any idea how much surplus you think might be available for the charity side of things?'

'Sorry I have no idea, we'd have to do some serious financial planning to get any kind of thoughts. Have you also thought about the other properties like Strathard and the forestry in Canada and the property in London?'

'We definitely want to keep Strathard,' Sebastian confirmed and Serena added, 'yes we love going up there.'

'You will need to keep some other profitable assets then just to run Strathard. You know that costs about three hundred thousand pounds a year to run which in anybody's book is a somewhat expensive holiday cottage!'

'I know,' Sebastian nodded, 'and it probably seems a bit hypocritical to want to set up this charity and yet keep the Scottish estate which is after all a rich man's playground.'

'You have of course a lot of assets held in your name anyway so you can do what you want with them in theory. But as they effectively are all going into the same pot as the trust income, then I don't think you can really start channelling that money away from the estate without the estate going bankrupt. So, although you have these ideas, I do beg that you don't do anything yet. Between us all we will find a way forward.'

They both agreed that nothing was going to happen immediately and they would look at the possibility of somehow keeping the estate intact as a basis for what they wanted to do.

CHAPTER 16

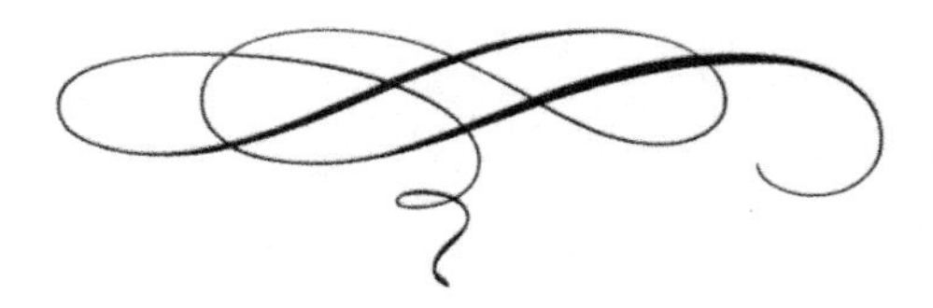

I didn't feel like going back to the office immediately so I drove up to Frampton Hall to spend a while in the imposing yet silent environs of the heart of this family's home. I found Hole in his pantry cleaning Sir Charles' riding boots.

He looked up.

'Hello, Mr Hole,' I said.

'Hello, Mr Aden,' he replied.

I looked at the boots. 'It's a rather odd job to be doing,' I suggested, 'I would have thought those had been packed away?'

'I like to keep Sir Charles' boots properly fed,' he replied, 'leather of this quality needs feeding and looking after rather like a plant.'

'I suppose it does,' I said, 'but it's unlikely that anyone's going to wear them.'

He looked at me. 'You never know, maybe Sir Sebastian will take up riding again,' he offered, 'he knows how to ride and used to have ponies when he was younger.'

'He may do,' I suggested sadly, 'but I can't see it at the moment.'

I didn't dare say anything to Mr Hole about the discussion I had just had with the current baronet and his wife. Not only had we had a confidential conversation but the revelation would likely give Hole a heart attack.

'Where are the dogs – they're quiet?'

'They're with Mrs Jubb in the kitchen. She's offered to take them for a walk this afternoon as I need to go to Bury to purchase some pipe tobacco.'

Hole possessed an impressive array of pipes on his desk and like most pipe smokers had a particular brand of tobacco that he smoked. After a lifetime of service in grand houses he had developed a passion for a particular tobacco that had to be ordered especially by the tobacconist in Bury St Edmunds. Hole was not disposed, he told me, to purchase that dreadful compost that they sold in the village store.

I left him sorting out boots remembering that one of the ingredients he used to feed them involved obtaining a jar of blood from the butchers and reflected that if Sebastian's plans came to fruition not only would Hole be out of a job but probably it would be the end of his career. I doubted there were many positions left that required a butler to mix a special potion of dubious origins to use on his master's riding boots.

I had a thousand thoughts spinning around in my mind and felt that spending an hour or so wandering around the staterooms and looking at the paintings and furniture would perhaps sift them into some kind of order. It was totally beyond my comprehension that anyone would voluntarily give up all this I thought, looking around. The was a weight of responsibilities but a privileged life and yes, it did cost a fortune to run the house but Sebastian had a fortune to do it.

If he didn't want to though it was pointless, I could see that.

I walked from room to room taking in the art that covered the walls and all of it was of fabulous quality and much of it was priceless. Rembrandts, Canaletto's, Vermeer to name only a few. The quality of the collection was world-class and it was depressing to think of it being presumably sold and split up. Museums, art galleries and significant private collectors would no doubt love to get their hands on even one of these paintings and again I couldn't understand why Sebastian wanted to throw away his family's heritage. It was a sobering and melancholy thought. I could reason with him in the sense that by not having an heir would itself be immensely disillusioning and therefore maybe by selling everything now he did in some way have control over the family's future. Maybe in the sense that a charitable trust could ensure the Buckley name would continue indefinitely.

My mind turned towards more practical matters of how we would deal with the situation. For the time being Sebastian and Serena and myself were aware but soon others, like the trustees, the solicitors, accountants and no doubt a whole host of experts in their fields would be required to advise us. It would be the biggest dismantling of a landed estate in decades, possibly since the end of the Second World War.

As I had mentioned to Sebastian, the trustees would be the first call and a lot would depend on their views and how he handled them. Although he was the beneficiary of the trust, in legal terms they owned a lot of the assets and Sebastian had no control over them. Sebastian now owned Frampton Hall and its grounds, its three hundred acres of parkland and the Frampton Stud which extended to another hundred acres adjoining the park. He also owned the majority of the contents of the house including half the paintings. The rest were owned by one of the trusts known as the Frampton Trust Settlement who owned about three and a half thousand acres of the farmland. The Frampton Hall Estate Settlement owned the other six thousand acres roughly speaking and most of the village of Frampton.

Sebastian personally now owned Strathard Estate outright and, although I wasn't sure, I believed he owned most if not all the shares of the Canadian timber company.

The property in London which extended to a sizeable chunk of Chelsea, was predominantly made up of let houses, offices and shops which provided a disproportionately large amount of income compared to the rest the estate. That was all owned by the Buckley Family London Settlement. Sebastian needed to take account of that due to its significant income.

I took the main staircase up to the first floor. The staircase was twelve feet wide and rose gracefully sweeping to left and right on the first floor with a galleried landing which circled the complete staircase hall. The gallery was again lined with an array of beautiful paintings no less grand or important than those in the staterooms downstairs. I went into some of what were referred to as the state chambers which were the grandest bedroom suites used by visiting nobility and sovereigns. Queen Victoria and Prince Albert had visited in the eighteen forties on a number of occasions to attend shooting parties. Several rooms had been redecorated and refurnished at that time to accommodate their visits. Inevitably called the Queen's suite the furnishings were as one might expect at the height of the Victorian era. I found them quite heavy and overbearing but this was of course the great days of Empire and reflected the taste of the time.

A much earlier Royal visit had occurred in seventeen eighty when King George the third had been entertained on a passing visit, as the monarch and his entourage were touring East Anglia. Again, a suite of rooms had been redesigned and decorated for his visit and the King's Suite was of a much more elegant and comfortable decor than the Victorian one. The Chinese bedroom was created and furnished following a previous baronet's tour of the Far East and interestingly held many cabinets of Oriental porcelain which I had been told were unique in their quantity and quality of any private collection.

And so it went on. It was hard to believe that this all might go. Although I was only an employee, I had a real attachment to the place and the family. I felt disheartened. I was relieved from my melancholy thoughts when I bumped into Hole in the long corridor.

'I thought you'd gone to Bury St Edmunds to get your tobacco?' I said surprised.

'No I haven't departed yet. I've been delayed as I'm on the search for one of the poodles. Mrs Jubb let it out of the kitchen we can't find it.'

'Oh dear,' I said, 'well it's not in any of these rooms,' I advised, 'which one have you lost?'

'It's Monty, the black one. He's a terror for wandering off and he never comes when he's called. I did tell Mrs Jubb to keep them on the lead if they weren't in the kitchen but I think it somehow escaped.'

Although Sir Charles' dogs had been very obedient with him, they rather ran rings around both Hole and Mrs Jubb. They possibly sensed that they were now the rightful owners of the house and these people were their servants. I supposed they were right. I have to admit that despite the fact that I should have helped find the dog I left them to it and returned to the estate office. There was a lot to be done as usual but I was distracted by the scenario that been presented to me earlier that morning. We would need to arrange a trustees meeting with some haste and Sebastian and Serena had said that they would make themselves available at early notice to fit in with the trustees.

That in itself was going to be a problem. The trustees were all busy and important men in their own fields and apart from the quarterly meetings that were arranged in advance, getting together at short notice would be a challenge. No doubt Sebastian's ideas would galvanise them to make haste if they possibly could.

Trustees meetings were formal arrangements and attended by the three trustees, the baronet, myself and usually the estate lawyer and accountant. The December meeting which traditionally took place just before Christmas was a more relaxed affair and centred around an expensive boozy lunch at a London club. The other three tended to be formal business meetings and whilst we could be assured of a decent meal, they tended to be more sober gatherings.

CHAPTER 17

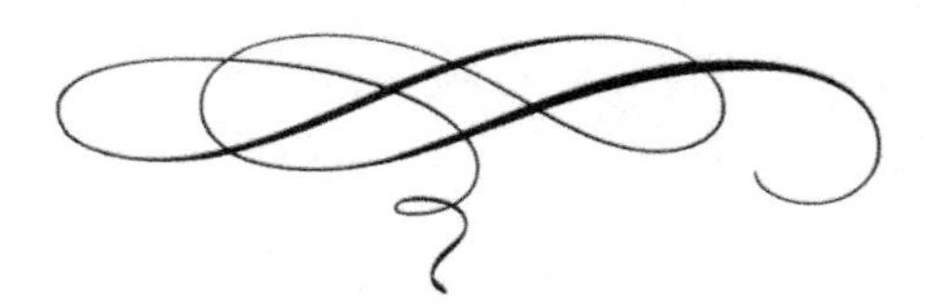

The trustees had been carefully chosen by Sir Charles as apart from their responsibilities as guardians, he rightfully wanted people that he could trust with their views and decisions with regard to the future of his family's assets.

With good fortune a new trustee had been appointed relatively recently who was a close friend of Sebastian's and proved helpful in the ensuing discussions. Peregrine Clark-MacDonald was a feisty entrepreneur with a rational attitude to the estate business.

He succeeded an old friend of Sir Charles, Lord Ivor Nowton. When Sir Charles appointed his trustees, they were, like him, relatively young or middle-aged men at the prime of their business acumen. As the years passed these loyal and trusted friends became less sharp and decisive. With wisdom Lord Ivor had decided to retire and his successor took his place.

Lord Ivor had in his day held a senior position at the Bank of England and was a well-respected financier. Sadly, as he aged his memory declined and he had claimed the nickname in the press of Lord Nought-On and his contributions to trustees' meetings had become, if not helpful then unusual. At his final trustees' meeting he had proposed for instance that the trustees should invest in a company that produced ladies nylon stockings which had rather surprised everyone. When asked why he felt this was such a good investment for the future he had replied that he not only thought the trustees should move into more wide-ranging investments but also that nylon stockings had a multitude of uses. They were wearable as ladies' stockings but they could also be used for placing over one's shoes during snowy conditions to prevent slipping.

Lord Ivor, a lifelong friend of Sir Charles, owned a neighbouring estate and in earlier years had been a valuable source of knowledge as he shared his experiences of owning and managing his estate bordering Frampton. In later years he developed some eccentricities which initially didn't seem to affect his judgement in important estate decisions but his lordship's appearance did not inspire confidence.

He took to arriving at trustees' meetings in the Strand in London wearing his bespoke Savile Row suit but spoilt the look because he'd wear a pair of bright green trainers with a red stripe down the sides, clutching his documents in a Tesco carrier bag.

Even Sir Charles had agreed at the time that perhaps it was time for Lord Ivor to relinquish his post.

Peregrine Clark-MacDonald had proved to be an inspirational choice and as he was of similar age to me, we had struck up a bond that was to prove useful in the deliberations over Sebastian's intention. It helped that he was a friend of Sebastian's. The other two trustees, Sir Frederick Millay and Mr Simon Bird were both still of astute mind. One was a landowner the other was a lawyer. It gave a fairly balanced approach to discussions particularly because Peregrine was not from a wealthy family although his ancestry was practically blue blood. The mix of characters and their experiences gave the trustees' meetings a real sense of deliberation.

The trustees would usually be joined by the estate lawyer, Elton

Carruthers, senior partner in Carruthers, Alton and Birtwistle, who were reputedly the finest trust lawyers in London. He was a man of immense knowledge and chaired the meetings with skill and precision but he had no sense of humour whatsoever.

The accountants that the estate used were again a London firm, Brown and Gray Limited. They were represented by a partner called Andrew Gray. Mr Gray worked closely with the Buckley family's bankers and stockbrokers juggling the finances with a skill that enabled the family and the businesses to prosper.

The severity of Sebastian's announcement fortunately galvanised everyone to agree an urgent meeting which was convened in the state dining room at Frampton Hall. On this occasion Serena also joined the meeting though more as a support to Sebastian rather than being able to add much to the conversation. Hole had kindly got the room ready for the meeting which, despite the continuing warm spell and the electric fire, was perishingly cold. The meeting was scheduled to last for most of the day with a break at one o'clock for a light lunch provided by Mrs Jubb.

Once everyone was seated in the formal surroundings of the impressive room and appropriately being watched over by Buckley ancestors peering down from the walls, we made a start. I gave an opening welcome and thanked all those coming to Frampton at such short notice on behalf of the estate and Sir Sebastian and Lady Serena.

I handed over the chairmanship to Mr Carruthers.

'Sir Sebastian, Lady Serena and gentlemen,' he began, 'thank you Mr Aden for your welcome and as we all know we are here under most unusual and extreme circumstances to discuss the wishes of our beneficiary Sir Sebastian,'

'As trustees we were appointed by your late father Sir Charles with the intention that the various trusts were to ensure the financial stewardship of the assets that belong to the Buckley family.'

He went on. 'We are now advised that the Buckley family will cease in this present line after the passing in due course of Sebastian and that in readiness for such time, which we hope of course is many decades away, we are to dismantle the trusts as we know them and redirect those assets into a new charitable trust that is to be set up and in part run by Sir Sebastian and Lady Serena.

'We all know that with the demise of these trusts the Frampton Hall estate will no longer be a viable business as on its own as it does not generate sufficient income to cover expenditure. The single biggest cost is the running of this house and we also know that there is an anticipated four million pounds perhaps to spend on improving the wiring and heating system.'

The others were all looking intently at him and glancing occasionally at their papers which were on the table. I had prepared on Sebastian's instruction, a summary of the discussion that he and I had had the previous week about his preferred intentions looking forward.

Mr Carruthers continued. 'Whilst we must be considerate of the beneficiary and his wishes, I think it is also our responsibility to consider if there are alternative ways of supporting the beneficiaries' wishes whilst retaining the estate. By doing that I mean we organise the estate business so that it produces a big enough surplus to meet the needs of Sebastian's new charity whilst maintaining the fabric of this house, its contents and all the let property.'

There was a murmur of approval throughout the room although Sebastian and Serena remained quiet.

A considerable amount of discussion followed about how this might be achieved in practice but it was clear from the very basic figures provided by Mr Gray that particularly taking into account the death duties outstanding following Sir Charles' death and the cost of renovations to the Hall there would be little left over for much else.

Even when omitting the extravagance of Sir Charles' racehorses and the stud it didn't make huge amount of difference. Sir Charles had led such a frugal life in every other way that his racehorses had cost probably a lot less than most equivalent landowners would have spent maintaining a reasonable standard of living. Sir Charles had barely gone on holiday except to Strathard, drove around in a nineteen seventy Morris traveller estate, and had even been known to stop and pick up roadkill and ask Mrs Jubb to cook it. It didn't leave much room for manoeuvre.

Sebastian did not look comfortable in the surroundings.

'I sincerely appreciate all of you coming here and listening to what I had talked about in some detail to James. All that is important, but I much regret that I do not feel the need or that there is any wish on our parts to try and preserve the Buckley inheritance if that's what you want to call it. Looking to the future it basically doesn't meet our objectives.

As you rightly mentioned, Mr Carruthers, there is a massive amount of money tied up in not just the estate but also the house and its contents. There are a huge number of assets which are providing an income, more or less the entirety of which is spent on running this house. So we have a twofold problem really. If we sell the assets, they can produce a much better income. For instance, the art collection here is worth a fortune and grows in capital every year but produces not one penny. And then secondly this house is draining all the money. Perhaps different assets could produce greater income?'

He looked inquiringly around the room to see if people understood him.

Clearly they had and in essence they couldn't really question his reasoning. They were all thinking of how to protect and ensure the continuation of a family's landed estate. He conversely was openly wanting to sell it all with the resulting pot of money invested in ways that would produce a sizeable income to support the various interests that he and Serena had in mind for their charity.

The meeting continued with various twists and turns and discussions about all sorts of alternatives but I could see that Sebastian was not much inclined towards any alternative to his own mission.

At one o'clock the was a knock on the door and Hole came in with a trolley laden with sandwiches and a selection of drinks.

'Lunch is served, Sir Sebastian,' he announced.

'Thank you, Mr Hole,' said Sebastian. 'Gentlemen please help yourselves to some lunch and perhaps we can take a break for half an hour.'

The lunch was not a great success partly due to the strained atmosphere in the room and partly, and I was afraid it was my fault, I had failed to suggest to Mrs Jubb a suggestion of sandwich fillings. She had been at Frampton for so long that she continued to produce the kind of food that Sir Charles enjoyed and seemed indifferent to the fact that other people might prefer otherwise.

There was an abundance of spam and pickle sandwiches, egg mayonnaise and cress sandwiches, a bowl of pickled onions, a bowl of pickled eggs and a suitable number of sundae glasses containing what I knew would be Angels Delight mixed up out of a packet.

As well as soft drinks there were, incongruously, a couple of bottles of vintage Bollinger champagne in an ice bucket but sadly they remained unopened.

Once the meeting resumed the tone changed. Having spent all morning trying to persuade Sebastian change his mind or to find suitable alternatives or compromises they realised that none of these were going to succeed. Discussion now centred around how on earth the total disassembling was going to take place.

Mr Carruthers explained some of the basic law connected with trusts and he was supported by Mr Gray who likewise advised on tax implications and some of the ways that might be considered workable. Effectively the trustees would become mere pawns in the proceedings and lawyers and accountants would instruct them and me in the procedures.

The meeting drew to a close and after some very dispirited farewells people went on their ways. Peregrine was going to stay with Sebastian and Serena for the evening which I felt was probably a very sensible thing to do as if anyone could change Sebastian's mind then it would be him. The other two trustees were very upset, no doubt on behalf of their dear friend Sir Charles.

As I walked them out to their cars, they were indignant and angry about Sebastian's action.

'The man's a bloody disgrace,' Sir Frederick said. 'I mean this is not what his father would have wanted. He'll be turning in his grave. And it's not what we want as the trustees looking after this family for generations. My father was a trustee to Sir Charles' father and it's a bloody impertinence.'

'I agree,' said Simon Bird, coughing as Sir Frederick lit up a cigar. 'Always a lovely estate to visit, everything anyone could dream about. Don't understand the logic of it, that is if there is any logic. Perhaps he's come unhinged?'

Sir Frederick Miller had another go at lighting his cigar and after half box of matches succeeded in getting it lit. A lovely aroma enveloped us as he continued his diatribe regarding Sebastian's attitude. He lent against his Range Rover and pointed at the house.

'I agree he must be a bloody idiot,' he ranted, 'why would anyone want to give all this away?' He waved his cigar at the ancestral home and Simon Bird, who clearly disapproved of any sort of smoking, legal or not took a step back as a waft enveloped him.

'It's going to be quite a pickle to unscramble things. Can we avoid these dreadful circumstances if we try and keep the trusts intact and feed some of the money to his latest charitable cause?' he asked.

'I've already broached the subject with him now on two occasions,' I said, 'and it was mentioned in the meeting. The stumbling blocks are the value of the painting collections and the cost of running this house. The collections are worth a fortune but because they don't bring in any income and the house is a drain it's a double negative really.'

'One possibility I did put to him was whether we could open the house to the public so that it produces an income which would contribute to the running costs. People would be paying to see the paintings so it sort of deals with both issues.'

The two trustees nodded sagely.

Sir Frederick said, 'I don't think the trustees would have any objection to that idea at all,' he volunteered, 'what do you think Simon?'

'I certainly agree that it could be possible to do that. If so then we will have done our job to maintain things.'

'Do you see any problems?' he asked me.

'I think there are some problems but they could probably be overcome with planning. We will need to invest money to be able to open it to the public. Better lighting, fire escapes all that sort of thing and I suppose the inevitable tea room and gift shop would need incorporating. But is it going to bring in enough money?'

'We need to talk to people who open houses to the public and get some advice. If we could do it, we'd have to set up a new business separate from the rest of the estate,' Mr Bird considered.

Sir Frederick remarked, 'And that's if we can persuade Sebastian to do it because it seems to me that he just wants out of the whole thing. As I said earlier, he's not only mad but irresponsible.'

He climbed into his Range Rover and with farewells drove off across the wide expanse of gravel, through the tall stone gate piers that were surmounted by the family crest and then down through the park.

Mr Bird said to me, 'Well there is not much more we can add to this today. I'll work with Carruthers on the legal side and as far as the trusts are concerned your area will have to carry on as normal. We also need to keep everything confidential for now because any news of this will set hares running. Keep in close contact and we'll see what the next stage may bring.'

He climbed into his car, a more modest Volvo estate, which had a sticker on the rear window announcing that he was member of the Caravan Club. For some reason he didn't seem the sort of person that would go on holiday towing a plastic box.

CHAPTER 18

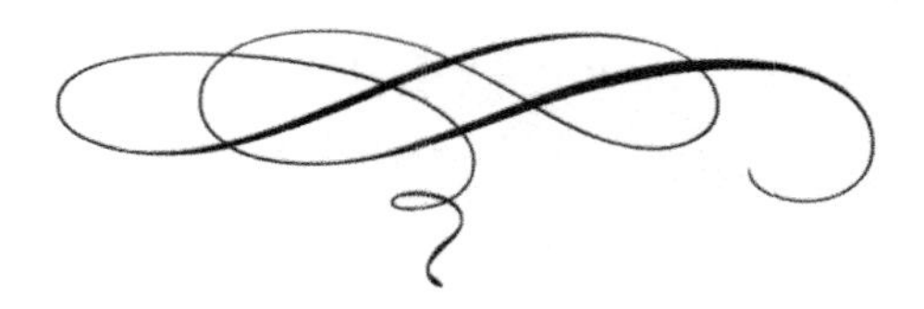

Sophie asked me how it had gone when I arrived home. Sworn to secrecy she knew the general gist of what was going on.

'It must have been a strange meeting but at least you've had everyone there and between you all it's now out in the open to be taken forward.'

'Indeed, it was rather fraught at times,' I said. 'I could tell that Sebastian and Serena were uneasy about the whole thing and the trustees were pretty upset actually. Angry even.'

'You can't blame them. Sir Charles appointed them to ensure continuity and Sebastian has pulled the rug from under their feet,' she remarked.

'It's a bloody mess,' I agreed, 'I cannot imagine how it's going to be a good outcome at all. We will have to see what happens next – there's a lot of planning and considerations to be made which all of a sudden will have to be pulled together to get to some kind of consensus as to where we go next.'

'Anyway,' Sophie changed the subject. 'I've got some good news for you.'

'What's that?' I asked.

'You know that Angus McKay was standing in for Sir Sebastian as chieftain of the Highland Games in Strathard?'

'Oh yes I did know. Sebastian felt that with all this on his mind and what may happen in the future, he didn't feel like doing his public duty just now. Even though coincidentally Strathard is probably the one thing that won't be affected by the upheaval.'

'Well Angus rang to say, and apologises that it's such short notice, that he can't make it because he's got to go into hospital for a small operation on his toe. He's asked the games committee, that if you were willing to accept would you be prepared to attend in his place?'

'I hope you said *yes*.'

It would be a lovely thing to do even though I didn't have quite the standing of a laird. 'He did say he'd been trying to get you at the office but I explained you'd been in a meeting all day with the trustees. I said you'd ring him this evening. Does he know about Sebastian?'

'No the trustees and Sebastian want it kept within the small circle for the time being and in any case whatever happens Strathard appears safe. They want to keep it which is some consolation.'

'That's encouraging. Why don't you ring Angus now?' she instructed.

I did so. He had already spoken to the games committee who were very happy that if I was willing and able then they would like me to act as the chieftain of the games that year.

The games were a week on Saturday so our travel arrangements had to be hastily made. I rang Sebastian to update him with situation and make sure that it was okay on his part as he had asked Angus McKay to stand in for him. I explained the reason.

He was fine with it and reiterated that he didn't want any word at all to be relayed from the trustees meeting to Strathard, not only because it wouldn't affect anyone there but also because none of us wanted whispers to start until we were entirely sure what we were going to do.

'We'd better see if we can book some flights tonight,' suggested Sophie. 'As we're only going to be able to go for the long weekend it's hardly worth driving up. Angus has assured me that the Lodge is available and one of the ghillies will meet us at Inverness airport and drop us off on our return. We can use the estate Land Rover whilst we're there so to let's see if we can get three seats on Fly Maybe.'

'Emma will love it as there's lots of things to do and she'll keep busy while you carry out your duties. I'm not quite sure what they are?' she asked.

'Angus has briefed me on the main points of the games and the committee chairman will guide me through the day. I do know that I have to read a welcoming speech at the opening ceremony.'

Fortunately, there were three seats available on the flight the Thursday before the games although we weren't seated together. The flight was only an hour and a bit so it was immaterial really. We had flown many times before with the airline company and whilst rudimentary it generally seemed to get most people safely to the right destination. Hardly ever on time but at relatively low cost.

Thursday soon came round and we packed as lightly as we could but even at the mild time of year it was highly likely that all four seasons would occur within the day so inevitably some luggage had to go in the hold. As I wasn't a Scotsman, I had no kilt or tartan so I decided the next best thing was the estate tweed, a suit which was not lightweight. It was effectively designed to be worn in the stalking season out on the hill when it could well be snowing and in sub-zero temperatures.

The chieftain's wife had no part to play whatsoever which was a relief to Sophie and she could enjoy a day without ceremony and look after Emma. She didn't need to pack any formal clothes as she was not on 'display' at the games.

Having not pre-booked our hold bag we were somewhat dismayed to find that paying for it on the day was an expensive mistake. It cost as much to send a suitcase to Inverness and back than it did for the three of us but there was nothing to be done about it.

At least we had got seats on the plane as it was completely full. We drove across to Luton and left the car in a short stay car park the cost of which was only marginally less than cost of transporting my suitcase five hundred miles. Our perfect if incautious timing meant we went straight to the departure gate.

Emma wanted to sit by the window so she and Sophie sat in the pair of seats near the front and I took one further back in the cabin. I settled between an elderly gentleman who appeared as though he might be a salmon fisherman, and a youngish woman who looked as though she been brought up on tatties and deep-fried Mars bars. She took up more than her fair share of the space but as the fisherman and I were of slight build we managed a fairly equal distribution across the three seats.

Once we were safely well away from Luton high in the sky, the trolley dollies bustled about with a variety of refreshments and free copies of the on-board magazine advertising holiday destinations and sun filled days on the beaches under palm tree umbrellas. Scotland didn't feature in that section.

I did have some conversation with the gentleman on my left and he was indeed a fisherman but not of the salmon variety. He was a sea angler. He was a wiry little man, a dour Scotsman on his way back home to Invergordon where he was based as an engineer on the oil rigs. He was a proud Scottish nationalist. In an attempt to explain how much I loved his country, its heritage and its landscapes I mistakenly let slip that I was on my way to act as chieftain of a Highland Games gathering.

This revelation caused him some consternation. Previous to this his dialogue been somewhat stilted but it now flowed in an unbroken cauldron, not quite of abuse but about what he thought of Englishmen. To take the role of a Highland chieftain in Scotland did not sit comfortably with him.

The conversation abruptly drew to a close and I reflected that I hoped there wouldn't be many people of a similar persuasion attending the games on Saturday or I might have to borrow a suit of armour from the staircase hall of the lodge.

Regretfully conversation to my right did not proceed in a fluid pattern either. I established that the young woman was on her way to visit her grandmother who had recently moved to a new bungalow in Culloden. An ironic destination considering my previous conversation to my left. Clearly it was an act of duty not pleasure, as she rather ungraciously let me know that she would much rather spend the forthcoming weekend in Luton. Given the choice of the two I would prefer to be in the Scottish Highlands but everyone was different. Her friends were there and she had also had to take two days off from her job as a shop assistant in the bakery in Luton High Street.

Without much to talk about we settled into silence, in as much as one gets silence on an aeroplane and I resumed my studies of the flight magazine. It had a little piece about every city that the airline flew into and I read with interest the article on Inverness.

The capital of the Highlands it stated, the most northern city in Great Britain with a population of around seventy thousand people. It was the base from which to explore the most remote Scottish Highlands; the nearby battlefield of Culloden where the English defeated Bonnie Prince Charlie, and the home of the grandmother of the baker's assistant from Luton although it didn't mention that; Fort George, built to suppress the Jacobean rebellion and the gateway to the great sporting estates of northern Scotland. There was also a number of distilleries mentioned, the annual summer events of the Highland Games and the origin of tartan cloth. Of course, it mentioned Nessie the Loch Ness monster, probably the most famous monster in the world. There were then a number of hotels and restaurants that were recommended, or I suspect paid to be included in the article, but it did indeed paint the picture of wonderful place to explore.

By the time I'd re-read the Loch Ness monster bit we were getting ready to descend into Inverness airport. The plane flew in over the Moray Firth and it was bouncing about a little due to the wind blowing off the sea. With some alarm, just as we were over the runway it accelerated fast and took off into the sky again with obvious anguish to the passenger on my right. My oil rig neighbour seemed nonplussed as surely he was used to the vagaries of Highland weather but the baker's assistant from Luton was decidedly perturbed. The pilot came on over the intercom and explained that due to a change in the wind he was having to approach from the other direction. It seemed to reassure everyone and a smooth landing was accomplished.

As arranged, we were met by one of the ghillies, Colin McKinnon who greeted us warmly. We had been stalking with him several times on the hill and he was an exceptionally skilled stalker. Many returning guests to Strathard would particularly request his presence and he was an old hand at collecting estate visitors from the airport.

'The first time an English chieftain has been so honoured,' he joked.

I laughed. 'I'm afraid they were scraping the bottom of the barrel.' I replied. 'As your new laird Sir Sebastian was unable to make it, as you probably know Angus McKay was given the honour this year.'

'Aye, aye,' he said smiling. 'And he's had to turn it down because of his toe.'

'Poor chap, it was bad timing but something he wanted to get sorted as soon as the appointment was available,' I agreed.

He drove us up to Strathard the scenery as ever changing and becoming wilder and more remote as each mile passed. Coming back to the glen was as enticing and enchanting as the first time. It was almost as if one was entering a different world and no matter how many times we visited, the magic remained the same.

We were as welcome as ever, the Lodge full of friendliness and we truly felt that Mrs McLeod was pleased to see us. She had prepared another Scottish feast in preparation of our arrival.

'The chieftain of the games is here with his wife and family. I could do no better than provide you with the proper provisions for a chieftain!'

We laughed. 'As always you look after us so well Mrs McLeod and we can't tell you how much we enjoy your cooking.'

'It's an honour to look after the chieftain,' she said and we all laughed again.

We enjoyed the evening being back at the Lodge and no doubt had too many drams but that was the norm of being there. We had the Friday to relax and finalise arrangements for the next day. I had to cobble together a suitable welcome speech for the games.

To my shame I had spent little time beforehand thinking about what I was to say so I spent Friday pacing up and down the drawing room composing a suitable speech. It was difficult. I wasn't Scottish, I wasn't a laird, but I had true love and feeling for not only Strathard but also the people that I had met over the years in the glen. Eventually I drafted something that I thought would be appropriate and passed it to Sophie who seemed genuinely reassuring that it was appropriate for the day.

On the Friday we ate again in the dining room and enjoyed Mrs McLeod's fine cooking and took a stroll by the loch with Emma before her bedtime. It was one of those fine evenings and the weather was clear, bright and warm with a slight breeze. If it wasn't for three hundred and forty days spent in cloud and mist then most people who visited Scotland would fall in love with the Highlands.

After a good night's sleep, having had the windows open allowing the Highland air to waft through the bedroom, and the sound of the river burbling in the near distance we felt suitably prepared for the next day.

CHAPTER 19

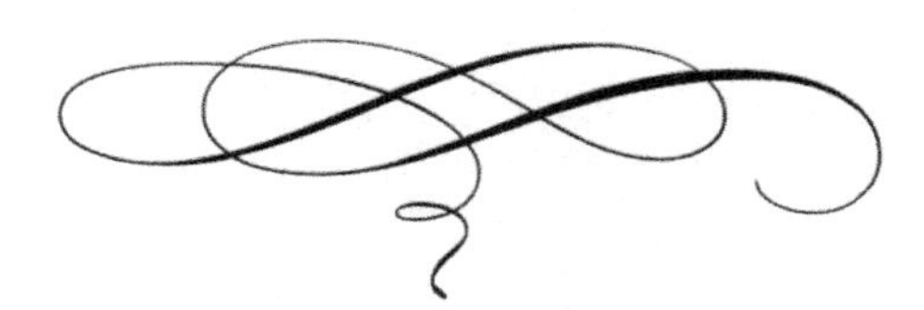

The weather couldn't have been more perfect. It was one of those days in the Highlands that are particularly memorable because there are so few of them. All the right ingredients were there. The sun was shining, it was warm with a gentle breeze to keep the midges away. Many Highland Games had been ruined by inclement weather and the resultant clouds of midges descending on competitors and spectators alike. This however was different. One could breathe the purity of the air which was so clean and scented with a faint hint of grass and heather drifting off the hills.

The games field was situated on an area of pasture by a bend in the river adjacent to the home farm and afforded spectacular mountain views both to the east and south. The grass was meticulously mown and marked out for the various events that were to take place. To one side of the field a long grassy slope provided a perfect position to sit on a picnic blanket and watch the proceedings. At the top of the slope were a number of small marquees hosting various local craft type activities and of course the beer tent. Already a large crowd thronged in front of it and the day's activities had not yet begun.

The opening ceremony took place at twelve noon and after much disorganisation everyone gathered around the ceremonial flag post.

Standing beside the pole I was introduced to the assembled crowd and welcomed as Chieftain of the Games. It was indeed a very special moment and I felt honoured to be there. I scanned the crowd and saw many familiar faces and was pleased that my fellow plane passenger from Invergordon had not come to heckle me.

After a very flattering and undeserved welcome from the chairman of the games committee I embarked upon my Chieftain's speech. I had prepared for it well in the end but did rely on my handwritten notes which I had placed beside me on a little table provided for that reason. I felt I was delivering my speech to plan when a slight gust of wind blew the sheets of paper into the listening crowd. There was a short halt to proceedings whilst willing helpers scrambled around gathering them back for me. I expect that plenty of people were enlightened at that point to the answer of the question often asked of Scotsmen, 'is there anything worn under your kilt?'

Having retrieved and reorganised the papers I continued without further interruption. After a polite round of applause, I was invited to raise the Saltire and declare the games open.

I had been presented as Chieftain with a ceremonial quaich, a delightful solid silver cup engraved with the names of previous Chieftains. It was an unimaginably lovely moment to read my name at the bottom of the list. The list was a testament to the many people who had been respected and loved in this splendid, isolated glen in the Highlands of Scotland.

Having undertaken the formal part of the day and the most nerve wracking, I was free to wander around the grounds chatting to people, both friends and strangers, visiting for the event. Despite the games being relatively small key in the Highland calendar and in such a remote location it was surprisingly well attended by people from wide and far including quite a number of Europeans and Americans.

Unusually there was even a group of journalists working for a famous German fashion magazine in attendance taking photographs for a feature on Scottish tartans. They were accompanied by two striking models dressed in tartan who enriched the scenery on a more immediate level.

The afternoon wore on, pleasantly sustained with estate grown venison burgers and a not so small and steady amount of whisky. Every now and then I was asked to present a prize and congratulate a winner but mostly it was a relaxed afternoon chatting with a variety of visitors.

At five o'clock when the final presentation was made to the various winners of the heavyweight competitions, tossing the caber, the sheaf, or hammer, the breeze dropped and inevitably the midges appeared. People started swatting the air or scratching their faces as the little monsters descended by the thousands.

The heavyweight games were taken most seriously and entered into by men who had trained hard and become proficient in their sport. Much like the quaich that I had received earlier, silver cups engraved with past winners' names were presented to their successors who had played impressively and fought with skill and determination.

I stood on the podium in the centre of the games field presenting the prizes as the Strathard and District Pipe Band marched up and down the field. Bagpipes and drums echoing through the strath. It was a magical atmosphere and one of the most romantic, thought provoking sites one could see and hear in such a setting. I'm sure people standing there could feel the deep patriotism of the Scottish people and particularly of the Highlanders.

With the midges upping their game and a few of the less hardy souls departing for home, the pipe major halted in front of the podium and asked permission to leave the field. A tradition that stemmed from the fighting between Highland clan chiefs. The clans' pipe bands would have been on the battlefield preparing for the fight and at the appropriate moment ask the Chieftain for permission to leave the field. The battle could then begin.

With the pipers marching off the field gradually the whole assembly of spectators, competitors and organisers departed having enjoyed a most wonderful spectacle and afternoon's entertainment in the remote glen.

It didn't quite finish there. In the evening, all the glen folk and any visitors that wanted to stay congregated at the hotel situated a little further down the glen. In a marquee on the lawn a dancefloor had been set up and a ceilidh band, The Jumping Haggis, had been engaged to provide music for the party. Although some of the dancing was a bit erratic a good number of Scots men and women really knew how to properly Scottish dance. In particular an elderly couple of chaps who were regulars at the games and had been mincing around all afternoon put on a good display of the Gay Gordons.

At one point the band stopped playing and the hotel proprietor came in to announce that Mrs Farquhar, who lived at the bottom of the glen, had telephoned to say that the local police patrol was on its way up the road. This was a nightly event and all motoring activity would cease until she rang again to say that the patrol car had left. Matters then resumed as normal.

I spoke to an American visitor who had the rather unlikely name of Audrey Autograph who remarked that this was an unusual state of affairs. I had replied that it might well be the case but as far as I knew there had never been any motoring disasters of any significance due to anyone having had a few too many glasses of whisky.

Following the most energetic and slightly inebriated version of the Strip the Willow which engaged everybody still present, the whole assembly joined hands and sang and danced to Auld Lang Syne, drawing the party to a close.

Breakfast the next morning was exceptional. Mrs McLeod had prepared what she described as a Scottish breakfast fit for a Chieftain and served haggis. It was a very kind gesture and served correctly, as she did, was a tasty dish. But in explaining the constituents of the meal to Emma she decided that she would rather have a bowl of Coco Pops.

It was with regret that we had to leave the glen that morning and return to the immediate matter of the future of Frampton Hall.

CHAPTER 20

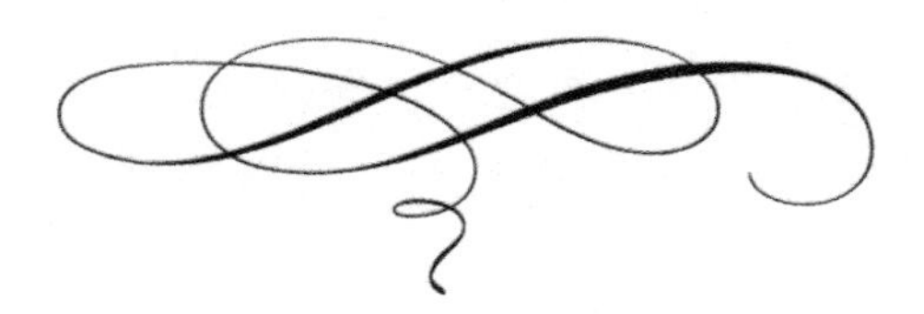

Back home life at Frampton seemed a bit strange. On the surface it went on as normal with all the everyday chores and meetings and dealing with paperwork. Underneath there was a frenetic activity as I worked with the trustees, the lawyers and accountants to consider ways of dismantling an historic landed estate. It was depressing and stressful. In a way I didn't want to be part of it because it was against my own inclination to rip apart something that had taken five hundred years to build and yet it had now fallen to be part of my job. The only consolation was that I might have some input in order that the whole thing could be manipulated in such a way as to cause the least controversy and distress to the many people that would ultimately become involved.

On Monday morning I drove as usual to the estate office and passing through the hamlet of Bridgend, which was not on the estate, I saw the Bridgend spectacle going about her daily work. The Bridgend spectacle was a lady of uncertain but considerable age who was the only female that I have ever seen who sported a full well-grown beard. No matter what time of day I went through the hamlet, she was wandering about, stooped, wearing an old Macintosh and carrying a number of carrier bags. I knew nothing about her and I often wished I did. Although I didn't envy her looks, I sometimes envied the simple way of life she had wandering up and down the road with her carrier bags. Goodness knows what was in them but they seemed to occupy her time.

I had only been out of the office for two days, the Thursday and Friday, and yet the paperwork was already mounting on my desk. The bills to pay, invoices to send out, rent demands to discuss and Sir Ian Glass' visit imminent. He had kindly fixed an appointment following my meeting with him previously.

Sir Ian had been to the Frampton Stud before but not for many years. He was impressed with the quality of the horses. He was happy to recommend a bloodstock agent who would sell the brood mares and even better knew of a likely job for the stud groom who would of course be redundant once all the horses had gone. Disposing of the thoroughbreds and the stud was very sad to see and although it would have happened anyway as Sebastian wasn't interested in them, it did seem like the beginning of the end. It brought the situation home to me with a feeling of despondency that was hard to lift.

The latest suggestion to Sebastian which came from Mr Gray the accountant, was to consider selling the Hall with its parkland and all the contents of the house which would relieve the cost pressure on the rest of the estate. It would release a huge amount of capital which could be directed to the new charity. Strangely, Sebastian had responded with the reply that it would feel like ripping the heart out of the estate and he would prefer to sell it all and retire gracefully. That view also put paid to any notions of turning the house into a country hotel, school or perhaps an old people's home. We considered every possibility, even as Sir Frederick suggested, a loony bin of which Sebastian could be the first occupant.

It was at this point that I think we all realised that Sebastian would force the issue through. We had spent several months trying to dissuade him, approaching it from different angles. Economically, socially, historically all these factors seem to have no influence on his decision. When you talked to him about inherited responsibility to those that lived and worked on the estate, he accepted it but was also of the view that those needs could be met by a new owner. He felt that doing what he had set out to do would benefit far more people than those at Frampton. He wanted the money invested in financial markets rather than in land and buildings as he believed they would be easier and cheaper to manage and administer. Historically, he said, he was the end of the line anyway.

The renovations at the Hall were put on hold, almost all the thoroughbreds at the stud had been sold and the last one would be gone by December. The stud groom had indeed been offered a very good job at Newmarket which he was delighted about.

Otherwise the estate went on as normal. Sebastian's trustees and professional advisers worked tirelessly to schedule a plan of action with which I was engaged. Serena and Sebastian had formally established their charitable trust and apart from themselves as trustees they also had appointed Peregrine Clark-Macdonald and Mr Gray, as he had an understanding of how the money would be effectively transferred from the Frampton trusts to the charity. There were three other people whom I did not know. They were, I understood, all well-known in their respective fields of expertise and included a former governor of the Royal Bank of Scotland, a civil servant senior in the Overseas Development Agency and a mutual friend of theirs who had been involved in delivering frontline relief efforts in foreign countries. At least one felt that the thing was in good hands and likely to be properly run. What was going to be a huge sum of money wouldn't end up being poured down a black hole in some mistaken attempt to relieve various tribes scattered across the African continent.

Whilst that black hole might have been dealt with, we had another black Hole to sort out in the Hall.

I received a telephone call from Mrs Jubb.

She was sounding slightly out of breath, 'Mr Aden please could you come up to the Hall immediately. There has been a bit of an accident.'

'What's happened?' I asked.

'Mr Hole has had an accident. Don't worry he's not dead but you might need to take him to the hospital.' She was her usual blunt self.

'Right I'll come straight away.'

'There's been some sort of accident up at the Hall,' I shouted to Anne as I ran out through the door.

I drove quickly to the house and parked outside the East front and hastily went to find Mrs Jubb.

She was in the corridor outside the butler's pantry.

'Where is Mr Hole? What's happened?' I asked.

'He is in here,' she replied and opened the door into his pantry.

He was sitting in his chair completely covered in soot.

'Are you alright Mr Hole?' I asked.

'Not really Mr Aden, I'm afraid it's my eyes. I can't see very clearly.'

'He was in Sir Charles' study', Mrs Jubb explained, 'and he heard something up the chimney so went to investigate. He was having a look and as he did so huge amount of soot came crashing down completely covering the poor man. And you should see the mess in the study,' she added.

'We'd better take you to A&E I think,' I suggested, 'it may be that the doctors can wash out your eyes or whatever they need to do.'

'Thank you, Mr Aden, that would be kind. But I can't possibly go looking like this.'

'Isn't it more important that we get your eyes seen to rather than what you look like?'

He was wearing his formal livery tailcoat and he did look like an extremely large penguin. He was also wearing a blindfold.

'Could you go and find perhaps a sweater and jacket for Mr Hole,' I asked. 'I think it is important to get your eyes seen to as quickly as possible.'

Mrs Jubb raced off and presumably went up to his flat to find some clothes. Once he had changed, I led him out to the car and made haste for the hospital.

'I'll guide you in,' I said, 'and then wait to see what they say. Hopefully, they'll sort you out and then I'll take you home. If not then I'll go back and get some overnight things for you.'

'That's so kind of you Mr Aden. I do appreciate it.'

'It's the least I can do,' I said. 'It's a damned nuisance for you and either bad timing or bad luck. It's a pity you had your head up the chimney when the soot came down.'

'Indeed, it was, Mr Aden,' he agreed sorrowfully.

After waiting for a couple of hours he was finally tended to by a doctor. I waited in the reception area trying to pass the time reading not very interesting magazines about celebrities on their holidays in far-flung places.

When he reappeared, the blindfold had gone and he was looking much happier.

'I'm much better thank you Mr Aden. Now that they've used an eye wash, I think they've got all the soot out and I can certainly see better now. My eyes feel as though they've still got grit in them but they say it'll disappear. Anyway, I'm allowed home. I have to go and get some eye wash and eyedrops with these prescriptions,' he said holding them out.

'Right that's excellent news, and I'm so pleased. Let's get the stuff from the pharmacist here and take you back home.'

Once he was back at Frampton, I suggested that he had couple of days off although, as expected, he put up some resistance. I insisted. He was well past retiring age and even though this hadn't been a traumatic accident, it was nonetheless unpleasant and uncomfortable.

'It won't do you any harm to have a rest,' I suggested.

'I am more worried about the dogs,' he said, 'as I don't feel quite up to taking them out for their walks.'

'Don't worry about them,' I replied, 'I'll take them with me and they can stay with us for a couple of days giving you a complete break. If you can tell me where the dog food is, I'll get all the necessary together.'

Following his instructions, I found dogfood, leads and a bed for them and loaded it all into the Land Rover. I didn't think Sophie would mind dog sitting to help out, even though I had never found them particularly friendly dogs. They always seemed slightly aloof. I left Mrs Jubb with instructions to prepare Mr Hole some supper and keep an eye on him.

'I'm afraid I have some visitors for a couple of days,' I told Sophie when I got home.

She looked at me questioningly.

I've got Sir Charles' poodles' and explained what had happened to Mr Hole.

'Poor old thing,' she said. 'I hope he is all right especially with everything else going on.'

'I'm sure he'll be fine but he was a bit shocked by it all. More to the point his eyes are quite painful.'

I let the dogs out of the Land Rover. They ran around the garden barking at our dog Bramble. After a lot of leg cocking, they settled and whilst I don't think they felt entirely comfortable or at ease they did at least know me as I spent so much time at the Hall. It seemed to satisfy them for the time being.

It did make me wonder though what would happen to the dogs when or if the estate was sold. It made me wonder what would happen to Hole. He had been with Sir Charles for nearly forty years, almost his entire working life and although I saw him on a daily basis, I knew very little about his family. Assuming he had one. It was something I would have to talk to Sebastian about because I knew that Sir Charles would have wanted Hole properly looked after. So much so that he had been left a small legacy. Sir Charles had given him £20,000 together with, rather obscurely, all his tweed shooting clothes and a case of particular fine claret which was still in the house cellar. I could understand the money which was kind but as Hole was nowhere near the same build as Sir Charles or went shooting, the tweed bequest remained a mystery. That was possibly why all the tweed was still in Sir Charles' wardrobe.

There would be other members of staff that we needed to look after. Many of the younger ones would no doubt find employment elsewhere but there was a retinue of older people who had been on the estate for a long time and would never find another job.

CHAPTER 21

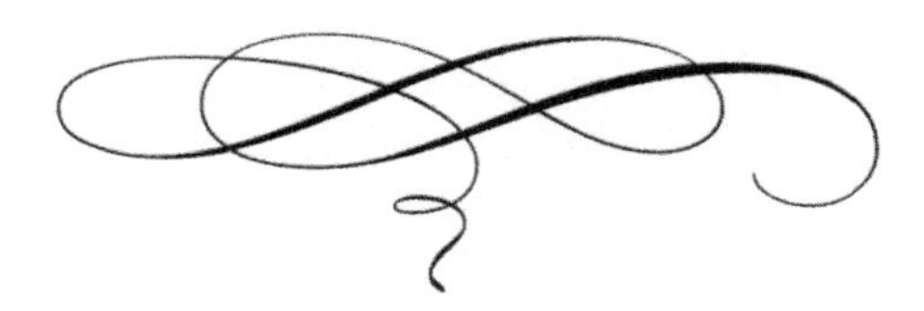

I had an appointment with a tenant farmer called Gordon King who was nothing like a king in a regal sense but reportedly king of his trade. He looked after his farm and always paid the rent dead on time but we would probably rather that he wasn't there. He had succeeded to the tenancy from his father and farmed a considerably successful stock rearing enterprise. It was one of the larger farms on the estate extending to nearly six hundred acres and he owned a huge number of sheep and cattle which he bought as stores and fattened over a period of time before selling them finished to the abattoirs. I daresay he made a good living out of it. The issue the estate had with him were his other two businesses neither of which he was allowed to operate under the terms of his tenancy.

The first was that he owned a fleet of lorries, mainly cattle trucks. The second was that he was a scrap dealer. If he made a reasonable living out his farming and haulage then I gathered that paled into insignificance considering what he made out of scrap. Although we could have forced the tenancy issue in a legal sense, we had rather undone our own position over the years by making use of his services. All our haulage on the estate, in particular from the Home Farm was contracted out to him and he also seemed to gather all the scrap from across the estate and take it back to his farm. Whilst his farm looked a complete mess at least you couldn't see it from the road and by default it meant the rest of the estate was more or less scrap free.

I knew that he wanted to see me to ask if he could buy the farm. He did this every year in the autumn without fail when presumably he had made a load of money from one of his enterprises. I did just wonder whether by the following autumn his wish might come true.

He was a bit of a rough cove and you would trust him as far as you could throw him. You could probably throw him quite far to be fair as he was a thin wiry sort of chap with a restless disposition. His restlessness meant that meetings were always held standing in his yard rather than in his house or office. Inevitably that led us to marching about through the scrap, mountains of the stuff everywhere.

'Why don't you get rid of some of this rubbish?' I asked.

'It's not rubbish, Mr Aden it's money,' he said, 'and of course it goes out from time to time but it depends on the market price. We have to sort it see,' he continued, 'different metals get different prices and the better it's sorted the higher the price I get.'

He pointed at a pile of copper. 'That'll go out soonest as the price of copper is sky-high at the moment.'

The ground was rutted where lorries and tractors had been shifting the scrap about and weeds grew with abundance throughout the area. It was a complete mess and covered the best part of three acres. There was just about anything one could imagine made of metal dumped in the field. Copper pipes, car batteries, old bicycles a few old cars even what looked like an old metal mill wheel.

'Is that a mill wheel, it's enormous?' I asked.

'Yes that's sharp of you, Mr Aden, that's worth a bit. It's cast iron and weighs five tons. I bought it out of the Smith's farm sale down in

Essex couple of years ago and just waiting for the right moment to sell it on.'

We progressed around the towers of scrap and every now and then he would stop and comment on some piece that he was particularly proud of. Remarkably he seemed to know the provenance of every piece. The top end of the field held a menacing looking machine which he explained was rudimentary type of crusher. Once the price was right he would shift whatever metal was appropriate at the time into the crusher and then load it onto his lorries to deliver it to whoever was buying it in the chain of recycling.

I couldn't help noticing as we left the field and return to the yard that he now had even more lorries.

'Eight lorries now?' I asked.

He laughed. 'I've got ten trucks now, a couple out on the road this morning and another going out this afternoon. All going up north to fetch a lot of sheep that I've bought to bring on over the winter. I hope you're not going to go on about me being in breach of the tenancy?'

'I point it out every time I see you Mr King,' I said, 'and every time I mention it you say you'll clear the place up and get it looking tidy which is really all we ask. But you never do it. In fact I think it gets messier every time I visit.'

'Now that's not a nice way to talk Mr Aden and it might look messy to the untrained eye but what you are looking at here is a well-run business. If it wasn't for all this, I couldn't pay the extortionate rent that you charge.'

I laughed. 'You could pay the rent out of the stock farming. You don't need all these lorries and scrap for the modest amount we charge.'

'Not modest at all, Mr Aden,' he said, 'modest, huh I'm paying seventy pounds an acre. I've put up most of the buildings on the place and it's only a basic little farmhouse. And there's no farm cottages for my men.'

'I wouldn't say your farmhouse is basic,' I retorted. 'It's a typical Suffolk farmhouse and it has five bedrooms and three reception rooms. I could let that for probably a quarter of what you pay for the whole farm. Well I could if it wasn't sitting in a sea of scrap as I expect no one would want to live here.'

'You speak some harsh words sometimes Mr Aden,' he said, 'beauty lies in the eyes of the beholder.'

I wondered what he did with all this money. He always wore the same clothes. A flat cap, green boiler suit and dealer boots which hadn't seen a coat of polish since the day he bought them. The only vague indication of making any money was a newish top of the range Mercedes. His wife, by the look of it had to make do with an old Renault and I wondered how she coped with living in a maze of chaos.

As if reading my mind, he said, 'come and say hello to the wife – she's in the house'.

Liz King who was busy in the kitchen came over and gave me a peck on the cheek.

'Hello James, how are you?' she asked. 'It's nice to see you. How are things up on the estate?'

'It's nice to see you too Liz,' I replied. 'We seem to be coping with all the changes since Sir Charles died and with Sebastian's ideas.'

She was not what one would expect a scrap dealer's wife to look or sound like. Not that there is a particular credential for such a person. Liz was an elegant well-spoken lady, witty and charming and a very popular and attentive member of the church choir. She maintained the house meticulously and the contrast between it and its surroundings was extreme. Rather like them as a couple.

When we conversed, it was James and Liz, outside it was Mr Aden and Mr King. If he was a bit of a rogue then she was the upstanding churchgoer. It made for an interesting visit and I'm sure a psychologist would find the whole set up a fascinating study.

'He won't sell us the farm,' he reported to his wife, 'won't even talk about price.'

She laughed. 'I don't know why you keep on asking,' she said. 'You know the estate won't sell so much as a square foot!'

'They sold old Harrison's farm earlier in the year,' he said.

'Yes, we did,' I agreed, 'but there were two reasons for that.' I explained. 'The principle reason was it's an off-lying piece of ground the other side of the main road but also the timing was such that with Sir Charles dying so recently we didn't want to throw a lot of money at it fixing it up.'

'If you need some money you know where to come. The money is in the bank waiting.'

That explained what he was doing with all the money. I expected there was an equal amount stashed under the bed based on any rumours I'd heard about scrap dealers. I refrained from enquiring.

'I better get going,' I said, 'it was nice to see you both. Perhaps when I come next year, you'll have all that lot tidied up.' We both knew of course that there would be no such thing.

I drove back to the office reflecting on Gordon King's annual request to buy his farm. If, as it looked increasingly likely, the estate would be sold then it raised the question of how we would do it. It would almost certainly have to be split into lots as the size of it was such that selling it as a whole would be most unlikely.

Sitting in the reception hall at the office was a man that I did not particularly want to see. Adrian Grimm.

When Sir Charles was alive, we had an in-house shoot on the estate. Sir Charles enjoyed the sport and entertained friends and neighbours to some high-quality shooting. As Sebastian had no interest in shooting we decided to let it, at least temporarily, and as a result of an advertisement in the *Field* magazine we had acquired Mr Grimm as our shooting tenant.

As in many circumstances people who interview well and come armed with an excellent CV and impeccable references turn out to be not quite what one was led to believe. Mr Grimm was one of those.

He complained about everything. The estate was always at fault if anything went wrong including, apparently, the weather. We still employed the shoot staff so had some control of what went on but Mr Grimm paid us for the pleasure running his syndicate shoot across the estate.

He was well spoken in a fabricated sort of way and according to the CV we had received had taken early retirement from his job as manager of a large department store in Chelmsford. I presumed it must have been quite a responsible position as it would have involved having a lot of staff reporting to him and no doubt millions of pounds worth of stock that he had to monitor, and targets to meet. Anything he said would have people scurrying around at his command and regretfully he carried on in the same manner at Frampton,

'Mr Aden I am sorry for coming in without an appointment but I've a matter of grave concern to discuss and really it is quite urgent,' he explained.

As he usually came in without an appointment, I didn't think the apology was either necessary or appropriate.

'That's fine Mr Grimm, tell me about it.'

Anne had offered me a cup of coffee as I had come into my office and although I was dying for a drink I gesticulated, which she saw and replied with a thumbs up. She knew that we must at all costs avoid the meeting becoming protracted.

'How can I help, Mr Grimm?' I looked at him wishing we hadn't made the mistake of letting him the shoot. He was an irritating man, not solely because he kept coming in with silly complaints but he was irritating to look at and irritating to talk to, everything about him was irritating.

He was irritating to look at because he would never look anyone in the eye and fastened his stares somewhere above one's left shoulder, he rarely blinked and talked through his nose. He was irritating to look at because he always wore a three-piece heavy tweed shooting suit with coloured shooting stockings and brogues creating the impression of a country squire. Overdressed except perhaps for when he was out on the shooting field.

'I'm afraid the timber haulage people are making a right mess of the tracks up in Bigwood,' he said. 'The ruts are so deep we can't get up and down in our 4x4.'

'Oh,' I said. 'I thought we had this discussion the other week?'

'Yes, we did but you've done nothing about it.'

'If I remember correctly, you're not shooting the Bigwood yet and I promised that we would get the ruts sorted out well before time.'

'We're not shooting up there yet you're right, but the ruts haven't been seen to and time is pressing. You know I've measured some of those ruts and the ruts are sixteen inches deep in places. I took a tape measure with me last time and the camera so I can show you what I mean.'

'I've been up there as well myself but until we get all the timber out there is no point levelling out the ruts.'

'When are you getting all the timber out by?' he asked.

'Like I promised, we would get this sorted by the end of the month and will stick to our word. You're not going in there beforehand anyway so really don't see what the problem is.'

'I'm just concerned that you won't do it. You know we pay a lot of money for the shoot and I should be very disappointed Mr Aden if can't get in there when we need.'

I was getting a bit impatient.

'This is the third time you've been in to talk about this particular issue Mr Grimm and for the third time I assure you that we will put it right before the end of the month. I am very aware that you pay a good rent for the shooting and as I said to you last time it's only fair that you can have proper access.'

'While I'm here,' he went on, 'I noticed that the shoot hut has got a leaking roof and one of the panes of glass is cracked.'

The shoot hut was an attractive converted barn where the shoot gathered for their drinks and lunch on shoot days. It was quite a sophisticated affair with a proper lavatory and kitchens and an open fire. Its use was included as part of the package that we had sold to Mr Grimm.

'I will get those seen to,' I agreed.

'Thank you, Mr Aden. When will you get that done please?'

'I'll get the builders to go up this week,' I assured him. 'Is there anything else while you're here?'

'I think that's all for now,' he said to my shoulder. 'Thank you for seeing me and no doubt I will be in touch soon.'

I had no doubt he would be in touch soon I thought as he left the office and made a note on my note pad to get the builder to go and sort it out.

Once he'd left and Anne had brought me in a cup of coffee, I settled down to wading through some of the paperwork on my desk.

The paperwork was building up more than usual because Sebastian had more or less succeeded in persuading everybody that his plan was going to be fulfilled. So, as well as all the normal work to do keeping the place running there was also a lot of background and preparation work to consider if the sale went ahead. Although the possibility was filtering out it was not a foregone conclusion. In addition to all that Sebastian had been advised that his own financial affairs needed to be reconsidered.

To some extent his and Serena's future was relatively straightforward compared to most people. They would continue to live at Bulls Place Farmhouse and keep their flat in Cambridge. They were adamant that they wanted to retain Strathard but they would need other assets to finance it. The London property, that I had little to do with, would provide enough income to run the three properties so they would be retained. The land in Canada and the timber business would also so be retained as Sebastian was keen to keep it as its remote location and ecological aspects interested him. I had gathered that the financial reserves of the timber company were over nine million Canadian dollars, about four and a half million pounds and were available to invest in adjoining forestry should it become available.

The much more difficult element in all of this was of course the Frampton Hall estate. In theory it could be split into hundreds of lots, every cottage sold separately but the advice was that that would put too much property on the market at one time and quite potentially depress the value. It was felt that private marketing of the whole estate or at least large parts of it should be attempted and if no buyer was forthcoming then we would have to reconsider.

The Hall itself would inevitably be the most difficult of all to sell because of its size. In reality it was far too big to maintain as a private house, unless of course you had inherited it along with the estate and been born to it, but it could perhaps be converted into something else. Some willing entrepreneur may be interested.

My more immediate concern was before we could do anything with that then we needed to deal with the contents which were in fact worth more than the estate, let alone the house.

I had a meeting with some influential and well-respected directors of the leading auction houses together with the curators of the country's most important museums and art galleries. I convened the meeting at the Hall to look at and discuss estimated values and more importantly how to sell them.

The trustees who were getting a bit fed up with running back and forth to Frampton had asked me to arrange the meeting and report on the outcome. All those that attended had been asked to write their own reports and then Sebastian, the trustees and myself would discuss amongst ourselves and decide the proposals.

There were eight people at the meeting plus myself and after coffee in the Yellow drawing-room we embarked upon a tour of the house. There wasn't one person amongst them who was not incredulous at the amount and quality of the paintings. Although it was common knowledge that the Buckley collection was one of the finest in the country there was no published inventory of the collection. We had an inventory of course and so did both the insurance company and a police department in London. Only some of the paintings were insured, the lesser value ones, the more expensive were simply too costly in terms of the premiums and the house didn't have either the security or fire arrangements that were required for insurance cover at that level.

The tour around the house was painfully slow as inevitably the visitors wanted to stop and discuss every painting in turn. After an hour we had only been into two rooms and bearing in mind that the old Masters and other paintings of note were located in four more state rooms and eight bedrooms, let alone the massive collection in the staircase hall I suggested that we pushed on a bit otherwise we wouldn't get around everything.

It was only the first introductory visit not one to catalogue everything. There would be no time left to discuss any ideas that any of them may have as to how we went ahead.

The house contained about three thousand paintings, many of them of no particular value or interest but there were approaching two hundred that were of some note and several dozen that were internationally important. The two gentlemen from the auction houses who although in competition with one another were in fact good friends had a particular desire to also look at the various collections and pieces of furniture. In the end it took all day to get round the house and so we decided that we would have to extend the meeting probably in London when we could discuss their thoughts. It was a bit of a nuisance really but having in mind the importance of getting things right, a trip down to London seemed of little hardship.

CHAPTER 22

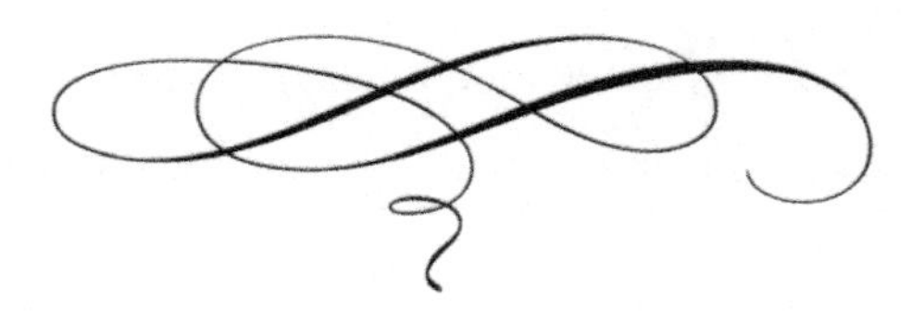

There was a screech of tyres as a vehicle braked to a sudden stop outside the estate office. Some banging of doors and Tony Williams, the gamekeeper, came crashing into the office.

'Mr Aden,' he panted his way straight into my office, 'we got a large group of travellers up on the sugar beet clamp near Home Wood,' he practically shouted.

'Oh, no,' I replied. 'I was hoping we'd avoided that lot.' That was going to please Mr Grimm. They were up near one of his pheasant pens.

There had been reports in the local newspaper about a large group of travellers who had been touring the area after being moved on from place to place but nothing had been said about them for several weeks now. I'd presumed that they had found somewhere but we had been on our guard in case they should be eyeing up anywhere on the estate. We had some a few years before and their visits were not something you would wish on anyone. Clearly our guard hadn't been good enough but in practice there was little we could do anyway as even if we locked gates they would cut through the padlocks. They would shift boulders that we put across unfenced openings and fill in ditches to get onto a suitable site.

'How have they got in?' I asked.

'The gates are missing,' he explained, 'so I imagine they cut through them and dumped them somewhere.'

'When did they get here do you know?'

'I think they must have arrived late last night. They certainly weren't there when I went to check the pheasant pens about eight o'clock. Looking at the mess you'd think they'd been there weeks.'

'Have you rung the police?' I asked.

'No, I've come straight down here.'

'Right we'll ring the police and go up when they get here.'

We both remembered the last time we had travellers and what a fortune it cost to clear up afterwards.

'The police never touch them for some reason,' I said. 'They seem to have certain rights that I've never understood.'

'I'll bloody touch them,' Tony retorted. 'I'll touch 'em with a bit of lead shot. That should see them off.'

'I wouldn't do that or it might see you locked up,' I suggested.

'They're no bloody good, I bet they don't pay any taxes, probably spend most of their waking lives stealing and then trashing the place.'

'You may be right, Tony, but we'll have to get the police to deal with it otherwise we may find ourselves in trouble.'

For once the police arrived remarkably quickly. Our bobby on the beat was PC Dave Duckling who as his name might suggest was a likeable benign fellow more adept at helping old ladies across the road rather than moving on a group of what may be an aggressive bunch of hardened crooks. Still the presence of officialdom would hopefully make some sort of impression on them and certainly better than just Tony and myself turning up.

'This'll be the lot from Harford I expect,' Dave said knowingly as though he was a senior detective.' We've been keeping an eye on them but they disappeared up Norfolk way for a couple of weeks so we thought they'd buggered orf. Not our problem of course once over the border.'

'Well whoever they are they're back by the sound of it and unfortunately they've decided to decamp here,' I said.

'Let's go and have a look then, we'll see what they're about. Jump in the patrol car with me.'

I couldn't imagine PC Duckling ever driving with blue lights flashing and siren sounding. He was a very methodical driver as ponderous in his operation of a motor vehicle as he was when walking the beat. He very carefully executed a three-point turn before setting off at a cracking pace. The speedometer pointed at twenty miles an hour as we sped down the High Street.

He was an excellent bobby though and as far as I understood everyone on the estate liked him, even our minor crooks seem to hold him in high regard. Whether that was because he never did anything may have been the reason but it certainly kept our local crime rate to a minimum. He was a big bear of a man and one could sense that if pushed too far he had the strength to handcuff any ill doers with ease.

We pulled up by the sugar beet clamp and got out of the car. There were eight caravans of various sizes but predominantly very large ones, quite a number of Ford transit pickup vans and some expensive looking cars. They obviously had a liking for BMWs. It appeared that they had settled in very quickly and a number of children were running around playing. Some chickens were scratching about and half a dozen evil looking dogs skulked around the campsite.

'Wait here for them come to us,' the police constable said so we did as we told.

'It's never a good idea to walk into their camp site,' he said, 'apart from those bloody dogs you never know what shit you might stand in.'

Sure enough within a couple of minutes four swarthy looking, thick set men came over to the entrance composed with menacing questioning stances.

They didn't say anything. What I assumed was the head of the group just raised his head inquiringly.

'Morning gentlemen,' said PC Duckling, though personally I wouldn't have used the word gentlemen. 'How long do you intend to being here? This is private land and you shouldn't be here.'

'We've got permission,' the leader growled.

'I don't think you have,' the policeman retorted. 'These two gentlemen with me are from the estate and you would have to have had permission from them which they haven't given.'

'Part of the estate is it? Owned by bleeding toffs innit? I'm sure they won't mind us being here, they've plenty of land to let us 'ave a corner.'

'I'm afraid we do mind you being here,' I said back, 'and I've confirmed to the police that that is the case and that we want you to move on.'

'There that's the position,' Dave explained, 'so I'll come back later and formally serve a notice on you to move on.'

The four men just stared at us. I'm sure it was a regular and routine occurrence for them.

'We got children and women with us and they've got rights.'

'They might have rights,' agreed Dave, 'but what you haven't got rights to do is camp here. Look at the mess you've made already. I'll do a rundown on those number plates on those cars. They're yours?'

'Some might be, some might not. We're proper law-abiding people.'

'You won't mind me making a note of all the numbers then.' He got out a notebook and wrote down such number plates that he could see from where we were standing.

There was evidence of some fires and burnt bits of metal together with a huge pile of leylandii hedge cuttings which I expected would end up being left behind when we did eventually get rid of them.

'I'll be back later to serve notices,' Dave said, 'in the meanwhile I want you to think about clearing orf.'

With that we departed. On the way back to the office in the car Tony suggested that we should do something ourselves and not wait for the formal legal process to work its way through the system.

'I think we should get Bob to come down from Home Farm with his muck spreader and drive through the camp,' he said.

'You'll get had up for that. I can't condone that sort of behaviour even though I can understand how you feel,' Dave warned him.

'But if we go about normal farming business and just muck the fields around the clamp, we'd be entitled to do that.'

Dave thought from moment. 'Well you'd be pretty near the mark doing that,' he said, 'but no one can stop you I suppose – might be a bit inflammatory.'

'Good idea Tony, let's get Bob down here. I should get some pig muck from one of the let farms, John Ravensthorpe will oblige, that might do the trick,' I said.

'I didn't hear this conversation of course and I'm not a farmer so I don't know what a normal farming operation is. I do the paperwork side of things and if I were you, I'd keep well away,' the policeman advised us.

Having dropped us back at the estate office he said he'd revisit later with colleagues and serve the requisite notices.

Tony seemed to relish the idea of spreading pig muck having been dissuaded from spreading lead shot. It seemed a fair enough way to deal with it I thought and it wasn't breaking any rules although could see it would be confrontational.

I wasn't there when the police arrived later in the afternoon with their notices but Tony had arranged with Bob the tractor driver who had by then procured a trailer load of pig manure to arrive at the encampment at the same time. With the official orders in hand and a trailer load of freshly steaming pig muck poised to be spread in the adjoining field, I understand that there was some suitably ripe language exchanged between the parties. The satisfactory result was that the travellers disappeared as quickly as they had arrived.

Such was life on a landed estate. The day after the travellers left, I caught a train to London and met the same group of people that had been up to the Hall to see the paintings. We congregated in some very smart offices of the auction house in the city of London. A boardroom had been made available for us on the twelfth floor of a modern office block with panoramic views of the city. It was interesting to see the Shard, St Paul's Cathedral, Canary Wharf and hundreds of other buildings making up a beautiful city landscape. The cars and the red double-decker buses looked like toys from twelve stories up as they scurried like ants through the maze of city streets.

We weren't there to look at the view no matter how interesting. All eight people had produced some fairly basic reports but they made a starting point for us to consider what we were going to do with everything. I was to summarise these reports in a single paper which would be discussed with the trustees and Sebastian. The main focus was on the most important and valuable paintings which would only be available due to their value and importance, to museums and art galleries or extremely wealthy individual collectors. There was some concern about a few of the paintings being sold abroad as it was felt by these experts that if it all possible, they should remain in this country. From Sebastian's point of view, it was another matter to think about and one that had rather escaped his and my attention.

The experts unanimously agreed that it would not be possible or sensible to put all or even a large proportion of the paintings on the market at one time. There simply wouldn't be enough funds in museums and art galleries or enough private individuals to buy so much within a short period. Their suggestion was, depending on how things evolved, that the paintings should be sold over a minimum period of ten years.

Assuming that Sebastian and the trustees accepted these opinions, which seemed entirely logical, then there was a further complication as to what would we do with them during that period. If the Hall was sold then obviously the paintings would have to be moved.

An eminently sensible suggestion by the director of one of the National Galleries mused that the paintings could be lent to several galleries over the interim years where they would be carefully looked after, be secure and of some public benefit whilst on display. I thought we could probably manage that idea and although Sebastian and Serena's new charity would not have access to all the cash straight away, it did mean that a continual and substantial income stream would exist for many years.

It was further suggested that the two leading auction houses would work on the project as a joint instruction due to the quantity of paintings and other collections. They would send a team of experts, which would change as different elements of the contents were examined and catalogued to record, photograph and compile what would be a much more detailed inventory than we currently held. Those inventories would form the basis of the eventual sales catalogues as and when ready to proceed.

An exceptionally good lunch of sandwiches and wraps delivered to the boardroom at one o'clock gave us a chance to view the cityscape and those in the know identified various landmark buildings across the city. The massive powerhouse of the city of London and its financial markets reminded me that there were plenty of wealthy institutions and individuals probably within a mile of where we ate our sandwiches who would be able to afford some of the Frampton treasures.

It was a somewhat bittersweet journey back home that afternoon travelling from the opulence of the wealth of the financial district to the baronial splendour of Frampton Hall. I travelled second class on the train in accordance with Sir Charles' preference who likewise had travelled second-class notwithstanding his fortune.

Second class travel and second-class stamps help a man keep his fortune he was wont to remark.

CHAPTER 23

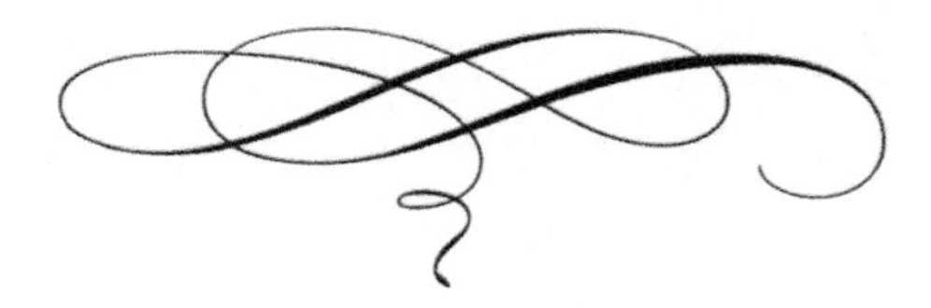

Sebastian and the trustees accepted all the recommendations made by the panel of experts and a month later a team arrived at Frampton. The work team were sworn to confidentiality as at that stage no public knowledge about the impending sale had been made. The team were introduced to the house staff as recording a new inventory which was required by Her Majesty's Revenue in respect of calculating taxes. To some extent that was true as there was the significant tax to pay in due course.

The team was led by a thin bespectacled lady called Dr Ann Lebowski. She could have been attractive but either chose not to or simply didn't realise it. She was slim, in fact very petite, with a face covered by the most enormous pair of spectacles giving her an owlish look and wore rather dowdy clothes. Her personality fitted her appearance and when I asked what her speciality was she said she didn't have one, her job was the senior cataloguer. It was her job to oversee compilation of the inventories and records. She brought with her two assistants, one was bright bubbly recently graduated girl called Camilla who had been educated at Roedean and now worked for the auction house. She was everything that Dr Lebowski wasn't in terms of looks and personality. She had long blonde hair, big blue eyes and a dress sense that could well have been influenced by fashion shows in Milan.

The third member of their team was a studious and serious chap called Toby who towered over the two of them and as if to hide his height, walked with a permanent stoop and spent a lot of time looking at the floor. He was middle-aged and clearly one of the most respected members of staff from the auctioneers. They had given Dr Lebowski absolute freedom over who she should choose to be on her team. The three of them oversaw the cataloguing, referencing and photography. Various experts in their fields seem to come and go when they were needed. For the first time in the history of Frampton Hall we put in place a basic visitor security process. Mr Hole kept a list and would know who was in the house and what they were doing. Quite often there were a dozen people involved at any one time and it would have been easy for an unexpected and unwelcome visitor to mingle in the throng and disappear with an heirloom.

The process had been estimated to take between two and three months so we had made arrangements to accommodate everyone at The Anne of Cleves in the village square which was both a convenient and comfortable place to stay.

Gail came into the office one morning and remarked that 'Camilla working up at the Hall was actually alright'.

'What do you mean alright?' I said.

'Well when I first met her, I thought she was stuffy you know, she speaks like Princess Anne.'

'Yes I suppose she does a bit but don't hold that against her. She does a very good job up at the Hall.'

'What I meant was, she does have a snobby voice but she's actually quite a good laugh. I've got to know her a bit as she's always down at the bar when I go in of an evening. She's a right looker too.'

'She's very pretty I agree. I would imagine she's turning a few heads.'

'I should say, the boys are around her like a load of flies to a shit.'

'How about bees to a flower?' I suggested.

'Yeah alright, more appropriate,' agreed Gail.

With her insatiable appetite for male company, I had on more than one occasion overheard her referred to as the village bicycle. She spent several evenings a week propping up the bar of The Anne of Cleves. With Camilla's ability to attract attention it was no wonder that the two of them had become acquainted.

'I'm surprised that she doesn't already have a boyfriend,' I remarked. 'She'd be a very good catch I'd have thought.'

'I think she's got a sort of on off chap that she sees at weekends when she goes home. He's a fund manager, whatever that is, and he seems to spend quite a bit of time at her flat in Fulham. It's a bit more off than on and she told me the other night that she quite fancied a bit of a rough rural type for a change,' she giggled.

'I can see where this is going and have no doubt that you will have a hand to play in it.'

Gail laughed with delight.

'It's such fun, a bit of new blood in the village and I think she's got her eye on Mark Elsey, you know the youngest son of the Elsey's up at Brook Farm. She's got taste I must say. If I was younger, I'd be after him. He's by far the best-looking bloke around here.'

'I thought he was going out with Katie Cartwright?' I asked.

'He is but she can't get out that much because she's got her baby to look after.'

Katie, the baker's daughter had had an unfortunate relationship with a youth from Bury St Edmunds a couple of years ago and at the age of eighteen was now a single mother living in one of the cottages.

It was a pity really that such a beautiful young girl had ended up in such circumstances and not quite as free as she might otherwise have been. Her parents were very supportive so at least she had a babysitter but clearly she couldn't be in the pub every night fending off unwanted attention directed at her boyfriend.

'It's not for me to say but if I was Katie, I would be thinking her bloke is getting a little bit too friendly with her.'

Gail who excelled in village gossip of the amorous theme informed me that Camilla was revelling in her new domain as the centre of attraction during the evenings and, as Gail was keen to explain, nights as well by all accounts It seemed as though Katie Cartwright did not choose her boyfriends very carefully.

I hoped that Camilla's nocturnal activity did not detract from the excellent work that the team were completing at the Hall.

With all this gossip about Camilla I asked what the other members of the team did during the evening?

'The lady with the large spectacles has her supper reading the Guardian and then disappears off to her room and the tall skinny chap has a couple of pints then takes his supper upstairs. They're boring really. And if there are any of the others with them who seem to come and go then they tend to eat in a group and spend the evening together. I haven't got to know any of them very well.'

They were getting on with cataloguing the contents of the house and it was becoming increasingly apparent that selling everything would have to take place in a number of stages. All the items that were being catalogued would, over a period of years, be sold in the London auction houses. This is where the majority of the value lay.

There were also the less important and less valuable contents. There were thousands of items which would be worth a considerable amount of money and at the end of the day even objects like crockery, cutlery and cooking equipment would need to be sold. There was garden furniture and garden tools, statues and other art in the grounds which had to be added to the list.

We formulated a plan. Once the updated inventory was completed of all the most important pieces then further cataloguing would take place of everything else. We felt that there may be some interest from the purchaser of the Hall in many of the items which led us to the timing of selling the estate. It also raised the question of how and when to go public with Sebastian's intentions.

This was a delicate and vital piece of the jigsaw.

A further meeting was held with Sebastian, Serena and the trustees where it was decided that the whole estate would be offered privately for sale on a confidential basis to known wealthy individuals and organisations that may be interested in acquiring it. There was an element of risk in this as even with confidentiality agreements in place rumours may start to circulate.

There were a number of specialist agents who sought out top end properties for retained clients and we approached them. The advantage in this respect was that their clients tended to be as secretive about their purchases as we were about the sale.

We began the process immediately. I made a series of appointments over two days in London to visit better-known agencies and prepared a resume of the estate. I allowed a month to prepare for the meetings as we had to have some idea of its total value. It was relatively easy to value the land and farms but it was also necessary to value each house and cottage in the village which took time. Those values depended on the type of tenancy the property was subject to, what income it generated and, in some cases, that there was vacant possession value. As we had discussed before it would have been impractical if not impossible to sell each house individually. Not least because it would flood the market. The preference was to sell the estate including the village although we realised that that would not result in necessarily obtaining the best price.

There were further considerations such as putting covenants in place to prevent an asset stripper acquiring the whole and then breaking it up for financial profit. Mr Carruthers looked into the legal position.

Once I had some reasonably accurate ballpark figures it became abundantly clear that the estate was unlikely to be sold as a whole. The values were just too great. It was interesting see how different they were from the probate valuations and the insurance valuations. Insurance values for the houses were of course based on rebuilding costs and the probate valuations based on assets that Sir Charles had owned at the date of his death. We now had to include the assets that Sebastian owned in his name together with the value of property that was held in the name of the trusts. It seemed more than likely that we would end up having to split the estate into various lots but nonetheless our first mission was to try and find a single buyer.

I booked a hotel in London for the night that I would be away. All the offices that I was attending were in the West End and hotels in W1 were eye wateringly expensive. I found somewhere a little less damaging to the north of Hyde Park in Bayswater.

I caught the commuter train in the morning which was an unpleasant experience. I did not envy those that needed to make the journey on a daily basis even though I was lucky enough to find a seat. Once we were past Colchester people were standing in the aisles crammed together like cattle in a lorry. The smell was dreadful. An odious cocktail of body odour, aftershave and perfume smelt worse than cow muck.

As we approached London the train became further packed with city workers. Many, both men and women dressed in suits had perfected the art of swaying with the carriage whilst reading their mobile phones or newspapers.

I had not purchased a newspaper at the station primarily because there had been none for sale. My mobile phone was a model of an age that did not entice me to read anything more than a text. For me, the novelty of travelling in rush hour was enough. People watching in an environment that one was not used to was an interesting experience.

A man opposite me was working assiduously on some matter with his laptop balanced on his knee. He was clearly an old timer and must have made the journey many times, even the interference of his neighbouring passenger knocking his arm with regular monotony as he turned the pages of his paper did not appear to bother him. The man sitting next me was reading a book. He was enjoying it and it was obviously amusing as every now and then he would lift his head from the pages and chuckle mercilessly at something the author had written. I glanced at the cover to make a note of its title, *You've Done What, My Lord.* I would have to look for that when I was next in the bookshop in Bury St Edmunds.

I enjoyed looking out of the window at the passing countryside which evolved into suburbia and then the city. I expected though that after a few hundred times of passing the same cemetery or rows of terraced cottages backing onto the railway it all became rather mundane.

At one point a wasp appeared in the carriage causing a diversion to everybody's concentration. Whilst some people were content to wave it away, others panicked. There was much jumping up and down, swatting and mild hysteria until an authoritative looking gentleman squashed it on the window with his newspaper.

We drew into Liverpool Street station, exactly on time. As we had passed a particular signal box, the masses drew to attention and stopped reading their respective material. Most people on the train must have calculated to the exact minute the time it took from when they left the train to arrive in their offices. Fortunately, I had allowed myself some leeway being unfamiliar with the journey and how long it would take me to get from the station to my first appointment.

I had intended to take the underground in the spirit of Sir Charles' homage to a parsimonious lifestyle. But by the time I dismounted from the train I had had quite enough of being crammed into a metal tube with hundreds of unknown companions emitting their own respective noises, smells and stares. I found the taxi entrance to the station and asked a cabbie to take me to Berkeley Square. He put down his copy of the Sun and started the engine.

Once I had settled into the back seat the driver slid open the interconnecting piece of glass between us and started a conversation much to my dismay.

'You down for a few days guvnor?' he asked having obviously spotted my suitcase.

'Yes,' I replied, 'I've got a couple of days of meetings in London.'

'Where you from then?'

'From Suffolk,' I replied.

'That's a lovely place,' he said, 'sometimes me and the missus go up there for a day out. It's not too bad a motor for us from where we live.'

I guessed that was my cue. 'Where do you live?' I asked not particularly wishing to know nor engage in conversation but realising that having started it was not going to end.

'I'm down at Morden,' he told me, 'so we just jump on the A12 and takes us straight out into the country. It's nice being in a bit of country, bit of fresh air and all that.'

'Yes,' I agreed.

'We go down the coast sometimes in the summer,' he carried on, 'down near Aldeburgh where there's lots of places to look at the birds.'

I thought that if he was a Sun reader there were probably other places more convenient for looking at birds, namely page three, but if he meant of the wildfowl variety then Aldeburgh would be as good a spot as any.

'D'you know what?' he asked me. 'For all the restaurants and takeaways in London,' he said,' I don't think there's better fish and chips than you can get at that chip shop in Aldeburgh.'

'Yes,' I said. 'I've been there, the one at the end of the High Street before it runs out onto the shingle bank?'

'That's the one guv. You been there?'

'Occasionally we take a trip out to the sea and enjoy the huge beach at Aldeburgh,' I explained.

'Where d'you live in Suffolk then?' he asked.

'I live in a little village called Frampton,' I answered.

'Oh we've been there and all. In't that where there's all of them old 'ouses built of wood? A bit of a square and pub in the middle?'

'That's right,' I confirmed. 'All mediaeval houses which are built of timber frames with lath and plaster.'

'It's beyond me how they stand up,' he said. 'I mean all of them bits of wood and that. I like something with some good old redbrick.'

'I suppose there's a place for both,' I suggested, 'but they have stood the test of time. Most of the village dates back to the thirteenth and fourteenth centuries.'

'Blimey that's bleeding older than me missus,' he chuckled.

I laughed suitably. Fortunately, we drew into Grosvenor Square at that moment.

'What number did you say guv?'

'It's the offices of Fiddler and White. I was told to look for a restaurant called Lugano's and their door is to the side of it.'

'Lugano's, yes I know them just round 'ere.' He obligingly drove me to the required doorway and I thanked him for his entertaining passage through London. I paid the fare with a generous tip.

'That's generous of you guv, 'ope you have a good day. Enjoy your trip to London.'

CHAPTER 24

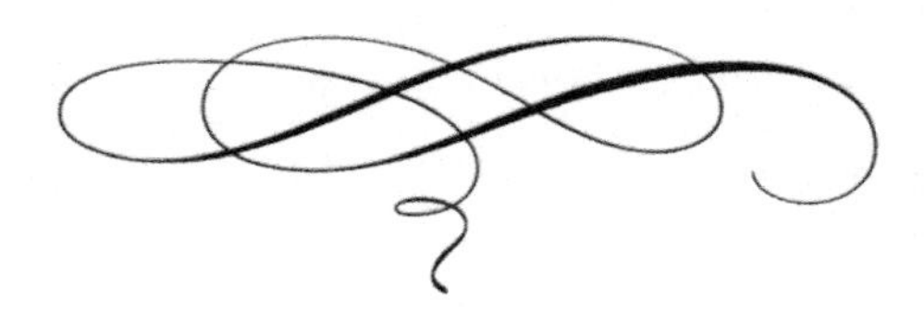

I walked into some prestigious offices. A spacious foyer with a marble floor, air conditioned and with comfortable leather sofas positioned next to coffee tables covered with expensive periodicals and the morning's papers. The girl behind the reception desk looked welcoming and enquiring. She had been selected for the job for her looks and demeanour.

The bright smile and body language were appropriate as she asked, 'Good morning, how are you?'

'Good morning,' I replied, 'very well, thank you. I've come to see Richard Brooke. My name is James Aden. He is expecting me.'

'Thank you,' she said. 'I'll ring him to let him know you're here. Would you like to take a seat?' And she pointed to the black leather sofas adjoining the periodicals.

I sat there reading the *Financial Times*. An appropriate paper considering the serious matters we were about to discuss.

He arrived from the left across the lobby from where I was sitting. We had been appointed someone with seniority as the man was in his mid-fifties, wearing a charcoal grey suit and exuded an air of confidence.

'Mr Aden?' he assumed.

'Indeed,' I replied, 'Mr Brooke?'

'Yes, thank you for coming to see me.'

'Not at all. I hope that we can have some fruitful discussions,' I said.

He led me to the lift which took us up to the fourth floor and his opulent well-furnished office.

'Would you like some coffee or tea?'

'I'd love cup of coffee,' I replied. 'Could I use your loo before we get down to discussions?'

'Of course. It's at the top of the stairs by the lift. I'll show you the way. You need a key pass to get through the door so I will lend you mine. I'll wait for you here and then we can go back to the office.'

I reflected that most of my clients visiting me at Frampton who needed a pee then more likely they'd do it in a hedge rather than need a pass. In the event a security man intervened and let me through.

The lavatories were impeccable and offered a choice of soaps and conditioner and cotton towels. We didn't provide either in the estate office. A bar of carbolic.

Mr Brooke had the polished overture of a man used to dealing with rich clients. Rich clients in the business world rather than in my own sphere of dealing with clients on a daily matter understanding their personal characters. Sir Charles and now Sir Sebastian were some of the richest people in the country and yet our relationship was one of informality, trust and integrity. I suspected that in this man's world dealing with rich clients was a matter of massaging and pandering to their whims. I didn't envy him his job but at that moment Frampton estate needed people like him to provide a solution to our situation.

'As you know I'm agent to the late Sir Charles Buckley and now his son Sir Sebastian who own the Frampton Hall estate in Suffolk.

Since Sir Charles' death we have had various meetings with Sir Sebastian and the trustees of the estate which have led us to consider the possible disposal of the estate in order to secure Sir Sebastian's future aspirations.'

He looked slightly taken aback. He would have expected some kind of large-scale sale from our initial telephone discussions but perhaps not the whole estate.

'Do you mean that Sir Sebastian wishes to dispose of the whole?'

'Yes, not only the Hall but the entire Frampton estate which, as you may know extends to ten thousand acres and the complete village of Frampton.'

He had done his homework but nonetheless looked surprised.

'Let me explain,' I said, 'Sir Sebastian is the last in the line of Buckleys and he has no interest in either the continuation of the title nor maintaining the estate which he sees as solely existing to fund the running of Frampton Hall.'

He looked at me inquiringly but offered no comment.

'So, we are in the position where Sir Sebastian and the trustees of various trusts are looking at selling it all. As I mentioned on the telephone this is a completely confidential discussion. We are hoping to find a purchaser who is wishing to buy into this sort of lifestyle, someone to take on the mantle of landed gentry and no doubt procure themselves a way of life. There won't be many opportunities for people to acquire such a prestigious and valuable estate.'

Richard Brooke sat there for a moment in contemplation.

'Highly unusual,' he agreed, 'and one that will create a huge amount of interest but I am afraid, even with our prestigious clients, it is unlikely that we would find a purchaser for the whole.'

'I'm not surprised to hear you say that,' I replied. 'However, we have decided to make first approaches in this discreet manner to your firm and one or two others to see if such a sale can be achieved. That is our preference but if it comes to nothing then some of your leads may be interested in significant parcels of the estate.'

'That is more likely,' he agreed, 'but we will start as you have instructed and make some enquiries. I totally appreciate the need for confidentiality as indeed will my clients.'

I passed him a copy of the terrier which detailed every property on the estate. Some of the properties were grouped together in batches with a figure as a total rather than putting a price against each cottage. At this stage it was sufficient to give an indication of value and for Mr Brooke to gauge his clients' opinions.

Along with the factual property terrier I had produced a description of the estate summarising the main elements and included photographs, a history of the family and the house together with a brief statement explaining why the present owner was wishing to dispose of it.

I explained that we had not produced a proper sales brochure but believed this document would give him and his clients an idea of what was involved.

He looked at it. 'Yes, this is very useful indeed,' he said.

'Depending on what comes out of these initial enquiries,' I went on, 'we may instruct an agent to act on our behalf for the sale. The values are only indications at the moment and as you can see, I've broken it down into various blocks which will give you an idea of how we have come up with this figure.'

'This quite sufficient at this stage,' Mr Brooke agreed. 'How we work is that once we have considered what you have shown me then we would make a telephone call or perhaps meet with some of our clients that we think might be interested. As I said earlier there will only be one or two who are looking at something of this kind of magnitude. Then if they are interested enough, I will contact you and the next step would be for them to make a discreet visit with me acting on their behalf.'

'That's fine and quite understandable,' I said. 'I would be happy to show people around although of course it would be more of brief tour rather than an inspection of each and every property. We can show them the Hall and grounds in some detail.'

I left Mr Brooke's office and descended back to the street.

My next appointment was at a similar firm who specialised in acting for high net worth clients. The office was only a ten-minute walk away and I had plenty of time between my appointments. I called in at a pleasant looking coffee bar to pass some of the time and sat there reflecting on what a strange mission I was undertaking. I was wandering around London with several sets of documents in my briefcase offering for sale what must have been the most expensive property in the country.

My second appointment was in a similar vein and a similar office. Very smart, understated and discreet. These were not your high street estate agencies but described themselves as private asset management consultants. My meeting was with Nicholas Jones and he was very different to Mr Brooke. I think he would have fitted well into a normal estate agency on the High Street and was a youngish rather smooth individual with an air of cockiness and wore pointed shoes. I regret that I did not take to him at all and was surprised that he was engaged in the type of business that he was. Compared to Mr Brooke's cultivated public schoolboy accent, Mr Jones probably originated from an area a couple of miles east of where we now sat.

My career in managing landed estates had meant working for the aristocracy and by association meeting their friends who tended to be of a similar background. Mr Jones reminded me that the people now with the most money were more likely to have made it in business rather than inherited it generations earlier.

'This is quite a spread,' he exclaimed as I showed him the papers. 'Big portfolio, big portfolio indeed.'

I couldn't remember Sir Charles ever describing his estate as a portfolio.

We went through the same conversations I had previously with Mr Brooke emphasising our wish to try and sell as whole but with the probability that we would need to split it up.

'Maybe, maybe,' he said, 'but I can tell you James that I'm looking after plenty of clients with money to burn. We'll put it about.'

'Discreetly,' I said. 'At the moment we are trying to keep this confidential and it would be most unfortunate if news of an impending sale leaked out.'

'Discreetly of course, discreetly,' he said. 'No problem. Most of my guys I deal with like to keep their business matters private so don't worry about that James. Don't always like to ask where the old readies come from,' he chuckled.

'It's a pile of money but tell you what James, you've no idea how much money they make in this city. Of course, a lot is coming from abroad and I've now got more Russian and Chinese clients than I have British.'

I knew as did the trustees and Sebastian, that it was quite possible that those with this kind of money would be foreigners. Quite how that would go down on the estate was anybody's guess and, more importantly, whether a foreign landlord would have the same philosophical attitude to owning a landed estate. Anyway, we were far from having to worry about that for the time being.

I decided on a light lunch in Fortnum and Mason rather than in a pokey little sandwich bar down some side street. The afternoon's appointments were in Regent Street and Jermyn Street both conveniently close by.

The afternoon was much like the morning and the two people I met were more along Mr Brooke's lines than Mr Jones'. The first meeting was with a man who could have been Mr Brooke's brother they were so alike but the second meeting was with a lady. She exuded charm, professionalism and I found her quite intimidating. I sensed that she had risen to her position in the company through fierce determination and ambition. She was certainly somebody that you wouldn't want to cross.

All in all, I thought, we had a good cross representation of agents now instructed. There were two more meetings the following day so I climbed into a taxi which took me to my hotel. This time the sliding glass screen stayed closed.

I arrived there relatively early at five thirty so having checked in and dumped my bag I returned to the foyer. I had seen some leaflets advertising local things to do and see. I was meeting a friend for dinner at a restaurant in Holland Park but it gave me a couple of hours to spare. There were as one would expect plenty of things to do although most of them would either have closed for the day or take up too much time. However I came across something that was quite unexpected and sounded rather appealing.

There was a local riding school offering one-hour rides in Hyde Park. I had never really thought of riding a horse in London and it felt quite an alternative thing to do especially when compared to riding on the upper deck of an open London bus which was a further option.

Looking at the map the stables was a mere five-minute walk away from the hotel so I made haste and went to find them. When I arrived, there were several people milling around in the most unexpected setting.

The horses were stabled in a mews yard behind some large grand houses. What was unusual was that most of the mews had been converted into cottages and interspersed amongst the cottages were random stables. The cobbled streets contained a mixture of horses tied outside the doors, motorcycles and cars. It was to my mind amazing that such a place still existed in the heart of London.

The last ride had gone out for the evening but a helpful girl said they could fit me in for a ride the next morning at eight thirty which worked well as my first meeting wasn't until eleven.

After a jolly dinner with an old friend from college and a rather late night, I slept well, was breakfasted and at the stables in good time the next morning.

The horse I was given was a bit of an old plodder and more suited to pulling a cart. Not something that I would have enjoyed riding at home but being on a horse in the busy streets of London, particularly riding along Bayswater Road before crossing into Hyde Park was an experience. Having to wait at traffic lights on a horse was not something I had done before particularly with a double-decker bus up its tail.

Once into Hyde Park everything changed. Miles of trails to ride along and there were a surprising number of horses out exercising. The park was relatively peaceful but it was strange to be able to see all the tower blocks and to hear the continual distant roar of traffic. It was a delightful change and I completely forgot that I was in London on business.

I concluded my other two meetings that morning, no doubt smelling faintly of horses which bearing in mind the property I was trying to sell did not seem inappropriate. I was able to catch a late lunchtime train back to Suffolk but it was a bit of a rush and having had nothing to eat I purchased a sandwich on board the train from the trolley.

The best they could do was a limp, tasteless cheese and tomato sandwich tightly wrapped in plastic. Quite unlike the previous day's lunch of smoked salmon and quail's eggs at Fortnum and Mason.

CHAPTER 25

Back in Suffolk the London trip seemed somewhat surreal because of the contrasting environments and being the first decisive step in selling the estate. Effectively it was now on the market and six agents had it on their books. Time would tell if anything came of it. I needed to attend to the next element of the dismantling of the estate. We had now sold the horses and closed down the stud which had not aroused any suspicion as it was common knowledge that Sebastian had no affection for them. It was inevitable.

The trustees and I had discussed the Home Farm. Sir Charles had taken a keen interest and liked to have his own stock and be involved with a hands-on farming operation. Sebastian, although he didn't say so, wouldn't know the difference between a dairy cow and a suckler cow. It was decided that we would disperse all the stock on the farm and turn it over to arable which reduced the capital and labour involved.

I arranged a meeting with local auctioneers Messrs Wood, Hunt and Ingram.

On a day-to-day basis the farm manager dealt with the auctioneers and would send livestock, both cattle and sheep, to the market every week. As this was a radical change we were considering, the disposal of the entire dairy herd, suckler herd and the breeding ewes the auctioneer came to see me in the office.

There was a knock on the door.

'Come in,' I said.

'I've got Mr Wood to see you for your ten o'clock appointment,' Anne said.

'Thanks Anne show him in and perhaps we should have some coffee or tea?'

Mr Wood came into the office. He was a shortish, slim fellow wearing a tweed suit with a spotted red handkerchief frothing from his breast pocket. I had expected a much larger man with the power to shout loudly over auction rings and a bullish stature to match.

'Good morning, Mr Aden,' he said in a cultured voice that made me wonder whether we had the right man. He sounded as though he sold fine art and antiques or possibly racehorses rather than cattle and sheep.

'Good morning, Mr Wood. Thank you so much coming to see me.'

'Not at all,' he replied. 'I'm interested to know what you have in mind here and hope that I can help you.'

'Well I hope so,' I said.' We have decided to change our farming practices and convert the Home Farm into an arable farm. It means that we need to sell the livestock and also the machinery that is connected with it such as the yard scraper, forage harvester and so on. We will still keep a few tractors and the arable equipment.

You probably know Sir Charles was very interested in the farm and has been succeeded by his son Sebastian who has a rather more hands-off approach.'

'I see,' he said, 'I wondered why there was a radical move to get out of the livestock business. I have to say is shame really because the Frampton Home Farm has always produced excellent stock which we have enjoyed having through the ring. It always attracts attention and good prices.'

'I know. It is disappointing but times change and we must adapt to them.'

'Indeed, indeed,' he said, 'tell me what you have in mind and the amount of stock that you wish to sell.'

Anne brought in the coffee. She poured it and offered Mr Wood milk and sugar to which he declined both.

'It will be everything,' I said. 'I have a list here from the farm manager which will give you an idea of what is involved. If you like we can drive down there and have a look to give you a better idea of what is involved.'

'Absolutely,' he agreed. 'Top-class. I am just considering whether it is better sold in the auction ring or whether it would be more advantageous to have an on-farm sale which tends to attract more interest as it's a little bit different.'

'We will take your advice but I expect that you're right, an on-farm sale will attract more people perhaps than the ordinary weekly auction mart. It also means we don't have the expense of haulage.'

He went on to explain his thoughts and set out his commission rates. He spoke with extraordinary speed and I reflected that auctioneers either speak at great speed or with great volume. There was no in between. He clearly liked the sound of his own voice.

Once he got going there was no stopping him and I was able to drink my coffee without interruption. His must have gone cold as he swallowed it in one gulp before we set off outside to the car.

'We'll go in mine,' he said pointing at an upmarket Saab coupe. We climbed in and I directed him to the Home Farm although it was clear that he been there before. The farm manager who had been warned of our imminent arrival was on hand to show us around the stock.

Some of the cattle were inside although most of the stock were out grazing in the fields.

'I don't need to see it all,' said Mr Wood. 'I have a pretty good idea from the list that you've given me as to what is what and some sort of idea of what it's worth. What we need to do is fix the date.'

'I'll leave that to you two,' I replied. 'To some extent the sooner the better but you obviously need some time to advertise the sale in order to drum up interest and get the buyers here.'

'Absolutely right,' he agreed, 'absolutely, and also need to get out my machinery chap who sells and catalogues that side of things.'

I was beginning to get a bit fed up with sales catalogues and values.

'Well I suggest that you come back with your machinery chap and have a word with our farm manager and prepare the catalogue so that we can get this underway. Sir Sebastian is keen we move on and frankly we might as well get everything sold and concentrate on the arable side as that seems to be the way we're going.'

'Jolly good,' he assured me. 'Leave it to me and will get it organised. In the meantime, if there's anything you want just give me a ring on my mobile. I'm afraid on the formal side of things we'll have to send you terms of business which will set out what we do and how much it will cost.'

'That's fine and I'd expect you to do that,' I replied.

He drove us back to the estate office in his Saab flooring the accelerator pedal on the straight stretches of road which had me stiffening in my seat.

A month later the auction took place. Another nail in the coffin as far as I was concerned but all part of the job that I was employed to do. The auction was a great success and attended by hundreds of people from miles around not least because they were interested in anything to do with Frampton estate.

On the day of the auction plenty of stocky, burly faced men arrived wearing the ubiquitous brown sales coats and marshalled animals, people and machinery into respective places and pens. The area was a hive of activity accompanied with a lot of shouting, people waving sticks and a general feeling that a carnival was about to begin.

As well as farmers there were machinery dealers, scrap dealers including our own home-grown scrap dealer Gordon King and rather a lot of weaselly looking men who I assumed were there for the day out. There were a fair number of women with their husbands or partners enjoying the occasion which was enhanced by the presence of a van selling bacon butties and hot drinks. The size of some of the ladies accompanying the various menfolk on the field led me to believe that most of them probably ate nothing but bacon butties attending such events along with their trips to the weekly auction market.

The auctioneers were a merry bunch and whilst there was no difficulty in hearing what they had to say it was sometimes more of a challenge to keep up with the speed of the action if one wanted to make any sense of it.

As proceedings got underway, I went and purchased a bacon butty from the van and devoured it with great relish. There was something rather fitting scoffing a bun over stuffed with fatty bacon standing in a field. It was quite understandable why they were doing a roaring trade.

The day was a long day but it was fruitful as everything sold. Even piles of scrap metal and old tools which could have been no use whatsoever to anyone were bought by someone. Some of the machinery achieved good prices although we had kept the best equipment to use as we converted the land to arable.

The livestock sold well and the Frampton dairy herd made strong money. After that day the Frampton Herd as an entity would no longer exist but the bloodlines of the cattle that Sir Charles had spent decades improving would go on to enhance the quality of other breeding herds throughout the country.

I was slightly disappointed but moreover sad that Sebastian had not attended the sale. He had to deliver a lecture at a conference in York that day which seemed either coincidentally convenient or manufactured.

CHAPTER 26

We had sold the stud, the racehorses and the livestock on the Home Farm. In itself that had taken a lot of organising and hard work by everybody involved but was only the tip of the iceberg considering what else there was to sell. We had been able to sell those without causing any suspicion as it was well known that Sebastian had never been interested in any of those ventures.

I had received some feedback from the agents in respect of my London trip and it was clear that the only client with enough money to buy the whole was a Russian oligarch. Unfortunately, he was intent on purchasing an estate either in the Cotswolds or West Country and the flat rolling acres of this East Anglian landscape did not appeal to him.

It meant that we had to consider how to split the estate up but try to keep some kind of heart to it. Once we had let our intentions be known to the agents there were some candidates who expressed an interest.

Discretion was still paramount and for the most part it was relatively easy to show people around without rising any suspicion. The hardest element was showing people the house as there were only a certain number of insurance brokers, archivists or surveyors that we could take around without questions from either Mr Hole or

Mrs Jubb.

Although we looked at the various possibilities of sensibly splitting the estate, in the end it would fall to whatever the purchaser wished to acquire. It was interesting to reflect on how these great landed estates had evolved and how in the present day there was actually very little interest in owning one. People may want the big house and park and maybe a substantial acreage around it but it seemed that owning too much land and too many properties was not on a rich man's wish list. Eight people came to view the estate and I managed to show them around on a brief tour under various guises of reasons.

Not one of them arrived in a Morris Traveller. Three came by helicopter, two in Rolls-Royces, one in a Ferrari and two in black Range Rovers with darkened glass.

None of them brought dogs with them and all of them brought wives or companions who looked as though they needed a multi-millionaire bank balance to sustain their appearances.

The relevant agents who had introduced these people to us accompanied the viewings and were able to deflect some of the attention. I felt as though I was prostituting the estate and was most uncomfortable about doing it.

Of the eight only three wished to return for a second more detailed visit. The first was a Chinese gentleman who, I was told, had the largest plastic making factory in China and when I googled his name saw that his estimated wealth made the purchase of Frampton Hall mere small change in his wealth. It made me wonder how someone could make so much money over relatively short period of time as it appeared that his business had only started in 1980. He had accumulated more wealth in just over forty years than the Buckley family, who would have been considered one of the richest in England, had acquired over five hundred years.

Mr William Chang spoke fluent English, his wife less so. They were personable enough but of such a different background to my own that I did not readily feel at ease with them. They were one of the party of viewers that came by helicopter, one of Mr Brooke's clients. The entourage included Mr Brooke and a couple of Chinese gentlemen who I was introduced to as advisers, whatever advice they might give I had no idea, and a very threatening looking bodyguard who definitely was not Chinese, standing at least six feet six tall and nearly as wide.

While showing them around the house I thought they might take particular interest in the Chinese bedroom but strangely enough they didn't. Maybe the Emperor whose bed the Buckleys had acquired was not of their political persuasion.

On that visit we had craftily arranged that Hole and Mrs Jubb would spend the day at Bulls Place Farmhouse giving it a complete spring clean. The cleaning ladies from the village had been given the day off much to their appreciation and the Chinese party were able to spend a good deal of time at the Hall. Most of their conversations were in Chinese so not only did I not understand a word, I kept having recollections of visits to a Chinese restaurant in Bury St Edmunds. A reflection on what a sheltered life we lived in Frampton.

The arrival of various helicopters had not gone unnoticed in the village. Rumours were starting to circulate though fortunately tended to lean towards film stars and that Frampton was being used as a possible location for a movie. The A-list stars were being ferried in and out.

The second set of visitors that came were as discreet as the Chinese were obvious. There were two cars full of them. Two black Range Rovers which quietly drove around the estate and scarcely ruffled any feathers. The interested party was a Scotsman who was a descendant of an old Scottish family which I thought boded well. Most of his wealth had come from the sale of his family's land holdings on the edge of Edinburgh which had all been built on for housing. The resulting hundreds of millions of pounds of profit was to be reinvested in land to avoid paying huge capital gains taxes. He seemed the most suitable contender with a background from a family of estate owners.

The third of the shortlist was stocky slightly arrogant businessman Tony Stoke. A somewhat coarse man. He arrived in a lime green Rolls Royce with his glamorous looking wife and no advisers. His agent, this time one of Nicholas Jones' clients, did not accompany him. He had a confident air of looking at something and if he liked it, he would buy it. He didn't quite go around the house kicking the skirting boards but I felt we were only slightly removed from kicking the tyres when purchasing a motorcar.

'What's the form with all this stuff in the house?' he asked.

'The plan at the moment is,' I explained, 'to sell most of the finer paintings and furniture at auction in London and to have a number of days of a house sale here in the grounds.'

'Any of these pictures being chucked in with the deal?' he asked pointing at a Rembrandt.

'Anything is up for negotiation,' I said, 'although that particular painting is probably worth more than the house so I'm afraid we won't be chucking that in!'

'Blimey,' he said, 'it's not my sort of thing – who's it by?'

'Rembrandt.'

'Oh right,' he nodded, 'I've 'eard of him'. He turned to his wife. 'Have to get a load more furniture and pictures if we bought this place,' he said.

'That's quite a nice one with the boats,' he remarked. 'I'd maybe put a bid in on that if it's not a rip off.'

It was a Canaletto of Venice.

'Darling I wouldn't worry about that. It's something we can do over time and it'll be very exciting to go on such a spending spree,' she enthused.

'Where do you live at the moment?' I enquired.

'We've got a big spread down near Dartford,' he said. 'Mind you nothing like 'ere. It's a big house but it's just in a residential area on the edge of the town.'

'It's the smartest address in Dartford,' his wife added, in case I was getting the wrong idea.

I hadn't realised there were any smart addresses in Dartford but refrained from saying so.

'What's the story with the couple of old dears we met coming in?' he asked.

I presumed that he was referring to Mr Hole and Mrs Jubb who we had not been able to remove for the day. I had introduced Mr and Mrs Stoke as recognised collectors of Italian porcelain, friends of one of the trustees who had arranged for them to come and see the Frampton collection.

I think the excuses were wearing rather thin by then. Luckily, their cover wasn't blown as neither Mr Hole nor Mrs Jubb were in earshot when Mr Stoke remarked, 'Blimey there's a lot of plates in 'ere,' when showing them the Wedgwood room.

Matters took a turn for the worse when we reached the state bedrooms.

'Fancy kings staying 'ere,' he exclaimed. 'What d' you think darling living in a house were a king stayed?'

'Yes this is the room that George the Third stayed in 1780,' I explained, 'and if we go through here this is the room that Queen

Victoria and Prince Albert used on several occasions in the middle of the nineteenth century.'

'Cor,' he said, 'it's a right royal house this,' then with a bit of a chuckle continued to his wife, 'wonder whether old Bertie had his way with her in 'ere.'

His wife tittered at the suggestive remark.

We carried on the guided tour which was always a long business at the best of times but seemed to be taking more time than usual.

Finally they had seen enough and went for a drive around the estate by themselves. They weren't particularly interested in the detail of the farms or how the estate was managed, more just that there was a substantial acreage which would show off the magnitude of their fortune.

I went to see Sebastian and Serena the following day to provide an update on where matters stood in regard to the sale.

'Come and sit down,' Sebastian invited me and led into their comfortable sitting room. 'How is it all going?' he asked.

'Well it's been a long drawn-out process,' I explained. 'There is certainly a mixed bag of people out there with this sort of money to spend. We've got three seriously interested people although none of them have made an offer yet'.

'That's good,' Sebastian enthused. 'Does it look as though we might have something on the table?'

'I hope so too,' I agreed, 'but as I said nobody has made an offer yet and after all the discussions that I've had with various people I still think it's unlikely that any one of them will buy the whole estate intact.'

'Oh,' he said, 'that is disappointing but you have always warned us that that might be the case.'

'Absolutely,' I agreed. 'It's just too much land and property for most people to either afford or really want to buy. I do think that we should consider some alternatives and maybe split it in some way although let's wait until we've had any offers, that is if we get any.'

'I agree with you,' Sebastian said.

Serena came in. 'Oh, hello James,' she said, 'how are you'?

I stood up. 'Fine, thank you Serena, and you?'

'Very well,' she replied. 'I hope estate matters are moving on, even if slowly?'

'It is a bit slow but inevitable really,' I agreed.

'Sebastian says we've had quite a few people looking around and we've seen some of the helicopters which is a bit of a giveaway isn't it?'

'I think we've managed to keep things under wraps. We might have to start thinking about something to say before people start drawing the wrong conclusions.'

'I don't think we're quite ready to do anything yet,' said Sebastian. 'I'd prefer to have something a bit more concrete before having to deal with all that.'

Sebastian was terrified of the press and being thrown into the limelight, the inevitable consequence when the news was finally released.

'Have you thought any more about relinquishing the title?' I asked them.

'Yes, we have. We've had a long hard think about that and certainly for the moment we've decided to take your advice.'

When the discussion had come up previously, I had suggested that it may be beneficial for their charitable work for them to keep the title. They didn't need to use it on a day-to-day basis.

'I'm glad about that,' I said. 'You can relinquish it at any time but once it's gone it's gone. Regards going public we'll wait and see if we have any bites, as it were, on the leads that we have. As soon as we do then we'll convene a trustees meeting and get Mr Carruthers and Mr Gray together. There's no point doing it until we have something on the table.'

'I think that's all we can do,' Sebastian remarked. 'We can discuss other options until the cows come home but until we have somebody genuinely interested it's a pointless exercise.'

We left it like that and had no other choice but to play the waiting game.

Waiting in the Square outside my office when I returned was a man in an open topped MGB GT playing loud French music. It was Dominic Brown. I was not pleased to see him. He was the reporter from our local newspaper the Edmunds Echo. We had met on numerous times as he was welcome at such events as the Frampton fete or the village Christmas Street fair. He was not so welcome when trying to discover stories about the private lives of the Buckley family. My last run in with him had been quite some time ago when he or someone he knew dreamt up some story about Sir Charles getting remarried. It was complete fabrication but he wasted a lot of time sculking around the village.

'Hello Dominic,' I asked, 'what brings you here?' He turned off the radio. For some reason he always had it tuned to a French radio station whether to improve his grasp of the language or for some other reason I never enquired.

'I'm hoping that you can let me in on a little secret James,' he chuckled knowing full well that was highly unlikely.

He sat in his car and I stood over it. He cultivated the demeanour of a slightly eccentric artistic individual with his hair tied back in a ponytail and he wore cravats. I guessed that he was in his early 60s and perhaps clinging to a youth much loved and not forgotten.

'I've been hearing about all these choppers coming in and out of Frampton and up at the big house,' he said, 'and heard a bit of talk about an A-list movie being made up there?'

'Is there?' I asked. 'What's the movie about?'

'Ha. Always the bloody same. Can't get blood out of a stone.'

'You don't expect me to divulge private matters about the estate, do you?' I retorted.

'Come on James you know I've got to do a bit of digging. It's my job. That's what I get paid for.'

'Of course I realise that and I have heard the same rumours about a movie. All I can say is that yes, if we were asked then the possibility is that we would entertain filmmakers here. But at the moment nothing has been arranged.'

I thought that was a reasonable answer which might keep the rumour alive but hadn't knocked it on the head or given him any factual confirmation whatsoever. Better that story than the real one.

'Well I'll have to accept that I suppose. While I'm here I'll have a scout round the shops for the local gossip about it. Someone else might be a bit more enlightening!'

'By all means,' I said, 'sorry I can't be more helpful but that's all there is to it.'

In the estate office work was still plodding on as always, keeping the show on the road. It was becoming much more difficult and stressful balancing the hidden agenda with everyday life. I dearly wished for something to change. Initially I had been appalled at Sebastian's actions but now that we were well underway, I wanted some decisive conclusions.

CHAPTER 27

'Nicholas Jones on the phone for you,' said Anne.

'Great thank you put him through.'

'Mr Aden, how are you?'

'Fine, thank you, and you?'

'Yes, I'm well thank you. Have you got a moment to catch up on the latest from our side of things?' he asked.

'Of course,' I said, 'I'll just push the door to.' I got up and closed the door in case anyone should arrive in reception and overhear us.

'That's better,' I said, 'how are you getting on?'

'I think I've got some encouraging news for you,' he said. 'You remember my client Tony Stoke?' he asked, 'One of me clients with a bit of cash to splash.'

'Yes, I do,' I replied, rather wishing I didn't.

'He has asked me to put a proposal to you, on behalf of the trustees and Sir Sebastian, but I should say from the outset that it is not at all what you are perhaps looking for.'

'I'm interested to hear it.'

'He is very keen on the house and a certain amount of land to go with it and would like to take discussions further. What he is not interested in is the whole estate and particularly not the village. He's a shrewd type but he's got the readies, if you know what I mean.'

'Oh,' I said hesitantly. 'That is a pity because as you know ideally we're looking to sell the whole.'

'Yeah I understand that,' said Mr Jones, 'but I need to provide my client's proposals to you in the best way just to see if there is any mileage in taking discussions further.'

'I absolutely agree,' I said, 'what does he have in mind?'

Mr Jones continued. 'He likes the area, he likes the house and it fits both his personal aspirations and his business sense. The offer that he has instructed me to put forward is that he would purchase Frampton Hall, the Park and as yet an unidentified area of land, but probably about two thousand acres. His aspiration is that he and his family can live in a grand house, which was they would achieve if they lived in Frampton Hall, but they would turn the majority of the house into a boutique hotel.'

I paused for a moment.

'It's not surprising that the house may have another use other than as a home,' I agreed, 'and it's an interesting idea to combine the two. Although it is far from what the trustees originally intended, I will of course have to put this to them and Sir Sebastian. Have you talked about some kind of price that he is prepared to pay?'

'Of course,' he replied. 'Depending on the exact acreage of land and what is included on the land then he's looking at a figure of thirty-five million. I can assure you he's got the dosh.'

My mental arithmetic quickly apportioned to being about twenty million for the land and fifteen for the house which did not seem unrealistic.

'Thank you for that Mr Jones,' I said. 'I'd be grateful if you can write to me with these proposals and I will in the meanwhile organise a trustees' meeting so that we can discuss it.'

We ended the conversation agreeing to take instructions from our respective clients. It was the only offer we had on the table, although of course we didn't let Mr Jones know.

I contacted all the other agents I had seen in London to see if there were any further leads before arranging a trustees meeting. There were none. Those that had visited the property had been highly impressed and were kind enough to give flattering comments but for various reasons it didn't suit their requirements. With the sort of money involved then I'm sure one would be very precise in one's requirements.

By the time I had spoken to everyone and others had rung me back it was time to draw the day to a close.

I rang Sebastian from home to tell him the latest and that I would organise a meeting with the trustees as soon as was practically possible. Unsurprisingly the trustees, Mr Caruthers and Mr Gray were able to rearrange appointments in order to get to Frampton before the end of the week.

As before Hole had arranged the state dining room for us although on this occasion, he decided to light the fire which gave the room a far better ambience than the electric thing he'd put out previously. To make matters even more enjoyable I remembered to speak to Mrs Jubb and we avoided the spam sandwiches for something more palatable.

Everybody greeted one another as we helped ourselves to coffee and then sat down around the dining table. We had a whole day to discuss the progress of all the different aspects that were under consideration. Usually Mr Carruthers chaired the meetings but on this occasion it was felt the mantle should be handed to me as I had been more closely involved with all the different discussions.

'Good morning gentlemen and Serena. Thank you all for coming at relatively short notice for today's meeting which is, I think, at last, going to set the map for the immediate future.'

There were some murmurs of anticipation around the table.

'Shall we start with the easiest. First the contents which are the most important in terms of historical and financial worth. As you all know we had a team of experts here cataloguing the better paintings and the collections and that has resulted in a very detailed record of everything we have here.'

'The process will be that the most valuable paintings, of which there are a hundred and sixty-five, and the different collections of porcelain and so on will be shipped to London and divided between the two auction houses for eventual sale. The auction houses will guide us on what to sell and when and, as I mentioned before, this process will take up to ten years. During that period some of the items will be stored securely in their warehouses and others, and this has to be decided by you the trustees and Sebastian and Serena, can be lent to museums and galleries for public display for the interim period.'

'Can you explain a little more how that will work please?' asked Sir Frederick.

'Of course. I understand that everything will be stored in a secure protected atmosphere until such time as it is either withdrawn and offered for sale or lent for public display. The trustees will be allocated a specialist from each of the two firms who will advise on a monthly basis on suitable sales, or requests that have come from museums and galleries to borrow paintings. At those monthly meetings, which can be over the telephone, you the trustees and Sebastian decide whether to take their advice or not.'

'Thank you,' said Sir Frederick.

'From the estimates that have been given from the auction houses and the teams that worked on it over the past few months, the total value of everything that will be sold through them is likely to be about £200 million.'

There were some sharp intakes of breath throughout the room.

'I had no idea they were worth quite as much as that,' said Sebastian.

The others looked suitably taken aback.

'Those are their estimates,' I continued, 'but bear in mind that the income from those sales will be generated over a period of at least ten years. Mr Carruthers is looking at how best to transfer the assets. That is, should they be sold by the existing trusts and the money be passed to your new charity, Sebastian, or are the assets better transferred to the new charity for them to sell? At the moment it looks as though it will be more beneficial from various points of view if the existing trusts retain the ownership.'

Mr Carruthers explained, 'In brief it is to do about tax and the way of minimising it but it has to be weighed up against the more onerous restrictions on working within a charitable trust which is overseen by the Charities Commission. It will be much more restrictive than if we, the current trustees, continue to own the assets and although I haven't finished working on this subject, I suspect that will end up being the best way forward.'

'The rest of the contents of the house will be sold by a joint auction of the two firms that are involved over a five-day sale held here at Frampton Hall,' 'I explained.

'It is a massive undertaking because there are simply thousands of items to sell. In practice viewing will take place by registered parties only. That is to say people that wish to attend the auction will need to provide their names, addresses and so on in order that we have some kind of security over the event. The items will be on display in the Hall and in several marquees in the gardens and the auction itself will take place in a large marquee on the terrace. As you can imagine the cost of this will be significant not least because security will need to be in place before we open the doors,' I explained.

There was discussion amongst the trustees over the mechanics of how it would all work and I answered as best I could though the details were up to the auctioneers.

'In summary that is how the process will work and although this sounds rather harsh, basically that is how we will empty the house. I have not got estimates of all the general contents even though some of them are quite valuable. They will be set out in a glossy catalogue in due course. All of you will receive copies of that but also the conditions of sale and expenses that will be incurred. You, the trustees and Sebastian will need to sign undertakings as owners.'

'Goodness it does seem rather sad,' Serena said rather unexpectedly. She did not say a lot at trustees' meetings, that is, if she attended at all, but the thought of selling the Frampton Hall's contents of half a millennium of history was perhaps suddenly dawning on her.

Sebastian looked quite subdued.

'What we are doing is sad,' I said. 'Literally turning the collections of generations of Buckleys treasures into cash, and I regret that I must put it as bluntly as that, because once this meeting is ended and we instruct the various people involved, there will be no going back.'

I looked pointedly at Sebastian. 'The Buckley family inheritance will be sold, all parts of it dispersed quite literally across the globe and it will never exist in its entirety again.'

I probably shouldn't have said it but I felt it was entirely appropriate to underline the fact that this was a momentous occasion. It had to be said when all the trustees, Sir Sebastian and Lady Serena were present because if there was any turning back then that was the time to do it.

There were some uncomfortable looks around the room but no dissuasion.

I continued. 'In terms of value the art and contents are straightforward insofar as I have explained this morning. However the sale of the estate is not so straightforward. We have approached all the main agents who may have clients interested in acquiring the estate. There is no one with either the inclination or the money to buy the estate in its entirety. We had all agreed previously that that was our preferred option but that option is not open to us. As it stands, we have one offer on the table which is this.'

I paused whilst all those assembled waited expectantly.

'We have a decent offer from Mr Tony Stoke who has come to us through Nicholas Jones who has offered, subject to further detail on both sides, thirty-five million pounds for the Hall, park and about two thousand acres. It does mean that we retain eight thousand acres and the village which we can deal with as a separate issue and I will come to that in a moment.'

I paused for breath. 'In essence the offer from Mr Stoke is sufficient to agree a sale in my view and we are partly achieving what Sebastian wished for at the outset of all this. The paintings and so on that are worth so much money can be converted to cash funding the new charitable trust. The house that soaks up so much from the estate can be sold. Your charity, Sebastian, will immediately benefit from a considerable amount of money and will continue to have substantial amounts fed into it over the next ten years. However it does mean that for the time being you will retain ownership of eight thousand acres and the village. Part is owned by Sebastian, part by the trustees, which will need to be maintained and managed but I think, in conclusion, it is a satisfactory outcome in the circumstances.'

Still nobody spoke and carried on listening intently.

'It also gives you all time to reflect on what to do with the rest of the estate. It will become more profitable without the cost of the Hall to run and either the income can be redirected to the charity or, bit by bit can be sold. I know for instance that some of the tenant farmers such as Gordon King will jump at the chance to buy their farms and I expect there are many people in the village who would buy their houses. That is a matter for consideration but I suggest for the time being it is left for future discussion.'

'That is my summary and my professional thoughts on how we proceed. I now need to take your instructions as between you, Sebastian and Serena as you have the final decisions and Mr Carruthers, Mr Gray and I will then work to those in the best possible way.'

Again, nobody spoke for a few moments and then Sebastian said, 'James thank you for giving us such a succinct and clear view of the position and I think we should all not only recognise your hard work but also come to some final decisions on this today as I do want to move forward.'

At that point there was a knock on the door and Hole arrived with Mrs Jubb and some trolleys laden with tasty looking sandwiches although I was rather disappointed to see a bowl of pickled eggs which clearly Mrs Jubb thought a necessary complement to a cold lunch.

CHAPTER 28

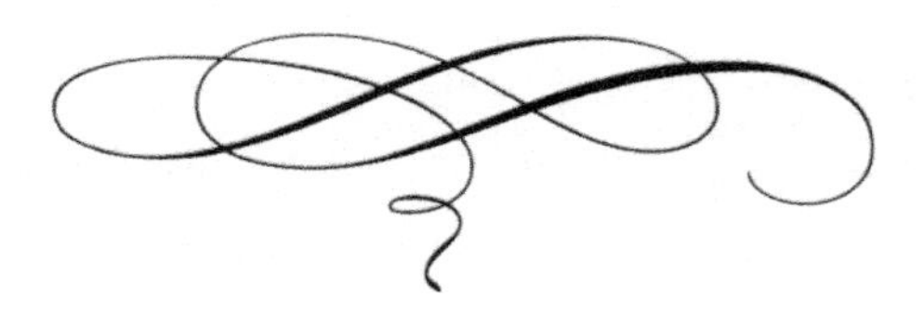

I threw some more logs on the fire not only to keep the place warm but also a bit more cheerful despite the chilly topics that we were discussing. The Buckley ancestors were peering down at us from the walls which emphasised the tragedy of our discussion. It made me wonder why Sebastian hadn't ever mentioned any of the family portraits.

'Sebastian,' I suggested, 'I was just thinking that a lot of the paintings in this room are your ancestors. Have you ever thought about keeping some of these and indeed any of the other paintings? If they're not suitable for Bulls Place Farmhouse then we can send them up to Strathard. There's certainly plenty of suitable places to hang them there.'

'No I hadn't really thought about it,' he mused. 'In a way I'm working out the details and trying to focus my energies on the new charity.'

'It might be worth your while at some point going around the house and selecting some things you'd like to keep? Either for Bulls Place or Strathard?'

Serena was listening. 'I think that's a good idea Sebastian. We haven't thought about it and whilst some of these paintings are a bit gloomy, so I don't think we'd want them, we may find some that we like.'

'Good,' I said, 'perhaps at some point before too long we can go round together and make a note of paintings or pieces of furniture that you'd like to exclude from the sale.'

The meeting resumed.

'To summarise where we are,' I continued, 'we have a plan in progress to deal with the contents of this house. Sebastian may well wish to keep some of the contents and move them to his house or Scotland but that is easily sorted and we will do that as soon as we get a chance.'

'We have this one offer for the house and two thousand acres which on the face of it seems to be acceptable.'

'A couple of questions James,' asked Peregrine. 'Presumably, you've met this man and I just wondered firstly what he was like and secondly do we know that he has got the money?'

'I have met him, yes Peregrine. He is not what you would call top drawer to be perfectly honest, in fact being a bit snobby about it he's a bit rough around the edges.'

'Not one of us,' growled Sir Frederick.

'No I'm afraid not,' I said, 'but that is no reason to dislike him and for all I know he's a decent sort of person. The fact is that he's from a different background and he's made his money out of business. Actually he made his initial fortune owning a factory manufacturing lavatory paper.'

I explained that first fortune led him into other businesses which from what I understood were linked to computer software and things like that.

'Good heavens,' said Sir Frederick. 'Fancy being able to make money out of loo paper.'

'They originate from Dartford,' I explained.

'Even more extraordinary,' exclaimed Sir Frederick. 'I see, not the sort of chap to have over to dinner,' he continued.

'Possibly not,' I said, 'but if he established an excellent shoot and invited anyone of us, I bet we'd accept the invitation.'

They laughed and Sir Frederick agreed. 'You're right there James,' he said.

'Anyway to concentrate back on the estate. Oh, and I forgot to answer your second question Peregrine, Mr Gray has carried out some extensive research into Mr Stoke's finances and discovered that he has far more money than he needs to be able to fork out the thirty-five million.'

'Heavens above,' exclaimed Simon. 'It beggars' belief how some people just seem to be able to make huge fortunes in relatively little time.'

'I know, I wish I could have done it,' commented Sir Frederick wistfully.

'So we will be left with eight thousand acres and the village. My view is that we continue to run the estate more or less as we do at the moment. We won't have the cost of running this house obviously and all the management that goes with looking after it. Then you can take a view. Gradually properties can be sold, either to sitting tenants who have expressed an interest, or you continue to hold onto it and the profits can be distributed as you wish. Most probable is a mixture of the two when we retain the estate and manage it but sell off bits when the time is right.'

'Of the eight thousand acres and the village,' asked Simon, 'how much of that is owned by the trustees and how much is owned personally by Sebastian?'

'There are fifteen properties in the village that Sebastian owns and the rest which amounts to about two hundred are owned by the Buckley settlement. With regard to the land it's little difficult to say at the moment because there has been no exact agreement over which two thousand acres are to go with the Hall.

'In my view there is an obvious block surrounding the house that seems suitable but we will have to be prepared to let Mr Stoke have his say. In broad terms there are likely five farms that belong to Sebastian which come to about eighteen hundred acres and the rest belong to the trust?'

'Would you be happy to carry on as agent?' asked Mr Carruthers.

'Yes of course, I'd be delighted. Very pleased to do that although I imagine that it would only take three or four days a week once the sale has gone through.'

'I would like you to stay,' said Sebastian which was kind of him.

'Thank you for that confidence,' I replied, 'and I hope that we can come to some mutually agreeable arrangement in due course.'

'As we are moving onto discussions more about the future now than the past,' Mr Carruthers questioned, 'would it be appropriate for Sebastian to tell us a little more about the charity and where we are with that? We are approaching a position where a lot of the capital receipts from at least some of the assets will be available. More to the point, for the foreseeable future most of the estate including the village are going to be retained by Sebastian and the trustees. From what I can gather, the profit if you like from this will be directed to the charity as the beneficiary rather than you individually, Sebastian.

'It might be helpful for us all to have an update on where you are with it. Obviously, I'm aware of what we've done setting up the charitable trust but the others may want to know as it's going to be intrinsically linked at least for a number of years.'

Sebastian shuffled about in his seat but he had been forewarned by Mr Carruthers as he had some notes in front of him.

'Yes, well of course that's an excellent idea,' he said.

'First I would like to thank all of you sitting here today and how much Serena and I appreciate the enormous amount of work that you have all done over the past months. It would have been impossible without you. The fact that we can't make a clean break of it is disappointing in some ways but it was maybe unrealistic to expect to be able to sell such a huge amount of property all in one go. So I'm happy that we will continue living at Bulls Place Farmhouse and the estate will still be owned by my family, such as it is, and we will be able to see where that goes in the future.'

Everybody was listening intently to what Sebastian was saying.

'We have achieved resolving the two greatest issues. Firstly selling this lovely house. It is lovely and we know that but it is such a massive drain on income. And secondly the impotence really of the art collection. That painting there, to the right of the window nearest the fireplace, James tells me that it has been valued at five million pounds. Personally, I don't like it anyway and nobody gets to see it apart from Mr Hole and the cleaners. I've also learnt that any single item worth more than five million isn't insured. So if it was stolen or went up in smoke then five million disappears and nobody has benefited from it, either when it existed on the wall or as ashes on the floor. We will now be in a position where that money is held in some other kind of safer form of asset and can benefit a great many more people.'

He looked around the room as there were murmurings of understanding although still a sense of not necessarily agreeing with his views.

'So to the trust that Mr Carruthers mentioned. He has kindly been working with us on the best way of setting up a charitable trust and it is now in existence. It will be known as the SABSER Charitable

Foundation and you already know those people who have very graciously accepted positions as trustees. The remit of the charity is deliberately quite far ranging although it does have two specific main directives.

The first is the significant investment of providing drinking water throughout the poorest areas of Ethiopia and secondly a global effort to support sustainable farming and forestry in Third World countries.'

'Those two projects are the ones that are of personal interest to Serena and myself, and that personal interest is what has driven us to this position. More importantly with the amount of money that will eventually fall into the foundation we will be able to see practical differences and improvements to truly thousands of people's lives in various parts of the world.'

There was a silence from those sitting there. It was probably the best speech, as it were, that Sebastian had ever made at a trustees meeting. He had summed up the reason for the demise of Frampton Hall and how the proceeds were going to be put to better use. Surprisingly, it humbled the meeting.

Even Sir Frederick looked as though he finally was coming to grips with Sebastian's ideals and might even change his mind about Sebastian's admittance to a loony bin.

Peregrine looked the least affected which was not surprising as he spent a lot of time with Sebastian and I don't think he ever really tried to persuade him to change his mind. At the outset some of us thought he was the best person to have any power of persuasion.

It seemed an appropriate time to draw the meeting to a close.

As before, Peregrine was staying the night with Sebastian and Serena. The others returning home.

I walked out with Sir Frederick and Simon to their cars. Sir

Frederick stood beside his Range Rover and as expected lit a large cigar.

'It could have been worse,' he said, 'at least most of the estate is intact for now. I have to say I still think he's wrong to be doing this but I can sort of see his reasoning.'

Simon was hopping around avoiding the clouds of smoke from Sir Frederick's cigar.

'It's a funny old situation,' he agreed, 'but in the circumstances I think everyone has done their best and although I'm certain Sir Charles would be devastated, none of us could have really done any different. What we can't forget is that Sebastian owns this house anyway so that's always been outside our control as trustees. And he also owns a considerable amount of the land.'

'We couldn't really have saved it,' agreed Sir Frederick exhaling a large plume of smoke that drifted across the roof of his car.

'Well perhaps they're the best results from everybody's point of view,' I said, 'partly satisfactory to all concerned and we must now put the final stages into action.'

'Yes, you're right, I'm afraid it's up to you James now to sort out the various sales. You'll work with Carruthers and Gray to get it all shipshape.'

'Yes, Sir Frederick,' I replied, 'most things are already well in hand and it was just a question of final agreement at this trustees' meeting in order to push the button as it were. It's going to take at least another six months to get everything in place and I suggest that we have one final trustees' meeting here at Frampton Hall before it is sold. In case we need to go through any other bits and pieces that need discussing.'

'Good idea,' he said. 'Let us know and of course if there is anything you want in the meantime just shout.'

With that he climbed into his Range Rover and sped off through the baronial gateway into the park. Simon followed more sedately in his Volvo and I returned to the dining room where Hole was clearing the room.

He straightened up and asked, 'What would you like me to do with the leftover sandwiches, Mr Aden?'

'I don't really know,' I replied, having been more preoccupied with the sale of over two hundred million pounds worth of the family's assets. 'Perhaps you and Mrs Jubb would like them for tea.'

'That's very kind of you, Mr Aden. I shall let Mrs Jubb know. However, I think we can reuse, as it were, the pickled eggs as they can go back in the jar for the next luncheon.'

There would be one more luncheon entertaining the trustees at Frampton Hall though I don't expect any of them were particularly bothered about the presence, or not, of a bowl of pickled eggs.

CHAPTER 29

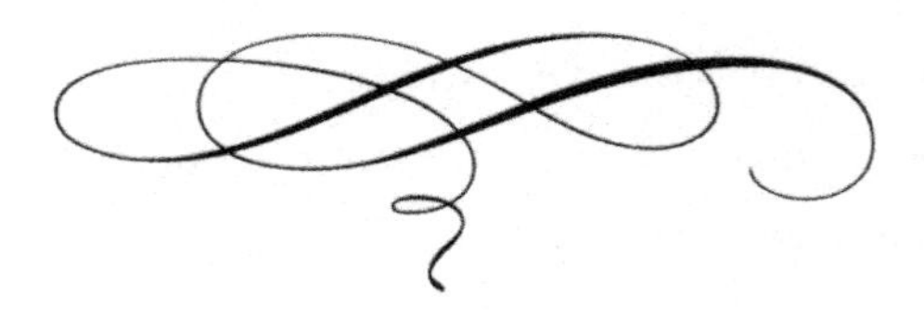

There was inevitably great deal of coverage in the press when it was finally made public that Sir Sebastian and Lady Serena Buckley were selling Frampton Hall and its surrounding two thousand acres. The fact that it was being sold to a lavatory paper tycoon led to headlines in the *Edmunds Echo* revealing, 'Baronet wipes clean' and in one of the nationals 'Sir Sebastian flushes it away'.

There was much more national and international press coverage on the news with regard to the contents. A number of the particularly more famous paintings were discussed at great length. The two auction houses had departments with media and public relations staff so dealt with all that on the estate's behalf.

Sebastian and Serena, in anticipation of the breaking news, had quietly departed to Strathard for a month out of the public eye.

The staff that were mostly affected were Hole, Mrs Jubb and the two gardeners. The gardeners were assured continued positions with the new owner but I went to see Hole and Mrs Jubb before the news became public.

Hole was in his pantry rearranging his pipe collection.

'Ah Mr Hole, have you a moment for a chat?' I asked.

'Of course, Mr Aden, please take a seat.' He sat behind his desk and despite the fact that only he and Mrs Jubb occupied the great house he still wore his liveried tailcoat as if the master of the house and a full contingent of servants were in residence.

'You look a little anxious if I may say so, Mr Aden,' he enquired.

'Do I?' I replied. 'Well I suppose I am. I'm afraid that I've come to tell you some rather difficult news.'

He looked at me inquiringly. 'I do hope that nothing has happened to Sir Sebastian,' he asked.

'No, no, not at all,' I said. 'Well not directly. But yes, in a way it is because of Sir Sebastian. There's no easy way to put this, Mr Hole. After a great deal of soul-searching Sir Sebastian and Lady Serena have come to the conclusion that they are going to sell the house.'

Hole looked shocked. His hands started to tremble and he tried to stutter some kind of question.

'I realise this is terrible shock to you and I'm sorry. I'm afraid though that there is really no other way I can tell you. What I can assure you is that the matter has been deliberated by Sebastian and the trustees for many months and they feel it is the right thing to do.'

'I, I, I'm not sure what to say,' he quavered. 'I, I …'

'Don't say anything for the moment Mr Hole. It's a lot to take in. Although I can promise you that I will explain in every detail what is happening and I can tell you that it won't happen overnight.'

'Sir Sebastian has particularly asked me to tell you that in respect of all you have done for his father in particular you will be looked after.'

As Hole was well past retirement age, he knew that he was unlikely to be offered a position elsewhere even if he wanted it.

'Does that mean that I will have to retire? Perhaps the new owners might take me on?'

'I don't think the new owners are the sort that would need a butler,' I said. 'More likely to need a minder.'

'Oh I see,' he said quietly and then, 'they're not landed types then?'

'No not like the Buckleys,' I confirmed. 'The kind of people that buy houses like this nowadays tend to be, shall I say, they've made their money.'

Hole said nothing.

'Looking on the bright side,' I continued, 'you'll be able to retire now Mr Hole and Sir Sebastian has offered you any house you would like in the village for the rest of your life together with a quite substantial pension. It means you will be comfortably off and able to enjoy a well-earned and worry-free retirement.'

He looked at me.

'That is exceptionally kind of Sir Sebastian and I'm extremely grateful. Though goodness knows what I shall do as I have been a servant to this house and family for over forty years. It's been my life and I have no idea what I would do with my time.'

'Well you'll have a while to think about it,' I suggested, 'as we don't expect to actually move out of the house for at least six months. It will give you a chance to choose a house in the village which we'll modernise to your requirements and you can think about perhaps taking up a new hobby?'

'It's very kind of you,' he almost whispered. 'I think if you don't mind, I should like to spend a few moments alone in my flat whilst I let this sink in.'

It was very sad to see him in such a despondent state. I went to see Mrs Jubb who was in the kitchen with the poodles.

'Hello, Mr Aden,' she said cheerily. 'How are you today?'

'I'm fine thank you, Mrs Jubb, and you?'

'Not too bad. Always busy though. There's no end of things to keep on top of in this place you know.'

'I'm sure there are, Mrs Jubb,' I said. 'Can I have a quick word with you on a private matter please?'

'Of course, Mr Aden. Where shall we sit? Would you like to stay in here?

'It's as good as anywhere I suppose,' I replied.

'Take a chair then, Mr Aden. Would you like a cup of tea?'

'No, I'm fine thank you,' I said sitting down at the enormous kitchen table. It was sixteen feet long.

I went through the same procedure as I had done with Mr Hole. She was surprised but less shocked than he had been.

'I did wonder,' she said, 'what with all these comings and goings. We haven't had so many people in the house this past year than we've had in the past ten years. To be honest I've been waiting for something like this. I never felt that Sir Sebastian had much of a liking for this place. Couldn't see him living here myself.'

'I think you're right. There has been a sort of reluctance to move.'

'Anyway,' Mrs Jubb continued matter-of-factly, 'it's not been the same since Sir Charles died and I'll be sad to go but I think the time is right.'

'Have you told, Mr Hole?'

'Yes, I have,' I replied. 'I'm afraid he hasn't taken it very well.'

'No I can imagine he hasn't. It was bad enough him losing the master but to lose the house as well he'll be very upset. I've only been here twenty odd years but he's been here over forty. It's been his life really.'

'I know,' I said, 'and I think it'll take some getting over for him but Sir Sebastian has offered him any house he'd like in the village and a pension. And the same goes for you.'

'My word, but that's very kind of him. I've often wondered what

I'd do when the time came. I've a bit put away but always thought that I'd be going to live with my sister. She lives in Scunthorpe which I've no liking for, so it'd be nice to stay in the village if Sir Sebastian means it.'

'He definitely does so I suggest you have a word with Anne in the estate office and start looking for a cottage that you may like. As I said to Mr Hole, I don't expect that we will be moving out of the house for another six months or so.'

After imparting the sad news to the two long-standing members of the household staff I wondered what we would do with the dogs. I suppose that Sebastian would have to take them.

To some extent I felt immense relief. Since Sir Charles had died there had been an atmosphere of something waiting to happen, if not across the estate then certainly up at the Hall. The emptiness of the house, selling the stud and the racehorses and then the livestock on the Home Farm had all been a gradual wearing at the foundations of the structure of Frampton as we knew it. Now that the important decisions had been made, it was in the public domain and key members of staff had been provided for we could start to look to the future with a degree of restructuring. There was plenty left, it was still a substantial estate. We would anticipate a different life with our new neighbours at Frampton Hall.

CHAPTER 30

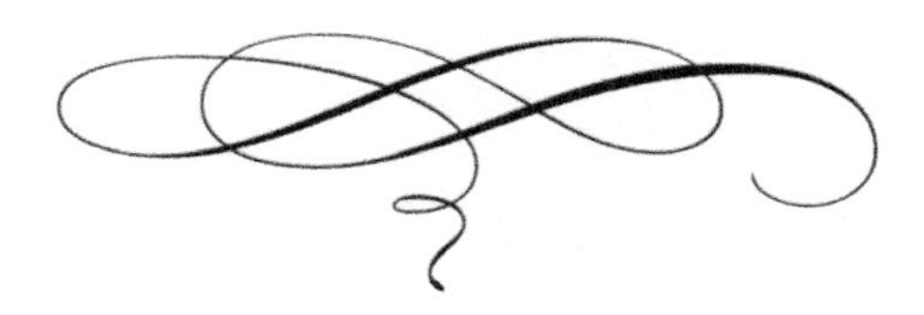

All the elements of the dispersal of the contents slid into place. Paintings were carefully removed and packaged before being transported to London. The house was stripped of its soul and as the weeks progressed it started to look like an empty shell with no living heart.

Once everything of note had gone the five-day auction was held in the grounds and the house was emptied.

Hole and Mrs Jubb moved to their respective cottages in the village which had been modernised to their own tastes and they seemed relatively happy in their new circumstances. Mrs Jubb seemed to take on a new lease of life. She hadn't joined the Frampton Cross Country Club but she immersed herself in other village activities.

Hole was not of that nature. Surprisingly one thing he had asked for a few weeks before leaving the Hall were the poodles. He didn't say so in as many words but I think he felt it was his final duty to Sir Charles to look after the late baronet's beloved dogs.

When the time came Monty and Napoleon went to live in reduced circumstances at Lilac Cottage and I saw them nearly every day. When Hole was walking the dogs, he would call in at the estate office without fail to see if there are any instructions for him. Of course, there were none but it was a pleasure to see him.

In anticipation of moving to Frampton Tony Stoke made an appointment to come and see me. I asked if he would come to the estate office to which he readily agreed and I watched arrive in the square driving his lime green Rolls-Royce.

'Good morning Mr Stoke,' I greeted him and showed him into my office.

'Morning,' he said, 'I'm Tony, don't forget. Everyone calls me Tony even on the factory floor.'

His gold jewellery jangled as we shook hands.

'Oh, yes sorry I had forgotten,' I replied. We had had a similar conversation on his previous visit just prior to him concluding the purchase.

'And Jim is it?' he said holding out his hand.

'I suppose so, but most people call me James.'

He didn't seem to hear me as I remained Jim.

Anne brought us some coffee.

'Thank you, Anne,' I said. 'Have you met Tony Stoke who is the soon-to-be new owner of Frampton Hall?'

'No not yet,' she replied, 'but I've heard a lot about you.'

He chuckled. 'I hope it's all good me love,' he said winking at her.

'Oh yes,' she tittered nervously slightly ruffled by his approach. 'Everybody is interested of course and looking forward to seeing what you are going to do up there.'

Just as well Gail wasn't in, I thought. She could never resist a bit of flirting.

'I bet they are,' he said. 'A new guvnor after five hundred years. And we've got a few plans in mind.'

I wondered what they were as we hadn't had much opportunity to discuss things in greater detail other than the extent of the land he was acquiring.

Anne left the room closing the door behind her.

I looked out of the window at his car in the Square. The flamboyant latest model Rolls-Royce with personalised number plate SH 1 T looked incongruous.

'I gather the sale seems to be going ahead as planned,' I remarked.

'Seems to be, Jim, seems to be. 'Course them bleeding lawyers take forever don't they. Every bleeding email costs fifty quid.'

'Yes, I'm afraid it does seem to be dragging out a bit. To be fair it's a lot of money, land and property so it was inevitable wasn't it?'

'I suppose that they'll get there in the end. Anyhow I've come to have a word with you about doing a bit of business with you. You'd better know what the plan is up at the 'all.'

'I'm very interested of course,' I said. 'I thought you were going to live in it as your house and convert part to a hotel?'

'Yeah well that's right and I'll explain the plan – I can't touch something without it turning a buck. What we've got in mind is that the bit on the left as you look at it from the front...'

'The West Wing you mean?'

'I don't know me north from me south Jim but if you say that's what it is then yes, it is.'

'That'll be where the family live and I'm bringing me mum and dad up to live with us. The main part of the house and the other side we will turn into what they call a boutique hotel. I wanna make a bit of money out of the place otherwise it will drain me like it did the last Lord.'

'It didn't exactly drain him,' I explained defensively, 'it was expensive enough to run that is true but fortunately they had the income to cover it.'

'You know what I mean Jim, everything needs to pay its way.'

'It certainly does,' I agreed. 'After all it's a rather large house in today's age for one family.'

'To go with the hotel, those stables out the back they will be converted into a spa and a gym and things like that with a covered swimming pool in the middle, so be like a top-class boutique spa hotel see. Very exclusive it'll be Jim, very exclusive.'

I thought there could be worse things that could happen to the lovely old house and with Tony's amount of money the job would likely be well carried out.

'The thing is Jim,' he continued, 'forget the hotel and all but there's quite a bit of ground that needs someone to look after it and I thought, well, who better to ask than the bloke who's in charge at the moment. I'm guessing you'll stay on here working for the Lord Sebastian for the rest of it? Maybe we could do a deal say, a day a week up at mine? You think about it and we can talk money at a later stage.'

'Thank you, Tony,' I said. 'Yes, I'm staying on here reducing my time to three or four days a week so let me think about it. It could work very well.'

'I'd better get going,' he said. 'I'm off to Norwich to see some computer nerd who's working on one of me programs.'

I went outside into the Market Square with the chairman of Stokes Toilet Paper and stood beside his startling green Rolls-Royce.

'You haven't remarked on the colour of me Roller, Jim,' he said as I looked at it. 'Most people ask but I'll tell you. It's the same colour as what is used for the Stoke toilet paper wrapping which made me my first fortune.'

'I thought they'd be some explanation for it,' I laughed.

'Yeah, a lot to thank for that first business,' he remarked, 'now look at me, I'm a toff, a boy from Dartford, now Lord of the Manor.'

With that he purred out of the Market Square and I watched SH 1 T slide down the Market Passage.

ABOUT THE AUTHOR

Rory Clark is a land agent and author who has worked on landed estates and is now a partner in private practice in the Derbyshire Peak District.

He trained at the Royal Agricultural College, Cirencester and began his career at Badminton in Gloucestershire, then at Althorp in Northamptonshire.

After many years in Suffolk he moved to his present home in Derbyshire.

He is descended from the Clan Colla and the Lords of the Isles and can trace his own ancestry back 1,800 years which gives him both an interest and knowledge of family dynasties.

OTHER BOOKS BY RORY CLARK:

YOU'VE DONE WHAT, MY LORD?: Hilarious tales from a country estate (2013)
AN ENGLISH COUNTRY MANNER: More true stories from a Suffolk country estate (2013)
STYLE AND MANORS: Rustic tales from a Suffolk country estate (2013)

Printed in Great Britain
by Amazon